TAKING
SIDES

by A. J. Huckman

For Emily

CONTENTS

SYNOPSIS

"Taking Sides", is A. J. Huckman's comedy, a thought-provoking novel that follows Hannah and Henry Burden on a calamitous holiday in Cornwall.

Vividly portrayed scenes feature the interplay between the pompous, ranting and opinionated Henry, and his balanced, calm and collected wife Hannah, as well as real and imagined aspects of Cornwall's landscape and history.

The narrative is richly laden with the protagonists' thoughts and feelings: how they perceive people and events differently; reflect on their own relationship; interact with other amusing personalities; and consider how to resolve dilemmas, always with hilarious consequences.

Some of the underlying themes highlight and debate the pernicious and corrosive effects of prejudice and discrimination, and expose the ironies of stereotyping. We only have to watch the news to know that humankind would be better off putting differences aside, valuing one another, and just getting along.

Whether it is debating questions of moral rectitude, or challenging uncivilised, inept or inapt behaviour, Taking Sides is an engaging novel that continually invites the reader to consider:

Whose side are you on?

CHAPTER 1

Friday, 12.57 pm

The half-term holiday begins in a few minutes, but the class of adolescents is uncommonly subdued. Perhaps the story dominating today's headlines is making them reflect on how close they come to provoking unbridled rage in the teachers they so casually irritate:

"BASEBALL BAT BLOODBATH!"

What degree of humiliation did the youths from a neighbouring school inflict on their mentor, until tolerance exhausted, he suffered a psychotic episode, releasing his frustrations with a baseball bat?

> "Oswald Pickles, aged 46, taught Art and Religious Studies at the school for 5 years, and had been a teacher since 1985. He had only recently returned to work after treatment for a stress-related illness..."

The fact that he taught these two subjects, considered by some students to be soft options, that could be flunked without shame, was one thing. It was quite another to be an authority figure with serious mental health conditions: depression and anxiety. Not necessarily being visible afflictions, his vulnerability must certainly have become widely known; perhaps disclosed by an indiscrete colleague wanting to curry favour with students; or a loose-lipped parent who knew someone with privileged knowledge.

The endearingly named Mr Pickles has already been arrested, interviewed and charged, and will stand trial for attempted murder at a Crown Court in another county in six months' time. There's a picture of him in the paper: Flaccid, middle-aged, nervous, balding and broken, looking guilty before the jury has even been sworn in.

I have little doubt his defence counsel will claim diminished responsibility in mitigation. The prosecutor will focus the jury's attention on convicting him with their evidence of premeditation: a receipt for a baseball bat purchased by the defendant that morning. Crystal-clear CCTV footage of the distinctive Mr Pickles at the till, and leaving the store with it; ex-colleagues testifying that he had no interest in baseball, or indeed any other sport. A parade of neighbours who will describe him as "uncommunicative", "socially remote", an "odd-ball".

Then of course there will be a plethora of emotional, juvenile witnesses brought on to take the stand chronologically, to tug at the jurors' heartstrings, and who may even enjoy being the centre of attention.

Next, the blood-spattered baseball bat will be produced with a flourish, covered in stickers: one colour indicating Mr Pickles' dabs; others showing the finger and palmprints of students who tried to defend themselves.

The prosecution counsel will argue against Pickles' defence of 'diminished responsibility', highlighting the unreasonableness of the force used, introducing to the jury the effects and consequences of the injuries he inflicted on his most persistent antagonists: toothless mouths drawing food through straws; rebuilt skulls and jaws clamped and caged in wire until they've re-set.

Some violently rock their upper torsos back and forth, drool dripping from their chins, their specialists working hard to control their post-traumatic stress. Maybe their condition is irreversible. Insensitive by-standers laugh at them. The irony is that Mr Pickles' tormentors now know how it feels to have *their* physical and psychological difference cruelly mocked.

The full, ugly drama will be reconstructed in the theatre of the courtroom. The defendant doesn't stand a chance. Goodbye career, home, pension; and if he has one, goodbye wife.

The mainstream media is focussing its attention on the rehabilitation and recovery of Oswald Pickles' victims. The Young Offenders' Bureau, (or YOB to give its unintended, though arguably appropriate acronym), is particularly voluble. YOB is a loony, left-wing child welfare organisation, renowned for petitioning the government to grant under eighteen-year olds immunity from prosecution on the basis that they are too young to form criminal intent, or understand the consequences of their actions. Conversely, YOB also champions the argument that the legal age for voting should be lowered to sixteen years.

YOB is very keen to highlight the fact that whilst many of the pupils who witnessed these assaults are not physically injured, they will nevertheless suffer long-term psychological trauma. YOB does not refer, in any of its representations, to the physical and psychological damage sustained by Mr Pickles, as a consequence of his many years of being relentlessly assaulted and bullied by his victims, which eventually provoked him to respond so violently.

The 1 pm bell tolls, heralding the end of the

spring term. My pupils await my permission to stow their books and leave the room. I suppose I have Oswald Pickles to thank for the unprecedented power I hold over them. I can't resist delaying that permission for a few extra seconds. Their observation of the delay proves that the balance of power now lies in my favour. Respect is returning to the classroom; not because of some politically inspired initiative to mend Britain's undisciplined, broken society, but a teacher's savagery, induced by sustained abuse and humiliation. Challenge me at your peril!

I perch my reading glasses on the end of my nose and peer over them sinisterly. "You may leave...quietly & efficiently".

Having returned briefly to the staff room to lock away my books, I prepare myself for the intricate series of counter-surveillance manoeuvres that have been such an important feature of my journey home from work, for nearly fifteen years. "Why would a teacher consider this to be necessary?" you may ask. Well, I can assure you that I am not in trouble with the police or an organised crime syndicate, and my happy marriage to Hannah precludes any need for a private detective hired by a divorce lawyer to log my every move. It is simply this:

At the end of his second day of teaching at Frimlington High School, Cyril Hodgkiss, one of our Mathematics masters, failed to notice a posse of five, acne-peppered soap-dodgers waiting at the gates. It was the objective of their leader, sixteen-year old Travis Grausam, to determine whether Hodgkiss drove a car to work, and if so, establish where he parked it. This would inform phase two of the operation: puncturing the tyres, accessorising its roof, bonnet and boot with upturned dustbins, and redecorating it with sprayed or scratched graffiti. Identifying and trashing a master's car, provided plenty of scope for causing him significant inconvenience and personal financial loss.

Cyril was oblivious to their scrutiny as they followed and tracked ahead of him, setting up ad hoc observation posts to anticipate and report his progress to others engaged in the conference call set up on their mobile phones. They pursued him so effectively, that at least one of them reported to have 'eyeball' on him at any one time. Being devoted disciples of 'Spy Cops' on Channel 27, they had conquered the practicalities of covert surveillance rather more masterfully than their studies of GCSE Mathematics.

Even though they failed to locate and trash Cyril's car, the operation was hailed as an unmitigated success. Grausam and his crew had unearthed information that afforded them greater scope to inflict a broader and more creative range of harassment: They had followed him as he walked home!

63 Acacia Gardens became the target in a campaign of misery that far excelled any of their previous endeavours. Cyril was baffled why he received late night pizza deliveries, taxis he had not summoned; visits from stoned teenagers in the early hours, asking where was the party promised on the social networking site, Face-Space? He also had to explain to his wife that he had not ordered the parcel of hard-core pornographic material she received in the post. His protestations were not believed. She had suspected for some time that refusing him access to her foo-foo for the last six years, had resulted in some unsavoury, alternative outlet.

It was only when he mentioned his experiences

in the staff room three months later, that some of the more streetwise teachers highlighted his mistake to him. Cyril wanted to move to another house, but he was in negative equity. He would just have to ride it out until the little sods found another target; and after all, he had made good use of the pornography.

One year later it stopped; but not after his tormentors celebrated his fortieth birthday by sending him a gift-wrapped cardboard box containing a dog turd, beautified with a card that had been stuck into it like a wafer at a jaunty angle, proclaiming, "Happy Birthday, you old fart!"

I change into my jogging kit, say my goodbyes to my colleagues, and randomly choose one of three exits to the outside world. I cast my eyes up and down the road, scanning the horizon, middle- and near-distances for Travis Grausam. I've little doubt that he is skulking in the shadows, maintaining safe separation from his foot soldiers, yet very much the General directing operations via his iPhone.

I set off at a keen pace to thwart any attempts of interception by bicycle or moped-riding youths. Five miles later, having taken sudden turns down alleyways, reciprocating my route, and running around the block, I finish the two-and-a-half-mile journey home.

Confident of having eluded a skilled and resourceful enemy, I hug Hannah on the doorstep, and dart upstairs to shower and prepare myself for the six-night caravan holiday in Cornwall.

CHAPTER 2

<u>One month ago</u>

I've just endured another day, trying to impart knowledge and insight to a class of pubescent GCSE Law students. I think I know how the Alchemists felt when trying to turn base metals into gold: It's equally impossible turning shit into brains. I returned home via a town five miles away to evade a particularly conscientious posse of stalkers.

There has been one bright moment: Ensconced in the private enclave of my home-study, I've just finished marking twenty-eight excellent dissertations on defences to the offence of Theft, as defined by section 1 of the Theft Act 1968.

It's amazing how adept these young essayists are at mastering the subjects they think will be useful to them in life. The *it-wasn't-me-you-can't-do-that-I-know-my-rights* generation has become more sophisticated and inclined to challenge authority: "If you think I did it, prove it!" Even when they know that you *can* prove it, they rely on liberal-minded governance brushing problems under the carpet, rather than dealing with them robustly. This is not a step forward for mankind, and I am uncomfortable with my role developing a culture that allows blank denial or self-justification, rather than acceptance of blame or responsibility when shortcomings or mistakes are identified. It's hardly any wonder that the bar of acceptable conduct has slipped so low and so quickly.

I shake off the onset of depression at the state of society to clear my mind for the part of the day to which I've been most looking forward: planning the half-term caravan trip to Cornwall.

Working with children means that enjoyment of my personal time is defined by how completely I can avoid them. My wife is a sales person, but she feels the same way. We both believe we would feel differently if we had been blessed with a son or daughter, but that has not yet happened. It's just the fact that other people's kids are so very annoying!

I settle down at the dining room table with a stack of caravan and camping magazines. I begin by starring only those claiming to be 'Adults' Only' sites, to maximise our opportunity for seven days' peace and quiet. Eventually I distil the choices down to Godleven Point on the north coast of Cornwall, two miles west of St Ives: *"A remote cliff top setting overlooking the Atlantic, and a short distance from a quiet Cornish village, with a pub and small supermarket"*.

Perfect! I access their site plan on-line and select an isolated pitch away from the shower blocks, the dog-walking paddock and the outdoor swimming pool. I enter my credit card details, and within a few minutes the pitch is ours for six nights.

Next are the lists. I am a great believer in lists. By sitting down in a comfortable chair with a mug of something hot, or a glass of something cold, a clean sheet of A4 in front of me and a pen in my hand, I derive a considerable sense of accomplishment and pleasure from compiling a list. A list allows you to feel as though you've taken the first step towards organising or achieving something significant, without expending much energy at all. A list now, is that first step of preparation that will save time, effort and money later, and that sinking feeling when you remember that you've forgotten to pack some vital item. Without a list, the water butt may be remembered; but what good is it without the filter? Or the remote control which is required to tune-in the TV?

Before I discovered the practical and therapeutic qualities of 'the list', I remembered to pack the main items but forgot the vital accessories, thereby rendering them useless. The result of this 'listless' existence was the need to buy more stuff on arrival at the site, when I knew I already had several, nearly new, and virtually unused versions at home. Apply the same principle to the grey-waste drainage system, security equipment, battery, gas bottle, and heating units, and it often tripled the cost of the holiday.

Having completed the inventory of what we must buy and take with us, it's time to decide what excursions or activities will sustain our interest on any given day. *This* list must be sub-divided into hot, fair and wet weather options. Hot weather is always the easiest: the beach! Yet the opportunity for sunbathing in Cornwall at the end of May is unlikely.

Fair weather requires us to visit some garden or other tourist attraction; but frankly, when you've seen one daffodil or rhododendron bush, you've seen them all! And as spectacular as St Michael's Mount is, it's all a bit of an uphill struggle when the alternative is sitting in our second-hand Bailey Unicorn Cabrera caravan with a cream tea, watching DVDs, playing on the Xbox, or reading a good book. But those, alas, are the wet weather options.

There is, I notice, an opportunity to see a live performance of Dirty Rotten Scoundrels at the open-air Sable Theatre. Two tickets cost thirty pounds for a matinée. I know Hannah isn't keen, but going to the theatre alone is like going to a restaurant alone: sad and pathetic.

So, having filled the itinerary with a diverse array of time-fillers that are based on the clemency of the weather, I secretly hope that it will either be very hot, or very wet.

I am Hannah Burden, Henry's wife. Henry has hidden himself away for several hours now, deciding where, what and how we shall spend our half-term break. I wonder if he has included in the itinerary any of the excursions that I enjoy...you know: shopping, going to the cinema, perhaps visiting a stately home, arboretum or show garden. He certainly hasn't asked me.

Henry and I met at the University of Bristol seventeen years ago, and we've been married for nearly five years. We would have married sooner, except Henry likes to be very sure about absolutely everything he does; for things to be done 'just right', and in full consideration of all the details and their impact; in accordance with logic, pros and cons, time and space. Henry isn't obsessive...more paranoid-obsessive-compulsive. You may be getting that general impression already; but he wasn't always like this.

When we met, I was an eighteen-year old undergraduate studying Sociology and the History of Art. Henry was two years older and studying English and Law. We both arrived in a relatively uncloistered university environment from structured, educated and middle-class families, who protected us from the many repugnant realities of life. Our respective parents continued to cushion us from the kind of austerity they had experienced in their own youth, by covering the cost of our student digs and crediting our bank accounts at the beginning of every term with living and studying expenses. Their generous financial support supplemented the meagre sums we earned working in bars or insurance companies during the holidays.

We perhaps took our parents' kindness for granted back then. But with the passage of time and life experience, one develops a less nave acceptance of the value of money; the efforts and sacrifices required to accumulate it, and how quickly it is spent merely sustaining basic living standards.

As a university student, Henry masked his post-adolescent inexperience by gaining popularity combining humour with forthrightly expressed, deeply embedded and extreme class-based prejudices. It was a daring style in a period of burgeoning obsession with political correctness, and condemnation of anyone who referred negatively to well-established stereotypes.

I particularly remember one occasion when he completed an application form and equal opportunities questionnaire for a joke. It was for a job as a Communications Officer with the local council's social housing department. He had no interest in getting the job; he just wanted to see how seriously it would be received. The fictitious, illiterate applicant proclaimed the fullest range of religious, political, dietary, physical, mental, sexual and ethnic diversities, and insisted that his childcare needs necessitated abstraction from the duties of work, for three out of the five days where attendance was required.

Henry published in the university's 'Rag Mag' both the application form and the council's reply, in which the applicant was short-listed to be interviewed. The magazine's editor also featured the council's proud assertion that as an equal opportunities employer, it would neither prejudge nor discriminate against the applicant's desire to be a Communications Officer, despite his inability to speak, read or write coherent English, or because he was unavailable to work for sixty percent of the time! Henry never attended the interview, claiming that he was suffering life-changing injuries following a slip of the scalpel during a back-street, vasectomy operation.

Appearing to exude a level of confidence and worldly knowledge that was envied by others, Henry won many friends and female admirers. Those who censured his opinions or were jealous of him, usually expressed their annoyance in huddled cliques. They feared that more direct demonstrations of disapproval of him might attract social ostracism, or worse, render them as objects of Henry's attention for ridicule. Yes, Henry Burden was as robust and self-assured as my father, but with an edgy, cheeky, rebelliousness that appealed to me deeply.

My first opportunity to speak with Henry, alone and without an audience was on 1st October 2002. We found ourselves standing next to each other in a queue for tickets for Spandau Ballet who were to perform at our Students' Union. We later established that neither of us particularly liked the band, but realised this was one of the biggest and most iconic groups of the '80s, and we might regret it if we didn't go.

"Well then…" I said casually; "do *you* always believe in your soul?" I cringed as I said it, not just because I had failed to preface the question with anything that placed it into any conversational context, but because I realised Henry clearly didn't recognise the line as being from one of Spandau Ballet's most famous hits. Now that I recall it, what does this lyric actually mean? Is it something to do with having confidence in the structural integrity of your shoes?

Anyway, it must have meant something to Henry, because he coughed nervously, unable to look me in the eye, and replied in a subdued yet sincere voice. "Well Hannah, I guess not. I can be a complete and utter arsehole sometimes".

You may consider me a little sappy, but I was smitten! I had never been a part of his entourage; not even on the fringes! I was a first-year under-graduate, and he was a final-year graduand! So how did he know my name? This was *Henry Burden*, whose social acceptance and inclusion many students eagerly coveted, to hear his outspoken and satirical take on the day's news or hall-of-residence gossip! He was not just *talking* to me; he actually *knew my name*! *Henry Burden*, openly showing genuine humility to a mere fresher, whose best and only friend was an anorexic Quaker called Chastity, an undergraduate in Food Science, who extolled the health benefits of drinking her own urine at least once a day.

But after 'breaking the ice', neither of us was able to risk embarrassment by prolonging the conversation and saying anything else we might regret. We were aware of each other's presence at the concert a week later, and we both failed to take the initiative to talk or have a slow dance at the end.

It was several weeks before Henry approached me in the canteen at lunchtime to ask me out on a date. In my nervousness, (and on Chastity's advice that Henry would consider me a sluttish crack-whore if I said "yes" too quickly), I declined his offer.

As I rebuffed him, I felt like I was having one of those nightmares where you can't physically respond quickly enough to a prevailing threat: having leaden legs when trying to evade a pursuing tiger; or pulling on a parachute's unyielding ripcord as you hurtle towards the ground. Only this was something I *wanted*; something I *dreamed* about, and my voice was letting me down.

I watched Henry's face change from nervous anticipation to red-faced embarrassment. Yet still I couldn't correct the glaring mistake by turning my unintended "no, thank you" into a truthful and sincere "yes, I'd love to". Then, worse still, I failed to offer any explanation for my refusal, to let him down more gently. I wasn't even able to concoct a fictitious excuse; and I could hardly divulge the real rationale: Chastity's puritanism. What would he think if I did? "Sorry Henry; I can't go out with you the first time you ask me because you'll think I'm a tart. You'll have to ask me again after a respectful period has passed; perhaps in a few months; or maybe a year would be more virtuous?" He would have considered me a complete idiot!

I was shocked by the apparent apathy of my rebuttal. As if in slow motion, he turned and walked away, his head bowed down dejectedly. And I just stood there floundering, blathering like a blithering idiot, panicking as I looked from Chastity (who was solemnly nodding her approval), to the retreating figure of Henry, to Chastity and back to Henry, in rapid succession.

"*No!*" I screamed; my hands outstretched like an angler proudly estimating the length of her catch. "...*Of course, I meant yes!*" Henry stopped, turned slowly towards me, smiled and nodded tentatively, then retreated. The crisis had been narrowly averted.

Chastity and I never spoke again. I heard on the grapevine that she now has four children by four different men, and lives on sporadic alimony and child-support allowances. So, she represented less chastity than promiscuity.

We chose the cinema as the venue for our first date, where the latest reincarnation of Thomas Hardy's "Mayor of Casterbridge" was being shown. The alternative option had been a visit to a pizza restaurant to take advantage of a 'two-eat-for-the-price-of-one' offer. I remember swaying

Henry's choice in favour of the film. I had already achieved at least two precedents of appearing foolish when talking to Henry; so, I reasoned that it was safer meeting him at a place where conversation was prohibited.

Afterwards we went for a drink at a pub, where I risked there being a third occasion of saying something daft. We animatedly discussed to what extent is the film's protagonist, Michael Henchard, the master of his own downfall? I gave examples of Henchard's flawed character, condemning him as a man in whom little merit could be found.

I was struck by Henry's ability to acknowledge my critique, whilst expressing alternative perspectives. Henry explained that whilst Henchard's original sin and impetuousness had been the main causes of his ultimate downfall, he possessed some admirable qualities. I realised that the causes of Henchard's fate were not as unambiguous as I had supposed. I feared Henry would see me for the intellectually incompatible fraud I felt myself to be, and that he wouldn't want to see me again.

I needn't have worried. It was Henry who suggested a follow-up date, and soon we were enjoying that collaborative sense of being that requires contact with one's 'special other' several times a day by phone or text, if not in-person. We became so mutually in-tune that we often experienced 'engaged' signals when we phoned each other...not because we were talking to someone else, but because we were dialling each other at the same time. Synchronicity!

I started to realise that the *real* Henry was very different to the one everyone thought they knew. The irony of our respective perspectives on Henchard's personality were not lost on me. For someone who was so sensitive to the complexities of Henchard and his interaction with the folk of Casterbridge, Henry had little concept of social anthropology in his own life. He had been indoctrinated by an antiquated public-school system that promoted academic and sporting achievement, but failed to develop its progenies' ability to understand, accept and interact with those from more utilitarian backgrounds, whose own experiences and priorities were different: intelligent, but not necessarily academically intelligent.

Henry was merely camouflaging the chink in his armour, believing strongly in the adage that attack is the best form of defence. He was completely unfamiliar with the experiences of those who were from different backgrounds, who represented the majority, and he supposed their tougher lives meant that they were street-wise and sufficiently intuitive to see and expose his relative naivety. So, he mocked unrelentingly the absurdity of anything that didn't conform to his entrenched ethno-centrism. His acerbic comments were his protective armour.

In time, I realised that most people didn't find him witty at all. I was maturing quickly, and fathomed that it wasn't cool for irreverence to be feared; very few people wanted to be like him.

I suppose that having recognised others' perception of Henry as a boorish bully, some may consider that I shouldn't have developed our relationship at all; but I was intrigued. I knew that he was increasingly broody, not because he was ruminating about everything that was wrong with other people and the world, but because the false persona and tirades were difficult to sustain.

My mission was to make him understand he must be himself; that pretending to be someone else was not making him happy or popular; in fact, quite the reverse. It was not going to be easy encouraging him to drop the self-assured arrogance and bluster that had attracted me to him in the first place. I was confident that if Henry was sensitive enough to reveal to me the disguised qualities of a man like Michael Henchard, he could learn to recognise that compassion is a positive and amiable attribute, not an affliction to be disguised. I wanted others to see Henry as I saw him.

CHAPTER 3

Friday, 2.00 pm

Standing outside on the driveway, Hannah convinces me that the windows are shut, the iron, cooker and hob are off, and the front, back and garage doors I've checked three times are still locked, and haven't miraculously sprung open as soon as I turned my back. She claims I have an obsessive-compulsive disorder, which I strenuously deny.

We climb into the Volvo, (minus caravan, but more about this shortly), buckle our seat belts, and simultaneously exhale long breaths. We sit motionless for a few seconds, independently wondering what it is that we've forgotten to do.

"Did I unplug the toaster?", I ask.

"Yes".

"The computer?"

"Yes".

"Cancel the milk?"

"Yes, Henry".

Another a few seconds of reflection..."Let's go".

"Right".

We're off! I start the engine and turn from the driveway and onto the road, before having to stop again.

Before setting off for Cornwall, I spent the previous hour shoe-horning our clothes and equipment into the car, and our Cannondale bikes onto the roof-rack. The result would have impressed a quantity surveyor, but not necessarily the local constabulary. Our ten-yard journey has caused the precarious internal load to teeter before toppling noisily. I am now wearing a pair of my wife's knickers on my head, and a bra in my lap.

You may wonder why we haven't hitched the caravan yet, having packed into our car as much of our gear as the laws of weight and balance permit. Well, the restrictive covenant in the deeds of our house specifically states that we must not lower the tone of the neighbourhood by keeping any commercial vehicle, vessel, caravan or motorhome on our driveway or at the kerbside. Apparently, an Englishman's home is not his castle, after all. This requirement was further reinforced by a Mrs Cavil from the local residents' committee, or as Hannah and I prefer to call them, the Dormouth Neighbourhood Taliban.

Nearly a year ago, one of their number, if not Mrs Cavil herself, spotted the Volvo's tow bar within minutes of our arrival at our new home. It fell to Mrs Cavil, one of the Taliban's activists, to post an excerpt from their monthly newsletter through our letterbox. It stated unambiguously and unequivocally:

"The Pines district of Dormouth is proud of its awards for being aesthetically enviable. Residents are encouraged to avoid risks to its outstanding reputation by:

1. Placing large, ugly encumbrances such as motorhomes, boats, caravans, and other trailers into storage.

2. Parking work vans elsewhere. Trades personnel working on your home may park on the road if absolutely necessary, for periods not exceeding 8 hours during the working week and daylight hours only.

3. Employing a gardner, if horticulture is not your thing.

4. Regularly painting window frames and cleaning your panes.

5. Putting out your bins on the morning your refuse is due for collection, and hiding them away again immediately afterwards, or at least the same day.

6. Not siting a hired skip for more than 24 hours; and if you must do so at all, ensure that it is appropriately lit. One of your neighbours had an unfortunate accident recently when she cycled into one during the hours of darkness, and dislocated her knee.

N.B. The Committee is able to supply you with an approved list of landscapers and window-cleaners if you require."

Honestly, had we known of this overbearing, prescriptive, patronising interference beforehand, we wouldn't have bought the bloody house. *"Large, ugly encumbrances"*? It affronted *my* sense of decency seeing Mrs Cavil's elephantine backside, waddling down my driveway.

Hannah and I discussed this matter in earnest: should we make a stand? What could they do about it if we ignored their rules? Would we become social outcasts? Did we care, if that was their attitude? Could we be sued for breach of contract? What defences could we offer? Contravention of our human rights based on their prejudice and discrimination against a minority group: caravanners! After much deliberation, we took the path of least resistance and scoured the internet for storage sites that same afternoon.

One of the downsides of organising something in a hurry, is losing one's objectivity. As you have already seen from my meticulous planning of this trip, I like to prepare well in advance of any given commitment. I don't take kindly to having the will of others thrust upon me suddenly and unexpectedly. That was the position in which that busy-body placed us, on a day when we were moving into our new home, and had many other more pressing priorities to consider.

Being forced to choose a caravan storage site so quickly, meant that I was neither able to shop around to find the most competitive price, or find a location nearby that could accommodate the caravan that same day.

Having re-packed our equipment, we've travelled fifteen miles east of our home in Dormouth on the south coast of England, to the working farm on the outskirts of Ashbourne, where our 'van is stored. It's ideally situated if we are heading for a holiday location to the east; not so great if we are destined to go north, west, or southwards across the English Channel to France! Today we are travelling to Cornwall, one hundred and sixty five miles to the west.

I am now driving along the narrow country lane leading to the farm, long grasses whipping our extended wing mirrors. I should be experiencing a warm glow at the thought of six days' rest. Instead, I have the sinking feeling I always get when facing the prospect of returning along the same lane, caravan in tow, and facing some defiant lorry driver, who resolutely refuses to move over or reverse.

Anyone who is not used to reversing a caravan will know that it is an appendage with a will of its own. Reverse with the car's steering wheel deflected left, and the trailer will turn right, and vice versa. Totally illogical! Even if you get it right but forget to 'relax' the turn, the trailer will suddenly jack-knife. I try to memorise where the lay-bys are situated, in the hope that on the way out with the caravan on the back, I can pull in to let traffic pass, so that I am not forced to reverse.

I've turned from the lane and we're heading down a rough track that leads to the storage area. The Volvo is bouncing in and out of rain-filled potholes, coating the carefully waxed paint-work in a syrup of liquefied cow shit, urine and mud.

Having parked and removed the caravan's cover, hitch-lock and wheel-clamp, I install the battery and gas bottle. Hannah unloads the clothes, food, and some of the accessories, and installs them in the 'van.

When I look inside, the sight of Hannah cheerfully froo-frooing the soft furnishings makes me start to relax. Many women really do possess the art of making everything look and feel better, just by primping, plumping, preening, and symmetrically redistributing objects to their own liking.

Now it's my turn to impress her by demonstrating my masculine power and ingenuity, and perhaps get her in the mood for some hot trailer lovin' this evening. I raise the corner steadies with the crank, and lift the cast iron wheel clamp into the boot with a grunt. I am enjoying putting on a show. It's the modern-day equivalent of impressing your woman by wrestling a mammoth to the ground, just using a lasso and upper body strength. Next, I reverse the Volvo, bringing the tow bar in line with the caravan's hitching eye.

"It never ceases to amaze me how you always manage to judge that so perfectly", she coos.

I bristle with pride.

"Yes, you haven't hit the caravan for a couple of years now".

Slightly deflated, I remove my shirt to recapture the mood.

"Oh, and you've reduced the size of your moobs since you cut back on the beer!"

I hesitate. Do I draw attention to her use of the word "reduced"? No. That would merely reinforce her view that my man boobs still exist; albeit in a more diminutive form. I shake off her dubious compliment, and bend down towards the hitch.

"It's so much quicker to lift it on to the tow bar", I say in a slightly deeper voice than normal. I grasp the plastic-shrouded galvanised steel in my hands. Lifting seventy-five kilograms when the axle provides a fulcrum is not as arduous as one might think, but Hannah doesn't need to know that.

"Henry, no! Remember the Lake District?"

It's too late. Searing pain flashes across my lower back. I'm locked at right angles, and any attempt at movement, even to the slightest degree in any direction, makes me scream like a referee's whistle.

"Stay still love; I'll get the Neurogen gel".

"I'm going nowhere!" I yell, but the effort of shouting causes my postural muscles to go into a spasm that feels like I've been cleaved in two. I collapse onto all fours on the stony floor, whimpering like a puppy. Within seconds I feel Hannah's hands expertly manipulating my lumber region. So much for hot trailer lovin'. How humiliating!

"Should we call off the holiday darling?" she asks, genuine concern in her voice.

"No way!" I reply defiantly, relieved by the rapid effect of the cold, high-dosage of Cyclobenzaprine that Hannah has massaged into me. Grabbing the Volvo's tow bar, I haul myself, gingerly, to my feet. Standing like a question mark, I point and issue instructions to Hannah.

"That needs to go there. The green thing needs to pop up, so we know the caravan is attached to the car properly. The stabiliser needs to come down, Then, the wires..."

"Henry..." she says. She doesn't need to say anything else. There is no admonishing frown or raised forefinger. Women can impart their precise feelings, intentions or desires, merely by stating your name. That one word, although uttered calmly and quietly, was imbued with all the menace of a cobra standing above its prey, just before it strikes.

"Yes dear", I whimper submissively, crawling onto the back seat of the Volvo to try to find a position which will alleviate the strain on my aching back.

Within minutes, Hannah is adjusting the driver's seat. "Right. I've tested the lights and checked all around. Everything is set and ready to go. I'll drive us there. It'll give you a chance to relax".

"Ugh", I groan, agitated at the thought of Hannah guiding our beloved Volvo and twenty thousand pounds' worth of caravan out of the farm, down that infernal lane, and onwards to the furthest reaches of the Cornish coast. But I'm too weak to protest. Sometimes you're in too much pain to fight. I position my head between the two front seats, so I can keep an eye on things from the back.

"These potholes really are quite easy to avoid, darling. You just have to slow down a bit, that's all".

I begrudgingly admit that Hannah is expertly manoeuvring between the dips and gullies caused by the hydraulic action of large, tractor tyres and a bitterly cold and wet winter.

"Yes, well don't get too complacent. Remember you've got to tackle the lane next", I say mischievously, before the possibility dawns on me of damage being wrought to the caravan's fragile pine-framed, foam-in-filled, ply, aluminium and fibreglass walls.

"More haste, less speed", Hannah says, smiling. "It'll be fine".

As soon as we turn from the farm track onto the lane, a boy-racer emerges from a blind bend ahead of us. He's travelling at least forty miles per hour faster than is appropriate to the circumstances. What was once a small, white, two-door Peugeot, is now a burnt orange, skirted, flared-wheel-arched, pulsating stereo speaker on absurdly low-profile tyres. It is still fitted with its original, one-litre engine; but what the owner hasn't told his insurer is that it has been re-bored and turbo-charged to produce an additional fifty horsepower.

Seeing that his way ahead is blocked, he brakes hard and lifts the hand-brake to bring the rear end around slightly, having just cleared the bend and a turn-in big enough to accommodate his little car. I wonder how many times he has practised that manoeuvre at night in supermarket car parks. I wait for him to reverse back into the passing space. He stays put.

My eyes dart to Hannah. How will she deal with this? Will she reverse the car and caravan? Our last passing point was several hundred feet behind us. Hannah appears unfazed. She is still smiling her relaxed smile, continuing towards the Peugeot at a steady and unprovocative ten miles per hour.

"But how are we going to…?"

"You'll see", she says calmly and confidently, still smiling.

Hannah halts, the Volvo's bonnet now forty feet

from the Peugeot's. I peer ahead from my place between the two front seats. The other driver's head is shrouded in an oversized black hoodie. His hands are gripping the top of his steering wheel. I hear the rasping of his exhaust as he blips the throttle of his pocket rocket.

"Hannah, perhaps you should reverse."

"Patience darling". Hannah raises her hands upwards for the benefit of our adversary in a manner that says, "What can I do? I'm a woman. I can't possibly reverse! You'll have to let me through".

But the yob stays put. The ungripping and regripping of his steering wheel becomes more intensified; the pulse of his rasping engine quicker and louder.

"Hannah, what if he forces his way past? There's no room. Think of the car and the caravan. Please reverse!"

"Patience", she sings.

And suddenly, all becomes clear: Just visible above the hedgerows beyond the bend is the cab of a five-ton Massey Ferguson at full tilt, rapidly approaching the stationary and obscured Peugeot. Careering around the bend, the tractor's driver has no time to brake before demolishing the back of the Peugeot, its heavy-duty mud tyres raking upwards onto the little car's hatchback boot. It comes to rest, pressing the Peugeot's chassis into the tarmac. I look again at Hannah. She is still smiling sweetly.

The farmer is now blipping his throttle, trying to reverse and disengage the chassis of his tractor from the Peugeot. The forward and backward motion of the leviathan gives the appearance that it is mating with the helpless little car, and shunting it out of our way. The tractor's front tyres take hold, and with much grinding of metal and tinkling of glass it reverses and disentangles itself.

Unable to open his door, the Peugeot driver angrily climbs out of a window, his puce face showing more frustration than my own when I once tried to teach Macbeth to 'Remedial English Literature, Class 3'. He struts and frets, hopping from foot-to-foot and stamping the ground. Forming his fingers in the shape of handgun turned 90° from its natural firing position, he jabs it aggressively in the direction of the farmer who is still in his cab. He is swearing, issuing insults and threats in a pseudo West Indian patois that makes him sound like the hardest gang-banger from South Central L.A. But I can now see that beneath his hoodie he is a rather typical, skinny, spotty, white lad, aged no more than seventeen years. In fact, he looks very much like one of the students from my remedial Shakespeare class.

I have always been a firm believer that in the face of conflict, you should act in a way that de-escalates the upward continuum of aggression, before it results in violence. I get myself into more than my fair share of conflict, so it is very necessary to have a strategy in case things go too far. Revenge can be taken later, when everyone else has calmed down and forgotten about it.

That is what I think the farmer is doing now. He may not feel the need to take retribution in the future, but by remaining in his tractor, and not engaging in a heated, face-to-face argument that would in all likelihood result in fisticuffs, allegations of assault, the involvement of the police, an arrest, an appearance in court and a criminal record, he may be trying to let the youth burn himself out, merely by responding calmly.

Unfortunately, in this case, it's not working. If anything, the youth is getting even more animated, perhaps interpreting the farmer's lack of engagement as indifference to the damage he has caused, or more likely, as fear. There is a certain kind of person who, on assuming that another is frightened of him, will behave with even greater bravado and braggadocio, not less.

Eventually, the tractor driver slowly unfolds himself from his cab, and climbs down onto the road. Six feet six inches of man-mountain towers above the irksome youth for a second, before simply handing over a dirty piece of paper, presumably with his insurance details scribbled on it. Without pausing for conversation, the farmer gets back into his tractor, re-starts his engine, and continues along the lane towards us, mounting the grass verge, to make room for us to continue.

As we pass each other, he doffs his filthy, moth-eaten hat, and greets us with a broad Wessex "Aft'noon". Hannah smiles sweetly and raises a hand in acknowledgement.

Passing the wreckage, I lock eyes momentarily with our conquered adversary: He is open-mouthed and speechless, clearly unable to comprehend that he is the architect of his own circumstances.

Approaching the bend, I check the extended wing mirrors and watch him slowly re-animate. The youth is straining his gaze towards the tractor; but all that is visible is dust kicked up in its wake. As he starts to swivel round towards our retreating car and caravan, we negotiate the blind bend before he can note our registration number.

I lie on the back seat for several minutes, observing the reflection of my wife's face in the rear-view mirror. She is still smiling that sweet smile, her shoulders occasionally rising and falling, unable to suppress her mirthful giggles.

"You knew that was going to happen, didn't you?"

I blurt out accusingly. "You knew that the tractor would not be able to see the car beyond the blind bend!"

"I don't know what you mean darling".

She maintains her quiet satisfaction. I don't know whether to feel intimidated by this woman's suddenly exposed capabilities, or be deeply in awe of her power to annihilate, without getting her hands dirty. One thing is for certain: Bad back or no bad back, her cool, calculated cunning is a real turn-on.

I nod off as soon as we join a dual carriageway; the Volvo's V5 diesel engine producing a low, flat, muffled hum that promotes sleep.

CHAPTER 4

Friday, 4 pm

After what I assumed to be a few minutes dreaming of Hannah the Warrior Princess in high-cut, red, string-sided bikini bottoms, a red and gold basque, and wielding a broadsword, I stretch and yawn loudly. Her earlier unambivalent and assured confidence in the face of conflict, has made quite an impression on me. I notice that Hannah is observing me in the rear-view mirror.

"You must have been out-for-the-count for an hour. How is your back?"

The rest has done me the world of good, and I had completely forgotten about my injury. I am more concerned about the aching strain in my trouser department caused by the erotic dream I've just enjoyed. I cover my ardour with Hannah's mother's travel rug, before realising that I'm making a wigwam. I quickly turn onto my side before Hannah notices.

"Oh, I'll grin and bear it", I reply manfully, adjusting my gentleman's area and disentangling my strangulated testicles from rucked boxer shorts. I change the subject: "How are we doing on diesel?"

"A quarter of a tank. We'll stop at the next service station. It'll give you a chance to stretch your back".

"Yes" I reply, wincing convincingly. "It'll be very painful, but I'll try". I look up at her reflection in her rear-view mirror with doleful eyes.

Soon the engine note is dropping, as Hannah changes down through the gears. I hoist myself up on to my elbows, and look out of the side windows at the diminishing rush of fencing and hedgerows on one side, and Armco barriers on the other. Before long I can pick out individual leaves of the bushes of a slip-road. Flora and fauna are soon replaced by gaudily coloured signposts proclaiming relaxation and replenishment at a main route rest area, but don't advertise the over-inflated prices that punish travellers who have little choice of an alternative, until they are inside the building and reach the head of a queue to pay.

"Here we are", Hannah says cheerfully. "And this one has extra long bays for lorries and caravans. We'll stop, stretch our legs, have a cup of tea in the café, then refuel on the way out".

"We can make our own tea", I blurt out, appalled by the prospect of paying over the odds for a lukewarm, Styrofoam cup of insipid brown liquid, instead of brewing our own with our on-board stash of Twining's, fresh milk, kettle, teapot, mineral water and china mugs.

"No, a change of scenery will do us good. We can uncouple and lock the caravan, and drive over to the building to save your back". I know better than to argue.

Hannah manoeuvres our train through narrow, traffic-calming twists and turns, over speed humps and onto a wide expanse of tarmac. Lines of juggernauts and trailers are parked nose to tail to our right. A cacophony of noise broadcast from an incalculable number of music radio stations competes with the roar of traffic on the adjacent motorway and the low, electrical hum of refrigeration units. "So much for this centre of rest and recuperation for the weary traveller", I say, but Hannah ignores me.

Lorry drivers stand around, shirts off or in dirty vest tops, hands plunged into trouser pockets or holding large, steaming mugs; cigarettes permanently clamped in whiskered mouths. Some sit on upturned buckets, playing cards at makeshift tables. One or two are boiling beans on single burner gas flames. Most of them seem sullen and morose, forced to observe the rules governing the hours they are permitted to drive before being required to stop and take a break. Those who run the gauntlet risk being spot-checked by the Ministry of Transport or police, and losing their licences and livelihoods. They follow us with their brooding, hostile eyes, so that we observe the demarcation between the spaces occupied by professional drivers in commercial vehicles, and those intended for mere pleasure-seekers with caravans or campervans. It looks like a motorised, third-world favela.

With some relief I spot the six elongated bays that have been designated for use by cars with caravans. There is only one bay occupied: the sixth. Hannah pulls into the first.

I look out of the side window from the back seat of the Volvo, and see the pot belly of a man emerging from the caravan in bay six. He is only wearing mustard and ketchup-stained shorts, white socks and open-toed sandals. His man boobs hang heavily in a wide, flaccid 'W' over a gut which sags pendulously over a belt that seems to cut deeply into his abdomen. A proliferation of greasy, sweaty, knotted pubic overflow carpets the area around his umbilicus. A woman follows him, presumably his partner. She is as anorexically thin and wan as he is morbidly obese and florid.

They obviously feel some affinity towards us as fellow caravanners, because they are walking over to our car as we are getting out of it.

"'Ello there. Ma name's Barry, 'n' this 'ere is the

wife, Maureen. We're down from Ber-min-gm".

He clamps the remainder of his half-eaten cheese-burger into his mouth, wipes his hand on his belly, and thrusts it forwards for Hannah to shake. Hannah, adeptly pre-empts this awkward moment with perfect timing, avoiding contact by occupying both of her hands picking up the nearest, heavy object...which happens to be me.

"Oh, lovely to meet you both. Sorry, I've got my hands full at the moment. I'm Hannah, and Henry here has managed to put his back out".

Barry and Maureen are standing together, peering down at me. Barry is noisily chewing his burger with his mouth open.

"Oh dear", they chime simultaneously in a nasal, Brummie whine.

A wet speck of chewed, sesame seed bun, beef, lettuce, onion and tomato lands on my nose. "Let me give you an 'and", Barry offers, and is already positioning himself to hoist me from the Volvo.

"No, really, thank you. I'm feeling better! Hannah and I can manage...please!" I beg. But he has already grabbed me under both armpits and is dragging me headfirst from the back seat, my face pressed against his damp, salty stomach.

He deposits me unceremoniously onto my feet. His suppurating stench is smeared over my face, oozing into my nostrils, mouth and into the back of my throat. I have no handkerchief, and wiping my face on my shirt will only double the opportunity for bacteria to thrive, and for the fetor to proliferate. Barry's body odour is that kind of primeval miasma that flourishes even after a boil-wash with soda crystals.

"There we are. Snow trouble 'enry. Backs loike to

be exersoyzed. Walk ararnd a beet an' you'll be as roight as rain in nah toime".

I feel tempted to comment on the irony of being lectured on the benefits of exercise by a man who looks as though he has never entered a gym in his life. Instead, I feign appreciation, and glance once more at the monstrous belly with which I have now, regretfully, become so intimately acquainted. I climb into our caravan to wash my face in warm soapy water and douse myself in Jo Malone, not that it will do any good.

Unbeknown to me, Hannah has uncoupled the 'van from the Volvo ready for our short drive to the restaurant building. The cantilever effect of my body weight being applied aft of the caravan's axis point, sends it crashing down onto its Alko chassis. I fly through the shower room door, coming to rest at the bottom of the cupboard, where I scream again in renewed agony.

Barry's body heaves into view in the doorway, blocking the daylight.

"Ya wanna unwoind ya rear steadies before ya get into the caravan 'enry; especially when you 'aven't got sufficient nose weight to counter-act adverse tilt. Ya lucky not to've damidged ya sub-frame tekkin a chance loike tha'".

Hannah reads the situation perfectly and pre-empts my torrent of highly personal, verbal abuse by manoeuvring herself between him and the door to our 'van.

"Thank you, Barry. If you wouldn't mind winding down the corner steadies, whilst I see to Henry".

Hannah seems to have got rid of him - sunlight suddenly fills the caravan.

"Why did you uncouple the caravan? Why did you have to engage that idiot in conversation?" I whisper

Hannah through clenched teeth. Why can't we just keep ourselves to ourselves?"

She ignores my questioning and remains outside the caravan, beckoning and urging me to get to my feet and move towards her.

"Slowly darling…that's it. We're going to leave the caravan here to drive over to the restaurant because of you back, remember?"

I grasp the inside of the door and raise myself gingerly. I am now standing upright inside the doorway of the caravan. Hannah moves backwards which I interpret as her signal that it is safe to exit. As I transfer my weight to the outside step, I feel the ground shake as the caravan crashes back down onto its front jockey wheel. I close my eyes and stand still for a few seconds. When I think everything has come to rest, I open them again. As soon as I do so, I hear the tinkling of glass as our carefully stowed, now dislodged glassware, dominoes itself to destruction. Barry didn't lower the steadies.

"Oh, deary me, Henry". It's Barry. He's back again, the metal winder in his hands. He's tutting and shaking his head, making his chins wobble. "I couldn't wind the rear steadies down until the van was level again…*obviously*".

Hannah can feel the heat coming off me, so she again takes the initiative and shepherds Barry back towards his own caravan. "Thank you, Barry. I think we can manage now", she says sweetly.

"Oh well, if you're sure 'annah", he says. "We'll be off then".

"Thank you, Barry. Thank you, Maureen. It's been lovely to meet you both. I do hope you have a lovely holiday". The words suggest sincerity, but there is something in Hannah's tone which suggests otherwise.

I glance at her sweet, smiling face, and notice the twitch of a nerve in her right eyelid that tells me unequivocally that Barry has even managed to upset the one person I have always believed it impossible to annoy. I move closer to Hannah, one arm draped around her shoulders as we watch and wave, smiling through gritted teeth as Barry and Maureen pull away from their bay.

CHAPTER 5

Friday, 5.05 pm

Forty minutes have passed, allowing us to stretch our legs, and refresh ourselves with exorbitantly expensive tea and cake. We've replenished our fuel tank, and I'm feeling better, although no more fragrant. I've taken over the driving duties and we're accelerating down the slip-road to re-join the motorway. I'm confident that the black Jaguar XJ looming in my offside wing mirror will move from lane one to lane two, which is clear.

Now I know I am obliged to give way to traffic on the major road; but when you're trying to join a fast road with more than three tonnes of car and caravan on a short slip-way, you need to join at a speed that is consistent with that of the vehicles on the main road. In this case, our optimum merging speed is sixty miles per hour.

The 'give-way' markers at the end of the slip-road are fast approaching, and I am still accelerating, my offside indicators blinking my intention to move to my offside. I urge the Jaguar driver: "Go on, move out. It won't kill you, move out!" But he resolutely remains in his lane, stubbornly refusing to budge. "Lane two is clear!" I shout, but he still shows no sign of deviating from his course.

Hannah casually glances over her right shoulder. "How do you want this to end?" she asks calmly.

"I want him to *move*...it's common courtesy to *move*!"

"It's his right of way darling".

I bury the accelerator pedal into the rattan mat, our vehicles steadily converging on a relative bearing, a four-second countdown to disaster. I make my move. It's now or never!

With a sharp, right-hand tug on the steering wheel, I swerve into the Jaguar's path, forcing its driver into a reciprocal, Mexican-wave-like shimmy into lane two. I keep my eyes on the road ahead, unconcerned with the forced, evasive manoeuvre of the other car. My peripheral vision tells me that it has drawn level with us to our right, so I defiantly raise the middle finger of my right hand.

For several seconds, the Jaguar remains level with our Volvo. Its driver hasn't overtaken, sounded his horn or attempted a retaliatory swerve to unnerve me, which is what usually happens after I teach another driver a lesson in roadcraft.

On this occasion, the on-going lack of any rebuttal feels all wrong. I look to my right, joyfully anticipating the sight of my adversary's apoplectic, indignant rage. But occupying the front seats of the Jaguar are two, burly men who are regarding me without expression or movement. They are dressed uniformly in black roll neck sweaters and Ray-Bans. Their shaven heads and clipped, black goatee beards and 'taches, make them look like Russian Mafiosi assassins.

My right middle finger withers like a penis exposed to a British winter. What had been a proud, one-fingered salute, calculated to be the last word in a titanic battle of wills, morphs into a surreptitious scratch of a non-existent itch on the tip of my nose. I dissolve into my seat, nervously glancing in my extended offside wing mirror to see the Jaguar smoothly decelerate, cross from lane two to lane one, and tuck into a following, unseen position behind my caravan.

It's like the scene in Jaws when the great white shark slips beneath the water. You want to believe that it recognises defeat and is turning tail, but you sense that it is still out there somewhere, and will be back for more. Beads of sweat are bubbling on my top lip and forehead.

"Well done love", Hannah says sarcastically. "You showed 'em what for!"

I check the wing mirrors periodically. After a few minutes, my focus on the road behind us becomes less intense: The Jaguar appears to have disappeared. Maybe it exited at the last junction. Was there a last junction? Yes, I'm sure there was. Wasn't it for Alphington? I start to relax, and breathe a sigh of relief, my heart beat slowing to just ninety beats per minute.

"You know it's still there, don't you?" Hannah says.

I again check both wing mirrors with renewed angst for the Jaguar; or even just its shadow...nothing. "Are you sure?" I ask, unconvinced.

"Well, I guess we're just about to find out".

I look ahead to the unsynchronised strobing of hazard lights of stationary vehicles ranked at the tail of a jam that blocks progress in all three lanes. I'm feeling unsettled, and release pressure on the accelerator to slow down and give me more time to think. If the Jaguar is still lurking back there, its occupants intent on doing me mischief, should I join lane two? I would be flanked by potential witnesses in lanes one and three; people who may provide some form of deterrent to my would-be attackers! I remain in lane one where I have an escape route afforded by the nearside hard shoulder.

Hannah observes my barely disguised anxiety

and smiles. "You know, you really shouldn't start these fights. For the sake of a few seconds' self-indulgence, they cause you such stress. Why do it if you worry about it afterwards? It can't do your blood pressure any good at all. Or your heart."

My eyes are so fixated on the offside wing mirror, I fail to notice that I've trundled too close to the rear of the lorry in front of us. I can't seek sanctuary on the hard shoulder even if I want to because I now have insufficient room to undertake the truck.

My wing mirror is quickly filled by the Jaguar driver who is advancing on foot towards my side of the car. I swallow nervously as he approaches my door. What is he doing with his right hand? He's reaching into his inside jacket pocket, that's what he's doing! My heart is thumping again, and I've forgotten how to breathe. This is it! This is how it happens! All those news reports of road rage incidents that end with the senseless murder of a (relatively) innocent motorist, who merely asserted himself with a bully, unaware that he was, in fact, a psychopath! How would this end? A bullet between my eyes, then Hannah's? A homicidal maniac would surely not allow a prime witness to my murder to survive, so that she could...what was the dubious expression...*finger* him? What have I done? What was I thinking? It was, after all, his right of way back there. Oh God! What a senseless way to die!

He taps on my side screen. I tentatively press the button to lower the window, just as he is removing a black object from his inside jacket pocket. "What can I do for you?" I offer innocently, before realising that my unintentionally patronising tone is more likely to annoy him than lead to a cessation of hostilities. He opens the black object, which to my relief is a wallet, and holds a silver and blue-enamelled badge in front of my eyes.

"I'm with the police. What do you call what you did back there?"

Relief floods my veins. "Er, erm...evasive action officer. A fox ran out in front of me on the slip-way...I had a split-second to decide whether to run it over and kill it, risk damage to my car and caravan, or subject you to the relatively mild inconvenience of changing lanes. As you are aware, I chose the latter".

The policeman puts away the badge, and places both hands on my doorsill. "You and I both know there was no fox, sir". He glances at the reduced but still substantial load in the back of the Volvo. "In fact, my boss managed to see everything from his seat in the back of our car, and reckons I should stick you on...I mean...report you for dangerous driving. And I don't remember that particular hand signal in the Highway Code. But I've decided to let you off with a stern warning."

Realisation and relief that Hannah and I are not about to be murdered, that British police officers are not likely to beat me up in front of other motorists, and the fact that he has already decided not to take the matter any further, all have a restorative effect on my bravado.

"Oh, does he now! Well, you and your boss clearly don't expend enough energy catching criminals, if you've got time to go around harassing innocent motorists". I look at Hannah for moral support, but she is looking out of her own side window. "In fact, why don't you tell your boss to speak with me himself, if he feels so strongly about it?"

The policeman removes his hands from the sill and stands up straight. "That won't be necessary, sir. I'm happy to let this pass with a few stern words of advice: Moderate your behaviour, distribute your load between car *and* caravan, and give way to traffic on the major road. Convictions for overloading and dangerous driving carry obligatory disqualification from driving and a hefty fine, to say nothing about the abusive and insulting hand signal".

"Thank you, officer. This is why we pay our taxes, is it? So that policemen can swan around in expensive cars intimidating other road users, dispensing road traffic advice, rather than catching burglars, rapists and murderers?"

Fissures are beginning to show in the officer's thick veneer of patience, honed after many years of having to deal with people expressing alternative points-of-view. I feel I have made my point, and now it's time to back off.

"It's precisely *because* we have more pressing business to attend to that I'm not going to nick you. Sort your load out, drive more carefully, and don't be offensive", he says, maintaining his professionalism through clenched teeth, clearly resisting his natural instinct to hoick me out of the car by my throat and rough me up a bit, before taking me onto the other side of the nearside Armco for a good kicking.

I watch him retreat in a straight-armed march to the Jaguar, his chin buried in his chest. I smile with satisfaction at having won the overall victory, and glance at Hannah who is staring forwards, her jaw set. "You don't have to have the last word, to have the *last* word", I say to her triumphantly, but she ignores me.

The traffic suddenly starts to move, and soon we're barrelling along at sixty miles per hour in lane one. I am suddenly aware of the dark shape of another car alongside me in lane two, matching our speed. I look to my right, and see the two plain-clothed officers in the front seats of the Jaguar, looking impassively at the road ahead. The rear nearside, black privacy glass rolls down, revealing an all-to familiar face glaring disapprovingly at me: the British Prime Minister! The principal minister of our sovereign; the head of our democratically-elected government is shaking his head at me in contempt. The tinted window rises, and the Jaguar accelerates away.

"I think *that's* what you call the last word", Hannah says dryly.

CHAPTER 6

Friday, 7.15 pm

We left the house over five hours ago. The sat-nav display tells us that we're forty-seven minutes from our destination, but I'm not 'counting my chickens' just yet.

I'm aware of the unreliability of these devices; I don't mean that they're particularly prone to breaking down at inopportune moments in the 'blank-screen' sense. I don't think my Navig8 XL has ever let me down in that way. I mean that after weeks or even months of efficiently guiding me to or from a particular location, it can suddenly mislead me, often at a critical stage in a journey. This deception undermines confidence; as when a life-long friend is discovered bending the truth or telling a white lie, and can no longer be fully trusted.

You never know when it's going to happen. Months may pass, unquestioningly following the sat-nav's bidding, arriving at your destination along the route it said it would take you, at precisely the estimated time of arrival. It can even alter its route mid-journey according to the ever-changing traffic conditions ahead. But the first time it orders you to cross a raging ford, or into a labyrinthine network of narrow, one-way roads, alleys, car parks; or sends you on a circuitous tour of identical buildings in an out-of-town industrial estate, you will never fully trust it again.

My mind's drifting because Hannah is still giving me the silent treatment after my contretemps with the British Prime Minister's close-protection team, who probably *were* armed with guns, after all.

Suddenly I'm stirred from my reverie by the slight urgency detectable in the sultry and seductive voice of my Navig8 XL, which I've secretly named 'Suzie'. Suzie rounds her vowels and annunciates with old-fashioned, BBC clarity; although her sentences are slightly disjointed: minor delays in delivery caused by the computer sequencing individual words from its lexicon. She also places emphasis on certain syllables, as though highlighting the most salient features and instructions.

"At the...*round*about...take the...*first*...exit", Suzie coos, albeit slightly robotically.

I want to obey her commands, but something doesn't feel quite right; what she is telling me to do doesn't sit well with my innate sense of direction. Memories of a recent, Suzie-related incident in Trafalgar Square three months ago, still make me cringe with embarrassment, although the counter-terrorism police were eventually fairly forgiving.

She repeats, "At the...*round*about...take the...*first*...exit".

I look at where she's sending me, and then at the other options. The tarmac of the road she is urging me to take is pristinely black; but it looks like it is heading south-east, and therefore in completely the wrong direction for the north coast of Cornwall. The one leading from the second exit is paler and sprouting weeds; entry is prevented by large red and white plastic barriers.

"At the...*round*about...take the...*first*...exit".

But the second, prohibited road seems so familiar from our previous forays to the Atlantic shoreline...and isn't that roofless, windowless building in the distance the husk of the Roadside Chef where we ate tasteless cheeseburgers on our way to Porthcredy Bay last year?

The third and last option is obviously wrong, because it is the reciprocal of the first exit, and leads to the north-east to Newquay.

"At the...roundabout...take the...first...exit."

Drivers in the line of traffic behind me noisily vent their frustration by sounding their horns, awakening in my mind in even starker clarity the nightmare of Trafalgar Square.

"AT THE...ROUNDABOUT...TAKE THE...FIRST... EXIT!" nags Suzie.

I feverishly scan ahead for other prompts to tip the balance of choice; to validate or negate Suzie's command. The arms of diggers rest on the teeth of their buckets like Hannah when she's exasperated with me, stands with a hand on one hip. Is it my imagination, or did Suzie's just challenge me in her slightly robotic lilt?

"WELL? ...WHAT...ARE YOU...WAITING...FOR?"

I reluctantly decide to take the first exit, and release the clutch pedal quickly. We lurch forwards onto fresh tarmac. We're flanked on either side by traffic cones, mounds of earth, plant, 'keep left' and 'men at work' signs; a falsehood as there's no one there, working or otherwise. Navvies are like Santa's elves - when do they emerge to do their work? Considering roadworkers are rarely ever seen doing any actual roadbuilding, surely this major construction of a new A-road couldn't have been completed in just one year?

I watch in despair as the road we took last year diverges so quickly away from us that within seconds it is at right angles to our course. My internal magnet keeps nagging me we should be heading due north-west, and I don't need reference to the sun to tell me that we're heading south-east as I previously suspected! Why do I always feel so compelled to follow Suzie's edicts, even when

I sense they are wrong? I just hope she tells me to stop or change course before we reach the English Channel, or I might just drive us to a watery grave.

I check the estimated time of arrival on Suzie's screen: 50 minutes. Surely that confirms it? We've lost three minutes, so we *must* be heading in the wrong direction! Hannah must also have noticed it, because she's speaking to me again, albeit icily, for the first time in a quarter of an hour.

"If you're concerned, why don't you turn off the sat nav, and refer to your map?"

"My *map*?" I repeat mockingly, laughing at the very suggestion that a technologically sophisticated, twenty-first century man such as I, would stoop to rely on such an archaic navigational aid. "I've spent the best part of one hundred pounds on state-of-the-art equipment, Hannah! It not only shows me, but *tells* me where I need to go and how long it will take to get there. Yet *you* want me to resort to the same method of orientation used by Christopher Columbus over five hundred years ago?!"

"Yes, well *he* discovered a new continent; but *you* can't even find the well-established north coast of Cornwall. So, stop fannying about and get your map book out".

"No...but...I...the...it...we... *One hundred pounds*, Hannah!"

She sighs. "Yes, Henry and the map book was *free* with last Saturday's edition of The Times. It will show you a schematic of the area's roads, which you can use to navigate back towards Godleven Point. A *map book* can't order us in the wrong direction!"

Hannah sounds so rational, yet I'm torn between her and my loyalty to Suzie; and the fact that I don't want to face any proof that I've wasted one hundred pounds. I know Hannah will robustly insist on map-reading, and that if she manages to put us back on-track, I'll never hear the end of it.

"Yeah, well, it's buried in the back under a mound of stuff", I say unconvincingly, as Suzie's display flicks up a new ETA: 53 minutes.

I glance at Hannah who is glaring at me with narrowed eyes and mouth. "You and I both know that's a lie..." she says, accusingly, "...because it fell out of the glove box when you pulled out your driving licence and insurance certificate to show the Prime Minister's body-guard".

I continue in silence for another three miles, hoping that a sign will divert us back onto our original course. I check Suzie's screen: 1 hour.

"OK...look for a lay-by, and I'll stop to consult the map book", I say in resignation, switching off Suzie's loudspeaker.

"No, keep driving", Hannah says authoritatively, removing the book from the glove box. "I'll navigate, and you concentrate on finding a suitable road on our right-hand side. We've wasted enough time. Look for signs for a bigger town like Langston, which is roughly to our west. Once we've got to Langston, we'll head north-west-wards towards Godleven".

I don't know whether she's being efficient and assertive, or controlling and patronising; but either way I am niggled by the helpless feeling of being lost. Aren't driving and navigating supposed to be *my* domains; isn't it an innate, instinctive male trait that harks back to the days of hunter-gathering? I can't criticise her logic, so I scan every road sign for any reference to Langston.

"There!" I say, noticing a junction ahead and to

our right.

"No, darling. That road is unsuitable for heavy goods vehicles, which may mean there's width restriction. It's best if we find another road".

No sooner has she said this than we pass another road sign for the next right turn:

"WIDTH RESTRICTION. ARTICULATED & LARGE VEHICLES USE NEXT EXIT, ½-MILE".

"Aha..." she says, "...I thought so".

"OK, well done Hannah", I say begrudgingly. She picks up on my tone.

"Oh, Henry. It's not a competition, darling", she says. "Take the next available right turn".

I follow her direction. Within a mile, we're already picking up road signs for Godleven Point, and the ETA is starting to count downwards again on the sat-nav. I should be pleased to be back-on-track, but I'm quietly simmering, incensed by Suzie's infidelity.

"Just update your sat-nav by downloading it with the latest information before we go on another road-trip", Hannah says, twisting her knife in her moment of victory.

The diversion to Langston is passing without incident. In fact, we're thoroughly enjoying this leg of the journey, not having seen this region of Cornwall before. Why are events often more agreeable when they're spontaneous and unplanned? My natural instinct tells me that they shouldn't be so. Dinner parties often lack vibrancy when one's had time to build expectations of how scintillating the conversation and company must be, or how fine the food, drink and venue.

The annual disappointment of Christmas Day bears testimony to this anomaly: After months of saving, planning, and demonstrating the logistical adeptness of a military commander, you succeed in seating three generations of your own and your wife's relatives in a modestly-proportioned dining room for lunch. But Uncle Tom, who started boozing on whiskey at 8 am, won't eat his dinner because you forgot to buy cranberry sauce. His profanities are offending Grandma Ethel, and the more she protests, the louder and more obnoxiously self-justifying he becomes.

The brood of kids, each lavished with gifts representing a quarter of a month's salary, are whining and bickering about whose turn it is on the latest generation of PlayStation. Hannah is a tearful and bedraggled bundle of nerves, incensed that the turkey is drier than the English summer of 1976, despite following the cooking instructions by ramming half a pound of butter between the skin and the flesh, and basting it every half an hour. The vegetables are colder than an arctic winter within minutes of leaving the pans, and she doesn't think she's made enough gravy. She loses all sense of proportion, convinced that by serving imperfect food she has single-handedly destroyed everyone's Christmas, and that *surely* that is the reason why everyone is behaving like a complete-and-utter twat!

No, this foray into the north Cornish countryside isn't like that at all. Our final approach to Godleven is completely unplanned, but it's bypassing the overcrowded tourist routes. The roads are clear, undemanding, and leading us through a rolling, emerald landscape. With the windows rolled down and the wind in our hair, we even feel like we're on holiday, finally!

Suzie tells us that we're just nine miles and twelve minutes from Godleven Point. It's time to phone ahead to the camp-site and ensure that everything is set for our arrival. Hannah obliges, as I'm still driving. It is approaching 8 pm. Last arrivals must be through the gates before 8.30 pm.

"Ah, hello there. Are you the warden? Oh, that's a lovely name Trevor!"

"'*Trevor*' is a lovely name?" I say in a half-whisper. Hannah slaps my left thigh and transfers her phone to her left ear.

"I'm Hannah Burden; just phoning to say we're only ten minutes away, and inquire whether there are any last-minute check-in arrangements". There is a twenty-second pause during which I can hear the distorted chatter on the other end of the line before Hannah replies. "...Er, yes, that must have been my husband Henry...Yes, he *is* still coming too. Would you like to speak with him? ...Oh, I'm sorry about that...Oh, ok, I'm *very* sorry about that."

"What's *that* supposed to mean?" I ask.

Hannah raises the palm of her free hand to silence me or threaten me; I'm not sure which. "Oh, I'm sure he didn't mean anything by it".

"Didn't mean anything by *what*?"

This time Hannah's flat palm moves rapidly closer towards my face. I instinctively flinch, yanking on the steering wheel and causing the caravan to shimmy, which I manage to control after three, heart-stopping oscillations.

"Jesus Christ, Hannah!" I shout, my pulse racing.

"Ok Trevor...I understand...yes, indeed...completely. We'll park in the lay-by and report our arrival at reception. See you shortly...yes...'bye for now". She terminates the call and stares at me in silence.

"What am I supposed to have said?" I ask, glancing at her with the injured innocence of an accused child.

"It's not so much *what* you've said; more a case of *how* you said it…Trevor obviously has a rather sensitive disposition. You appear to have offended him with your…directness".

"For God's sake Hannah. I spoke with him to confirm a booking, not invite him out for dinner. There's nothing wrong with a forthright, businesslike attitude. False sincerity is a form of deceit – why don't people ever respect my honesty?"

"Human nature isn't like that. You're more likely to win hearts and minds…*and* get what you want…if you try to be a little more…*empathic*. Soften them up before you demand service; or as in this case, "*the largest and quietest pitch furthest away from any people, animals, communal areas, vehicles and roads*", and demanding a "*substantial discount for an early reservation*"".

I bury my chin in my chest, sulking, concentrating on the road ahead.

Hannah breaks the silence, "Ah, here we are: next on the right…"

CHAPTER 7

Friday, 8.10 pm

I've turned right as directed, driven a quarter of a mile up a driveway, and we're approaching the gates to the 'Adults Only' campsite. As we get closer, I see that the entrance is shut, and the exit is open. We roll to a halt.

"What's the matter?" Hannah asks, looking up from the article she's reading on The Ecological Charity Project.

"Look!" I say indignantly, drawing her attention to the gates. "We phoned ahead just as Trevor requested, presumably so he would know our arrival time and make last-minute preparations…like opening the bloody gate to let us in!"

"Well maybe he got way-laid. He must be very busy - remember, it's half-term. It's just him and his partner Pat running this place according to the 'Getaway Guide'. Anyway, the exit gate is open; drive through that".

I select first gear and we move onto the opposite side of the driveway, crossing the threshold and entering the park via its exit gate.

Without warning, a black Dodge Ram 1500 Big Horn, trailing an eight-metre long, 'fifth-wheel' caravan, bears down on us out of nowhere. Presuming that he requires the lengths of two rugby pitches to stop, I stamp on the brake pedal to avoid a head-on collision. The load I reconfigured after my disagreement with the Prime Minister's protection officer shifts, and rains down on us from behind.

Although imminent danger has been avoided, the other driver draws attention to my fault in this near miss by sounding his four-tone, one hundred-decibel horns for five seconds. Now that might not seem like a long time, but it is four and a half seconds longer than any reasonable person would consider necessary, unless the user wants to scare the living daylights out of those in his line-of-fire, whilst inflicting on them immediate, temporary hearing loss.

As I raise my hands from my steering wheel to cover my ears to uselessly muffle the unnecessarily pro-longed din, I see caravaners fall off their deckchairs in fright. One septuagenarian lady suffers an involuntary body spasm, causing her to throw her tray of full tea mugs over her shoulder; a male is clutching his chest in what appears to be the preamble to cardiac arrest, if not the real thing. The tea-thrower recovers, yet the horns are still blasting, and I can lip-read her shouting, "WHAT THE *FUCK* IS THAT?"

"Sshh!" I say pointlessly in the direction of the black-tinted windscreen ahead, as if this will mute the deafening blast. But then I realise that the only way of silencing it is by reversing out of his way, through a nar-row gate…and I've explained how difficult that can be, es-pecially under stress.

I lower my driver's side window, select reverse gear, and focus alternately on the reflections in the off-side and nearside wing mirrors. My head has the appear-ance of a metronome. I periodically poke my head out of the window to check our separation from the gate. We slither falteringly backwards to the left and right like a confused snake, and continuing the reptilian analogy, I nervously flick out my tongue to lick my top lip, because everyone knows that this is conducive to enhanced concentration.

Satisfied that I've left sufficient room for this bully to pass, I stop and apply the handbrake. The truck's driver revs and moves forward, pulsing the throttle of the V8. The ground vibrates, blurring my vision. As it passes, a hairy, heavily tattooed, unfeasibly muscled arm unfurls from the driver's window. It is attached to a pug-faced Neanderthal in a white vest top. An adult female is sitting next to him, sneering at me. Then, not for the first time today, I am subjected to a fellow motorist's lack of appreciation for my assertive driving style. Only unlike the admonishing glare of our Prime Minister, Early Man closes the fingers of his right hand, which he jerks up and down in the vertical like he is shuffling a deck of cards. He does so with such violent force that I think better of responding with one of my withering and devastatingly witty snubs.

Writhing, seething with uncontained fury on the truck's back seat is an apoplectic, shaven-headed, eight to ten-year-old mini-version of the driver. I assume they are father and son. Whilst they are wildly animated, my own body feels paralysed by these assaults on my senses; only my eyes seem to be working. I watch the yoblet's mouth form unambiguous shapes that proclaim me to be a "COMPLETE, FUCKING WANKER!" as they pass and roar away from the exit.

"Are you ok?" Hannah asks eventually. She touches my arm tenderly. "It's alright darling. They've gone now. We'll check-in, set up, and enjoy a chilled Chardonnay within the hour...Henry?"

I shake my head, not blinking; a pool of drool forms inside my bottom lip and threatens to spill over onto my shirt.

"Henry, what's the matter?" Hannah says anxiously. "You look as though you're having a stroke...Talk to me!"

My head-shaking intensifies, and I flick dribble over my shoulders like a slavering Saint Bernard. "The kid in the back of the truck. He said...he said..."

"Oh, take no notice of him darling! What does *he* know? A precocious kid on holiday with his chav parents! Anyway, it looks like they've packed up and left for good. So at least you won't have to worry about another confrontation".

"No, it's not that...he said..."

"Well...yes...and I know the Prime Minister's look of disapproval suggested you are one too, but really Henry...*I* know you're not a wan-...well, I don't deny that you have your moments...but a *complete* one? No!"

"I'm not talking about what the kid said! I meant *Trevor*...he said...he *assured* me that...don't you *see*, Hannah? Don't you *realise*?"

Hannah ponders; after several moments her eyes widen, betraying sudden understanding: *There was a kid in the back of the truck.* We slowly face each other, before turning our attention to an enclosure equipped with swings, slides, see-saws, a roundabout, climbing frame, sandpit, and a collection of seats fashioned in the shapes of elephants, lions and tigers mounted on heavy-duty springs: an area reserved exclusively for unrestrained and noisy enjoyment by...*Children*!

Elbows clamped to his sides and hands raised, a man is trotting towards us. He is pursing his lips and shaking his head, and doesn't appear happy to see us. I switch off the engine and lower my window, as he skips to a halt and places a hands on a hip. I see from his name badge that we are about to meet Trevor de Cristifaro, in-person.

"You were supposed to wait outside until I opened the gate! Departures first, *then* arrivals! You'll *ruin* my system. There could have been absolute *grid*-lock! Honestly, I turn my back for *half* a minute and..."

"Never mind about that. This is supposed to be an Adults' Only site. Why are there kids here?" I wave a hand in the general direction of the play area.

Trevor is now standing beside my car with both his hands on his hips in indignation. He is wearing a khaki t-shirt and matching shorts that are at least two sizes too small for him. Sitting in my car, my eyes approximately level with his waist, the tightness of his trousers unfortunately leave little to the imagination. And is that the lower parabola of a testicle poking out from under the hem? I feel nauseous.

"It's *not* an Adults' Only site during the half-terms, Easter and Summer school *holidays*. We can't afford to exclude *families* during periods of peak *demand*. It *says* so on the *booking* form!"

"Well, I'm not staying here for six days of purgatory. We'll find one that is!"

"Suit yourself..." he says with a shrug that shows that he couldn't care less; "...but you *won't* find one, and your payment is *non*-refundable. Turn around via the *round*about over there."

He's pointing towards a large circular expanse of grass, where four adolescents have abandoned their game of football in favour of boisterously fighting over whether Tottenham or Arsenal is the best team.

"Henry, he's right. We won't find another adults' site at this late stage, and we've had a long journey. They're scarce at the best of times. It's 8.15 and will be getting dark soon. Come on; let's make the most of it".

My eyes narrowed and jaw set, I consider the options:

1) Forget the holiday; turn around and head for home, risking the wrath of the neighbourhood Taliban by leaving the caravan on the driveway for the night, and returning it to storage tomorrow.

2) Finding a farmer's field, and living frugally off a twelve-volt leisure battery.

Losing two-hundred pounds, and the prospect of surviving a week without running water, mains electricity or TV, is too much to bear.

"Come a*long*; chop-*chop!*" Trevor says impatiently, clapping the fingertips of his right hand into the heel of his left. "You're risking absolute traffic *mayhem!*" He nods in the direction of a car which is slowly advancing towards us and the exit gate. "Tut, tut, tut...de*cision* time!" he goads.

"Ok, we'll stay", I say magnanimously. "But I booked a full-service, hard-standing pitch in the quietest area of the site".

"So you *did*..." Trevor replies coldly, as though remembering the conversation with distaste; "...and very in*sis*tent you were too. Park over on the left and let these vehicles out...then go and wait for me in the re*cep*tion office so that I can check you in".

I do as I am told, whilst Trevor goes to the exit gate and effusively waves goodbye to the leavers.

"He showed some balls, talking to you like that", Hannah says.

"Yes, he did..." I say peevishly; "...in more ways than one."

I've been standing at Trevor's reception desk for five, tedious minutes. A couple from Hull are ahead of me in the queue, pondering whether they should extend their two-night stay to three nights. Having finally decided that they will book the extra night, they spend an additional two minutes securing Trevor's agreement that the cost of the third night will be reimbursed, should they change their minds by 9 am tomorrow morning. It appears that the reason for their forward-planning is their concern that neither they nor the two-person tent they purchased for one penny shy of thirty pounds will withstand a third night, should the weather become less favourable. They leave, chuckling as though they've won the lottery. Thankfully, I am the next in-line.

"I think I can help you to keep this short, Trevor" I say in a brisk and business-like tone that proposes *if you save me time, I'll save you paperwork.*

His eyes rise slowly from his computer screen; I can tell immediately that reducing bureaucracy and breaking protocol are not high on his agenda.

"Records are kept for a *reason*, Mr Burden" he replies prissily. "If you'd arrived any *later*, I would have asked you to return in the *morning*" he adds, looking at the clock and pointing to a sign prominently displayed on the wall behind him:

"THE 3 PM TO 8.30 PM DEADLINE FOR ARRIVALS IS STRICTLY ENFORCED. THANK YOU FOR YOUR CO-OPERATION".

It is now 8.25pm. I take a deep breath, for the sake of expediency. "Yes, yes, quite rightly so...but I can assist you by confirming that all of the details I originally submitted on the booking form are correct and unchanged: I haven't moved house, re-married or changed my phone numbers. We're still only staying for six nights, and I accept that the site accepts no responsibility if my property is lost, stolen or damaged. My wife Hannah and I still identify as female and male respectively, and we don't have any children with us. There we are; simple! So, you show us to our pitch without any further delay, allowing us an end to a long and tiring afternoon, to set up our caravan and enjoy chilled Chardonnay before bedtime. What do you say?"

Trevor's eyes return to his screen, unmoved: "Mr. Burden. Please confirm the spelling of your names, dates of birth, and details of your car, caravan, and registration number..."

I watched as the clock's larger hand clicked inexorably towards half past eight. I was petrified that he would suddenly end the unnecessarily laborious process, and require us to return at 3 pm tomorrow.

But 8.30 pm came and went, and I felt a surge of unexpected relief when he continued verifying our booking, before summarising the contents of a site map, leaflets about the centre's rules, facilities, opening and closure times, local amenities, transport links, tourist office, and suggested excursions to places of local interest.

I trudge back to Hannah and the car at 8.40 pm, feeling an inch shorter, a stone heavier, and more round-shouldered.

I slump into the driver's seat. "What on earth have you been doing in there?" Hannah asks testily. "It'll be getting dark soon, and I don't like the look of those clouds". She points towards the sky; but I lack the energy to even raise my eyes and follow the direction of her finger. Frustration has overloaded the circuitry of my central nervous system, forcing it to perform a partial shutdown. My mind and body have defaulted to a power-saving mode that protects my operating machinery, rendering me incapable of performing anything other than basic functions.

"Come along", she says, "let me take over from here. You look washed out, and you're going to need your energy to set up the caravan". We swap seats.

CHAPTER 8

Friday, 8.45 pm

Hannah brings our rig to a halt alongside our allocated pitch, which jolts me awake. I must have dropped off for a few minutes, but I feel strangely refreshed. We inspect the uneven patch of grass and level, gravelled concrete. Most caravaners know how irregular ground requires careful deliberation about the optimum orientation of the 'van, and judicious use of at least one, wedge-shaped levelling block. I booked a hard-standing pitch to avoid this faff. The grass is our adjacent recreation area.

We must consider movement of the sun relative to the windows, door, and any place suitable for positioning a table and chairs: Parking with the nearside door facing towards the east, and siting external furniture near to the door permits easy access to the 'van and the enjoyment of your breakfast in sunshine. Facing the nearside westwards may be convenient and preferable if you enjoy a glass or two of vin blanc whilst watching the sun setting, and maintaining accessibility to the door.

I peer up and scour a darkening, monochrome sky that obscures all evidence of the sun. The cartographer who drew the site's map omitted the usual compass that points towards 'north'; nor was the presence of the Atlantic considered worthy of representation. Both features would have enabled me to determine in which directions the sun will rise and set.

I cast my eyes around the field in vain, attempting to identify a pattern to how others have set up their 'vans to maximise sunlight. Couples are pottering about, either collecting clothes from lines, shaking their heads that they haven't dried, or sitting in jumpers and coats, determined to read their books outside in the failing light and dropping temperature as night approaches.

"Why don't you just ask someone darling?" Hannah asks, quite reasonably.

I mutter a reply. I don't want to risk being drawn into some tedious conversation with someone who will insist on talking to me for the rest of the holiday whenever he sees me. I trudge off down a sandy trail nearby, seeking higher ground to pinpoint the location of Godleven's beach and the sea.

Henry can be so infuriating. He'll spend half an hour finding 'north' relative to our pitch, rather than ask someone or check Google Earth. Still, it will give me peace to unpack the car, wind down the stabilisers, tidy the 'van, open a bottle of wine and start making a salad supper, unhindered. Henry can decide when he returns whether he wants to move the caravan with the tow bar facing inwards instead of outwards; then he can attach the fresh and grey water waste containers, fill the chemical toilet, and connect the electricity supply.

I think I was explaining how I recognised Henry's positive attributes, and decided to fix him rather than dump him...

As I got to know him, I realised that he was not the wit and raconteur I had first considered him to be. He used humour as a weapon, often savagely humiliating others whom he feared would criticise or mock his unfashionable bourgeoisie. His best form of defence was attack. But I remained attracted to him because he always showed me the sensitive, considerate and vulnerable side that no one else was allowed to see. Changing him was not going to be easy: Old habits die hard.

As university life and education transformed me from a mawkish girl into a confident woman, I noticed our university peers developing into self-assured, critical-thinkers too. Henry's sparring partners were starting to detect the motivations for his behaviour. They were becoming increasingly immune from his digs about their accents, clothing, tastes in music, or their leftist leanings, and they were either ignoring him or vilifying him. Henry's tactic was backfiring, and he knew it.

This was a seminal moment not only for Henry, but for our relationship. He was at a crossroads: He could either dig in his heels and carry on regardless, or realise that we had all moved on emotionally, intellectually and socially, and change his ways. If he hadn't chosen the latter option, I would have walked.

I suppose it helped that this sea-change in people's attitude towards him occurred in his third and final year of his degree. He had to apply himself to his studies for his combined honours in English and Law, instead of playing rugby, drinking, and going out on dates with me. Ensuring that he kept on track of his essay submission deadlines, revision, and writing two, ten thousand-word dissertations, reduced his exposure to social gatherings, and limited his opportunities to rub people up the wrong way.

Henry became outwardly business-like and sensible; not surprising considering the amount of work his subjects required. His resolution to knuckle-down and excel impressed me. When I later reached my final year, I felt embarrassed admitting to Henry that my dissertation was entitled, "*Sociological insight in comic books of the 1980s*". Henry's were, "*Should the defence of 'Diminished*

Responsibility' be extended, and how far should human rights influence any change?"; and *"How were nineteenth-century novels first received by their contemporary public and academics, and how has our understanding of these novels changed from a modern-day perspective?"*

He got a high, upper second. I got a first. Where is the justice in that?

When Henry graduated from Bristol University, I had completed my first year of three. My future was mapped out for me for another two years, but Henry was still considering where he would complete his one-year, Legal Practice Course (LPC), his next step if he was going to become a lawyer. It wasn't because he hadn't secured a place at a university. He had received firm offers from Bristol, Cardiff and Bath. It was because he wanted to simultaneously work part-time in a solicitor's office, gaining valuable work experience, earning whilst learning. Knowing Henry as I do, it was also a way of getting a taste of legal practice, so he could re-evaluate his own future if he didn't like it.

There were so many other Law graduates from good universities with first-class Law degrees, Henry found firms offering such internships fairly thin on the ground. After much searching, he found one in Cardiff, one in Bristol, and none in Bath. He joked that if both firms rejected his application, then at least he could apply to be a barista while he studied to become a barrister.

I was delighted that Henry was planning on remaining in the south-west, and if not in Bristol itself, at least within a commutable distance. Although he didn't say so, I felt this was a sign that he saw a future with me; although I suppose it could have been that he wanted to remain close to his family, who lived in Gloucestershire.

Henry researched and attended open days at the

two practices who were advertising placements: 'Wainwright & Associates' in Cardiff was a small, friendly firm specialising in Family and Criminal Law. It had five solicitors and two paralegals based on the fifth floor of a grey, high-rise office block. Built in the early 1960s, and suffering from terminal concrete cancer, it had an open-plan office subdivided by shoulder-high partitions offering no sound-proofing or privacy from adjacent desks. A small meeting room seating four could be used for confidential conversations. A single toilet was available for employees and clients. The hand basin also provided water for a kettle that had to be switched off manually to avoid a Vesuvian eruption of boiling water that would result in victims seeking a rival law firm to sue 'Wainwright & Associates' for damages. An under-powered desktop fridge, just big enough to hold a one-pint bottle of milk and a packet of Hob Nobs, kept its contents just one degree below the prevailing room temperature. The carpet was tacky underfoot, and the polystyrene ceiling tiles were broken, missing, or featured brown staining that betrayed an historic leak from the pipes or toilets on the floor above. They were offering Henry seven hundred and twenty pounds per month for twenty hours' work per week, for eight months.

'Uppingham & Snook Advocates of Bristol' on the other hand was based in a fashionable district in a four-storey, Palladian mansion in a crescent of identical, adjoining buildings of honey-hued stone. Each edifice was crowned with an architrave featuring classical scenes in deep relief, supported by two, soaring Corinthian columns. Its highly glossed, black front door was reached via a step from the pavement that led clients through an ornate black and gold-topped gate and railing, and along a flagstoned garden adorned with vibrant, seasonal blooms in ornately carved stone urns.

It was equally opulent inside. Original architectural and decorative features in plaster, marble and oak were tastefully and expensively complimented by reproduction antique furniture, exquisite rugs, carpets, wall-papers, and heavy, swag-tailed drapes. The chandeliers, wall and table lights complimented each other in style, all featuring tentacles laden with Swarovski crystals.

All members of staff dressed alike: Whether you were male or female, junior or senior, everyone was immaculately coiffured, and attired in tailored, conservative trouser suits, and dark shoes. But perversely, despite the firm's obvious wealth, 'Uppingham & Snook' weren't offering Henry any salary at all for the same commitment of his time.

I remember wondering which would option he would choose; how strong were his principles? I still didn't know for sure whether his improving social skills were a by-product of his preoccupation with his final examinations, or a consequence of a budding emotional intelligence. He was...*is* a fascinatingly complex character, and I enjoyed being a spectator. Yes, he was...*is* an intelligent, articulate, amusing man, and always loving towards me. But I needed to understand him completely to love him completely in return.

Oh, here he comes now...

"I got lost".

"Yes, I was beginning to wonder where you were, darling".

"I headed off in the wrong direction...wasn't until I reached a school, church and pub I realised that I was heading inland, not towards the beach..."

"Klutz. Don't get too settled. You've got to decide whether to move the caravan", Hannah says, passing me a flute of Prosecco, which has been chilling in our caravan's fridge since 3 pm.

"No, no, I've had enough for today. We'll leave it just the way it is".

"Well, just the electrics, TV, water, drainage and toilet to do then!"

"What have *you* been doing all this time?"

It's then that I notice Hannah has tidied or stored everything away, and prepared a dressed salad. She places her knuckles on her hips in a way that challenges me to say anything other than make an apology.

"Sorry", I say meekly, setting down my glass and going outside to finish setting up the caravan. I return fifteen minutes later to enjoy the wine, my meal, and what's left of the evening relaxing in front of the telly with Hannah. It's been a long and not particularly relaxing day. I fall asleep in the middle of the ten o'clock news.

CHAPTER 9

Saturday, 6.45 am

I prefer to wake naturally, nestled in Hannah's arms; passerines chirruping a soft, sweet soundtrack; bright sunlight spilling through chinks in the window-blinds and skylights.

Sadly, this is not the reality. Hannah is still fast asleep. We are both naked and her long, smooth limbs are wrapped around my legs in a manner that usually provokes early-morning love-making. She has managed to commandeer ninety percent of the bed's width. I'm teetering on the edge, muscles tensed to maintain balance and avoid falling into the narrow gap between the bed and wall, where I would inevitably become wedged... just like the last time. She's wrapped the duvet completely around her torso, leaving me exposed. The heater is synchronised with the alarm clock. The absence of a pulsing tone and the presence of frigid air tell me that it is not yet 8 am.

Her head is resting on my right shoulder. Her face is no more than a couple of inches from mine, chin pointing upwards, mouth gaping like Edvard Munch's "The Scream". But Hannah isn't screaming, she's snoring. Loudly. Every other intake of breath sounds like the last remnants of water gurgling down a plug-hole. She straightens her back, and belches in my face. It's not the minty toothpaste I tasted when I kissed her goodnight; but a primeval, acidy effluvium from the salmon, dressed salad, pickles and wine that have been digesting in her stomach. I recoil, stretching my neck like a drowning man seeking air above the water's surface.

She stirs; I freeze, waiting for the one movement that will allow my opportunity to reclaim territory. But she grips me tighter, groaning and smiling, moulding herself to the shape of my body, as though burying herself deeper in a pleasurable dream.

Her face is now pressed against mine, mouth still open. As the minutes tick by, her viscous drool oozes onto my cheek, drips gelatinously onto my chest, and collects in a pool in the hollow beneath my Adam's apple.

I slowly turn onto my right side to face her, and gradually move her head onto my upper arm, before raising my left leg to hook around hers, regaining valuable inches. She moans, frowns, still asleep, but yields. I gather some folds of the duvet, pulling them towards my upper body. It's not sufficient to cover me, but it's enough to blot the saliva that has dribbled from my chest onto the mattress. I wrap my left arm around her slim waist, and she turns to her right, and I cuddle like her like we are two spoons in a drawer. Taking my opportunity to free my arm before it goes numb, I steal back more duvet and glance at the clock: 6.55 am. It's too early to get up, and I think I've found a position favourable to re-couping more sleep. I kiss her back, and drift away...

"GET THEM SAUSAGES WHAT WE BOUGHT YES-TERDAY WILL YA? OIL COOK 'EM UP WITH THESE EGGS 'N' BOYCUN!"

My eyes flash open widely in shock, like I have gulped milk with bitter-tasting lumps in it. I'm instantly awake, stock-still, glancing nervously around the caravan's compartment to identify the source of a voice so loud and grating it sounds as though its owner is close enough to touch. Hannah is still fast asleep. I look at alarm clock: 06:59. I've managed just a four-minute nap.

A muffled female voice responds, but I can't hear what's she's saying.

"NO! THEY'RE INDER FRIDGE SECTION!" the man replies rebukingly, still shouting. Then, *"OOH, THAT WERE A LOVELY SHOWER! OI RECOMMEND EET BEFORE EVERYONE WYKES OOP & THERE'S A QUEUE AT THE BLOCK!"*

My eyes are narrowing, brows furrowed, lips pursed. I recognise that voice, but can't easily place it: flattened vowels; inappropriate use of verbs and relative pronouns; irritatingly lacking in emotional intelligence, or any intuitive social etiquette to grasp that people are on holiday and may actually want a bloody lie-in. Then it dawns on me...*Oh God, it can't be! Barry and Maureen!*

I twist away from Hannah towards the nearest window and gently ease up its roller blind. Peering through the gap, I scan the adjacent pitch for evidence to corroborate my fear, or put my mind at rest.

I can see an old, light blue metallic, Rover 75 estate. Well that doesn't help. I didn't notice their car at the service station yesterday – I spent most of the time bent double, on my hands and knees, nursing my back. Next to it is a white touring caravan of a similar vintage with the words 'Elddis' and 'Odyssey' respectively emblazoned above and below the front nearside window. I didn't have cause to register the make and model of their caravan either yesterday. I recall that it was white, but most of them are. I focus on the movements within it.

Smoke is rising from an open skylight, and my nostrils flare when I detect the heavenly fragrance of frying bacon. Crouched down, I shift from the bedroom to the living area of our 'van to try to get a better view though the hedge that separates our pitches.

Then I see him. Barry scratches his matted gut with his right hand, then reaches into his Y-fronts to adjust himself. He accompanies this action with facial contortions that betray high levels of concentration, then unmitigated pleasure at having found optimum distribution of his tackle in its confined space. He's holding a burnt wooden spoon in his left hand with which he's conducting a '70s glam rock song being played on a CD. Sniffing the fingers of his right hand, he turns down the corners of his mouth, which suggests that his early morning shower was not as thorough as it could have been. He moves away from the window and out-of-sight. I collapse against a kitchen cabinet, head lolling on my shoulders.

Hannah yawns, stretches, turns over and slaps the duvet next to her, checking for me. She frowns on finding the empty space and opens her eyes, re-focussing on me when it dawns on her that I'm sitting on the floor in the living area, my hands cradling my jaw to support the weight of my head.

"What's the matter Henry? What are you doing over there?"

"You're not going to believe who are our nearest neighbours."

"Henry, have you been drinking? Of course I know: the Pumfreys...Cressida, Norman, and their daughters Poppy and Rosie".

"No, not our neighbours back home. Our neighbours now, here, next door, over there". I jerk my thumb backwards and over my shoulder in the direction of the neighbouring pitch.

Hannah gathers the duvet around her naked body, kneels on the bed and lifts the lower edge of the blind to squint through a gap. "I can't see anyone. Just a caravan. You tend to get them at these places, Henry."

"OH FOR FOOK'S SAKE, MAUREEN. OIVE BROKEN THE FOOKIN' YOLKS ON THESE EGGS. OIL AVTA START AGAYYN, UNLESS YOU WONEM?"

"BARRY, NER! YOU KNOW I CANT EATEM LOIKE THAT. CHUCKEM INTHA BIN 'N' START AGAYYN!"

"OIVE ONLY GOT 1 LEFT, 'N' THE BOYCUN 'N' TO-MARTUZ IS REDDAY!"

"SEE IF YOU CAN BORRA SOME FROM NEXT DOOR. THE SOITE SHOP WONE BE OPEN YET".

Hannah slowly releases the blind, and we freeze, listening to thumps and crashes caused by Barry leaving his caravan. He slams his door, before walking over to ours. My eyes swivel in their sockets, checking the blinds are covering every gap; to ensure the entrance door is locked. All is secure! I slowly move onto my hands and knees to noiselessly crawl back into bed, where I plan to ignore the imminent door-knocks, and attempt to sleep for at least another hour. I freeze again, right in front of the door as I hear the crunch of Barry's footsteps on the gravel square that forms our pitch. He raps on the door with a happy cadence that takes no account of the fact that we could be asleep, it being only 7.03 am.

"'ELLO CAMPERS! ANYONE IN?"

He knocks louder this time, and my heart misses a beat when I hear the 'zip' of the door's window-blind rapidly rolling up into its spindle, its flimsy retaining spring unable to withstand the vibrations caused by Barry's ham-fist. I peer upwards with dread at the small square window, and watch Barry using his sausage-fingers to wipe away condensation caused by his breath.

"WELL OI NEVVA! ISS YOU, HENRY! WHAT YA DOIN' DOWN THERE? BACK STILL BAD IZEET?"

He gives me a little wave.

"WELL, 'URRY OOP. IT'S BRASS MOONKEYS OUT 'ERE! YOU GOTNEE EGGS OICAN BORRA?"

CHAPTER 10

Saturday, 8 am

The alarm clock sounds and the heater clicks on. Hannah and I have barely spoken ten words to each other for just under an hour. Numbed by our rude awakening, we've showered, dressed, and now we are staring blankly at Breakfast TV on BBC1 whilst sipping tea and eating bacon butties. We would have had a 'full English' breakfast, with poached eggs, sausages, hash browns, beans and grilled tomatoes, but we sacrificed our full punnet of eggs to get rid of Barry as quickly and politely possible. You can't have a 'full English' without eggs. It's just not done.

It could be any work-day morning, but this is the first day of our holiday. We feel heavy with disappointment. If things don't get better, the holiday is going to be a struggle.

"We've got to look on the bright side", Hannah says, picking a piece of gristle from her teeth with her forefinger and thumb, and inspecting it before flicking it into the kitchen sink.

I look out of the window at the dark storm clouds, just as the first rain drops start drumming on our roof. "Mmm".

"Holidays are what you make them".

"Yeah".

"Where's that list you made? Today is probably going to be a poor-weather-day".

I reach into a drawer and retrieve the plan I formulated on an Excel spread-sheet, handing it to Hannah who then spends a few moments considering the day's possibilities.

"Well, we can go for a drive to the coast and have a picnic in the car; or visit a museum or art gallery; or have a swim or a game of badminton at a local sports centre, then reward ourselves with a pub lunch; or we could have a lazy morning here until the weather clears, just reading our books, playing cards or a board game."

Neither of us are too enamoured by getting back into the car after the previous day's journey. We glance at the book shelf at our pristine, newly purchased hard-backs. I reach for them, and we spend a few moments reading the fly covers.

Hannah looks up from her book to see what I'm reading. "Oh, my friend Geraldine and I saw the film they made of that. It was really good. But I thought it was a bit predictable".

I nod but avoid eye contact and remain silent, not wanting to encourage her to say anything that could give away the plot. Hannah starts reading her novel, and I turn to the first page of my own.

"Yeah. Geraldine thought David did it, but I thought it was Charles", she says, absent-mindedly.

I toss my novel onto the table. Hannah looks up at me. "What's the matter?" she asks.

"You thought it was predictable".

"Yes, it was a bit".

"Geraldine thought that David was the killer".

"Yeah".

"But you thought it was Charles".

"Yes, that's right".

"Not a lot of point reading it now then, is there?"

Hannah becomes indignant, slapping her book

down on her thighs. "Oh for goodness sake Henry. Why are you so tetchy? I didn't give the plot away, I just said I thought it was a bit..."

"...Predictable; and you thought that Charles was the killer".

"Ur, yes".

A long pause ensues. "So who was the killer, Hannah? Was it Charles?"

Hannah bites her bottom lip, and can't maintain eye contact. "Shall we go to the cinema?" she asks, changing the subject.

––––––––––––––––––––

We've established that Hannah has seen all of the films being shown at the local cinema. Not wanting to spend the entire movie waiting for her to pre-empt a scene, forewarn an event that'll spoil my intended response, ruin the plot-line, or disclose the identity of a mystery protagonist, I suggest we do something else that doesn't involve using the car.

Having Googled the attractions available within walking distance of the caravan site, I discover the Godleven Tin Mine Museum is situated just over a mile's walk away along the coastal path. Hannah is surprisingly enthusiastic about braving the inclement weather, donning our walking gear, and educating ourselves about a subject which neither of us knows anything.

Having strapped on our walking boots, clad ourselves in Gor Tex over-trousers, jackets and hats, and tied our carbon-fibre hiking sticks to each wrist, we peer out to check for the presence of Barry and Maureen's Rover 75. It's not there. Satisfied that the coast is clear, we leave the cosy warmth of our 'van, lock it and pick up the trail I should have taken last night when I was looking for the sea and due north.

The well-worn path leads from the caravan site to a paddock, where our fellow caravanners are encouraged to take their dogs for exercise. I skid on a turd, my walking sticks flailing about over my head as I struggle to keep my balance and remain upright. It seems that re-trieving balls and rubber toys is not the only canine ac-tivity that takes place here with their masters. I scuff the foul-smelling sludge from my boots on the corner of a wooden bench. Payback!

Hannah tuts in disapproval; "Henry, what if a child sits on that?"

She really knows how to rob me of my little vic-tories. I give her my sticks and begrudgingly remove a cotton handkerchief from my pocket, using it to care-fully remove the mess from the squab. Pinching the hanky between my right forefinger and thumb, my little finger extended like a genteel lady sipping from a teacup at a tea party, I carry it at arm's length to the nearest bin where the offending matter should have been deposited in the first place. I use a gnawed stick to open the lid and drop it in. I sniff my right hand as a precaution, not ex-pecting the stench of a tiny dab of dog shit I have unwit-tingly transferred onto the heel of my right hand.

"Urgh! Urgh!" I say to Hannah, looking from her to my hand and back again. "Urgh!"

Hannah rolls her eyes heavenwards. "Go and wash your hands, Henry. Honestly, I feel like your mother sometimes, not your wife". We re-trace our steps to the 'van.

Hands scrubbed and disinfected, we lock the cara-van again. It has stopped raining, but the sky remains grey and overcast. We take a chance, and leave our walk-ing gear in the back of the Volvo, just as Barry and Maureen pull up in their Rover. Our hearts sink.

"ELLO 'ENRY! 'ELLO HANNAH!" Barry shouts. "WIV JUST BIN SHOPPIN' TO RE-STOCK PROVISIONS. ERA YA EGGS!"

Maureen hands Hannah a punnet of six, small, 'value' eggs; unworthy replacements for the extra-large, organic, free-range Burford Browns we 'loaned' them earlier. I bite my lip and clench my fists. Hannah thanks her through a strained smile.

"Werra ya offta?" Maureen asks, looking us up and down.

"A long walk". "The cinema", Hannah and I say respectively and simultaneously, to throw them off the scent lest they offer to accompany us to the tin mine museum. "We're taking a long walk to the cinema", I say quickly to disguise our inconsistency.

Maureen and Barry look at each other. "Iss a *very* long way to the cinema, 'enry", Barry tells me.

"Yes. Well, we fancy a *very* long walk, don't we Hannah?"

"Yes, we enjoy a *very* long walk now and again".

Barry and Maureen are looking at each other again, and then back to us. "Iss 'bout thirty mile to the nearest cinema, intit Maureen?"

"At least, Barry, at least". They look at each other again, and then back at us.

There's a pregnant pause. "Well, best we get a move on then! See you both later!" Hannah and I head off towards the paddock before they think of a reply. Their eyes are boring into our backs as we enter the paddock and pass through the first wooden kissing gate onto an overgrown sandy pathway, which I reckon will take us to the beach. As I close the gate, I can just hear Maureen's strident voice:

"WHY ARE YOU TEKKIN THE EGGS WITH YA?

Barry follows this with, "YAREDDIN IN THE WRONG DIRECTION FOR THE CINEMA 'ENRY!"

I pretend not to hear them, and put my arm around Hannah's shoulders as we disappear out of their sight amongst the Ammophila arenaria, dumping the cheap eggs into the next waste bin we see.

Having navigated dunes of heather, sea sandwort, cakile maritima and cord-grass, we reach an expanse of immaculate sandy beach that extends for a mile in each direction, north-east and south-west. The absence of any man-made structure, vehicle, device or mechanism, their sounds or smells, make us forget the weather and tribulations of our holiday so far. *This* is where it starts! *This* is living! I draw Hannah closer and we kiss before holding hands to walk to the firmer sand at the water's edge.

A quarter of an hour later we arrive at the end of the beach at an outcrop of rocks that have been exposed by a receding tide. Like children, we can't resist clambering over them to explore what the sea has left behind in their nooks and crevices. After half an hour we've identified what a fellow rock-pooler assures us is an unusually plentiful harvest of small crabs, anemones, sea urchins, a goby, two butterfish, a blenny, and almost a salad bowl of prawns and shrimps. But unlike children, we're able to look without disturbing them with nets or fingers. The encroaching lapping of the waves tell us that soon they'll be carried back out to sea.

Gazing towards the south-west, we see what we assume is the Godleven Tin Mine and museum perched near a cliff. The sturdy, square, grey-stone engine-house with a new slate roof seems perilously close to the cliff's crumbling edge. A tall, thin, refurbished, earthen-red chimney stands next to it, with three, large wheels that look like spiders' webs. I reckon they are the water pump that keeps the mine dry; the whims that raise the rock to the surface, and the ore crusher that prepares the rock for processing. At this distance their huge, brown frames appear to be constructed of wood, but must be of rusted steel. Pyramids of grey and black rock lie at the end of conveyors.

Further in-land, a modern, low-rise building, clad in weather-darkened wood and a turf roof sympathetically and unobtrusively compliments its environment. The kaleidoscope of primary colours of visitors' cars are the only unnatural and incongruous aspects of the scene.

We climb a zig-zag path carved over the centuries by footsteps in between the slate, granite and metamorphic rock. A sign greets us as we breach the rim of the cliff:

HARD ROCKS CAFÉ
40m ahead to your left

Glad of the opportunity for refreshment, and pondering what seems to be a blatant infringement of copyright, we study the renovations. Centuries of lichen and sulphates have been blasted from the rock used to build the engine house and stores; their stonework re-pointed with fresh lime mortar. Now that we're closer to the piles of rubble, they seem too high to have been deposited manually, or by nineteenth or early twentieth century engines. The white picket fencing that surrounds them are more telling of the influence of a twenty-first century health and safety executive, than the mine's original estate manager.

Manicured lawns are crossed via gravelled pathways; permanent wooden benches and picnic tables are dotted sporadically where visitors are afforded the best view of the sea and coastline. We have nothing for comparison, but recalling from our school days our studies of Britain's industrial history of the eighteenth and nineteenth century, this appears to be a sanitised version of the dusty, smoky, treacherous and unmechanised conditions endured by labourers when it was a working mine.

We approach the entrance to the restaurant, and I peer through the glass of the main door. Inside it's decked-out like a dark, subterranean mining platform, subtly lit by reproduction oil lamps. The low ceiling is buttressed with aged, sturdy, wooden railway sleepers, and food and drink orders are wheeled from the bar and kitchen to the restaurant on replica gurneys in the style of those which ferried boulders from the rock face to the shaft. The tables are slices of tree trunks supported by squat columns of stone. The bench seats have been moulded in plastic to look like rocks, and the floor is littered with sand to make the restaurant look like it has been hewn underground. Customers are eating from tin plates and slates with old fashioned cutlery. Only the music is contemporary.

It's only 10.10 am, but the walk has made me hungry. I casually peruse the menu posted outside the entrance. The restaurant's victuals are over-printed on the facsimile of a sepia production sheet, which shows that two tonnes of tin was valued at two hundred and seventy six pounds in 1805. My jaw drops like someone suffering from a temporomandibular disorder when I see the price they're asking for a cheese-burger and fries...which I approximately calculate is what over one hundred kilograms of tin would have cost in the same year.

"Henry, could you let go of my hand? You're

hurting me".

I release my grip immediately. "Have you seen the price of…"

"Come on Henry…I'm thirsty, peckish, and we're on holiday".

We enter the restaurant and wait briefly at the maître de's podium before being greeted by a waitress in her late teens. She's wearing a white miner's helmet with a motif over the brim that is more than reminiscent of the famous, plagiarised original, and a pair of red dungarees with the legs rolled up mid-shin, above a pair of hob-nailed boots. Her unnaturally bright, syrupy smile, and the perfectly inclined position of her head to one side exude such sincerity that she would put many of her American hospitality peer-equivalents to shame.

"Good morning? My name is Chardonnay? Welcome to the Hard Rocks Café at Godleven? What is it that I can be doing for yourselves today?" she says, her cadence rising inquisitorially at the end of every phrase.

I don't know whether I'm more irritated by the upward inflection, or her inappropriate use of the reflexive. Hannah must have gathered from my frown that Chardonnay's mannerisms have distracted me from answering, so she answers for us, mirroring the infectious upward inflection.

"A table for two please, Chardonnay?"

"Oh God, now *you're* doing it" I say morosely.

We follow Chardonnay to a table next to a glass display of a life-sized manikin dressed as a contemporary nineteenth century miner, smeared in mud and dirt, and with a doleful expression that makes him look like he could do with a holiday. A pick axe is in his right hand, a Cornish pasty in the other. His glassy eyes stare down at us miserably.

"It doesn't look like he recommends the pasty", Hannah quips.

"It probably cost him a week's wages if he bought it from here", I reply.

Chardonnay either didn't hear us or she's politely ignoring us. She hands us over-sized menus, which we glance at quickly before deciding what we want. "What is it that I can be getting you for yourselves today?"

"Me, myself and I would like a glass of chilled Chardonnay, please Chardonnay?" I say, mimicking her conversational quirks. Hannah kicks me in the shin under the table.

"And I would like a pineapple juice with lemonade and ice, please; with a "Miner's Monster-Melt Megaburger" to share". Hannah takes my menu and hands them back to Chardonnay. "Do you really have to find fault with everyone and everything?"

"They've decorated this place quite well", I say, looking at the various tools and receptacles fixed to the walls and ceiling, quickly finding something positive to say, to contradict Hannah's criticism of me. "Look over there…a kibble bucket. It's shaped like that so when it was being hoisted up through the shaft, it didn't catch on rough surfaces and tip out its contents".

Hannah looks impressed, considering the most practical, hands-on work I ever attempt is towing the caravan. "How do you know that?"

I shrug my shoulders. "I'm just a *mine* of information". Hannah doesn't need to know that I read the explanatory card displayed beneath it, when we were waiting to be shown to our table. Hannah has apparently missed my pun…or ignored it. I snigger self-indulgently to fill the void of silence.

There is a commotion at the entrance. A long-legged woman who appears to be in her late-twenties, with long, blonde, blow-waved hair, absurdly long eyelashes and excessive make-up; is fussing a teenaged boy and girl. I assume they are her stepchildren due to the age difference, but you never know these days. I read somewhere that underage pregnancy is as prevalent in certain areas of the UK as in some developing countries.

Apparently, the kids have been glued to their phones without a break for the last three hours. They are not paying her any attention, other than by tutting petulantly or telling her to "Geroff". Their indifference to her attempts to limit their time on-line seems to be increasingly irritating her. She calls out to her partner, who is an inch or two shorter than she is, and following them into the restaurant.

"Darren! Tell 'em! Princess an' Zack ain't takin' no notice!" Darren doesn't hear, or he's ignoring her.

The assumed stepmother is wearing tight white jeans with a mobile phone encrusted with crystals poking out of a back pocket, and a pair of pillar-box red, six-inch Louboutins. Her white halter top exposes her long neck, slim, smooth, tanned arms, and accentuates huge, impossibly round breasts that wobble as much as a brain surgeon in an operating theatre. Other than Botox-injected lips that are pursed in a permanent moue, her face is as expressionless as a reality TV star in an episode of University Challenge; but that could be the fillers in her forehead, cheeks and under her eyes. Hannah kicks me in the shins again.

"I am *here*, you, know! Do you have to ogle quite so obviously?"

"What? I was wondering what the fuss was at the door!" I rub my leg. I've been rumbled.

Darren is an orange-bronzed man in his forties

with dyed black hair. He swaggers ahead of his brood, apparently unconcerned by the disturbance they're making. He's talking loudly and self-importantly in thick estuary English, apparently to himself; but then I notice the Bluetooth earpiece hooked around his right ear.

"Yeah, mate. Telldder geezah to find two der same, and we'll stitch 'em togevva to make one, innit."

"I wonder what he's talking about? Making a 'cut and shut', probably" I whisper to Hannah. He certainly looks like a used car salesman of dubious quality: gold sovereign rings on his fingers, a heavy gold bracelet watch on one wrist, and a gold bangle of equal heft on the other. He waves his arms around unnecessarily as he talks, rattling his jewellery. The top three buttons of his black shirt are open, revealing a waxed chest, and a gold, ten-millimetre, Cuban link-chain around his neck. He's wearing black Oxford bags with pleats and turn-ups, and has draped the matching jacket around his shoulders like a mafia don. His black cowboy boots feature Cuban heels for extra height, and metal heel plates that clack on the flagstone floor drawing even more attention to him.

"Yeah, mate, yeah. Ketchup wivya laters, yeah? I'm darn in Cornwall wiv Wendy an' me kids". He presses the earpiece to terminate his call and respond to Chardonnay's greeting. "Allow darlin'. Best table inya arse fafforovus please". He peels a five-pound note from a gold money clip whipped from a trouser pocket, and palms it to Chardonnay. She leads them towards a raised booth with a picture window overlooking the grounds, and hands out four menus.

"Stop gawping, Henry!"

"But it's *fascinating*, Hannah. We're told we mustn't stereotype people; that making assumptions leads to prejudice and discrimination. But of course, that's all such rubbish. It's so often possible to *know* people without actually *knowing* them!"

"So, in what value-laden pigeon-holes are you consigning that family?"

"That's easy: He's brash, modestly educated, self-employed; probably a used car salesman, and on his second wife at least. She was one of his employees, recruited for her youth and looks, not her brains; or perhaps a waitress in a bar. And the kids...they're exactly what you would expect...spoiled, belligerent, disinterested, addicted to social media, gum-chewing brats."

"And you can tell all that after a minute's observation?"

"Yes, can't you see it?"

"Oh Henry, you are *so* prejudiced and discriminatory! You're just making excuses because it amuses you to highlight traits that don't conform to your idea of what is acceptable. Your attitude is archaic!"

"No it's not".

"Yes, it is. Being so judgemental is outmoded. Very 1950s. People are more aware and accepting of relative, personal difference these days. Your unqualified perceptions of them would change your interaction with them".

"What do you mean? I have absolutely *no* intention of having anything to do with them!"

"And why is that, Henry?"

"Because they're not my cup of tea."

Chardonnay places our drinks on the table, and tells us the 'Miner's Monster-Melt Megaburger' won't be long.

"So what's your point?" I ask Hannah.

"Oh, nothing Henry. You're a product of your class and upbringing. It's hardly your fault, really. It's just that I thought you had...oh, never mind. Cheers!" She sips her drink, and expresses her approval. "Mmm... fresh pineapple!"

I stare at her askance, frowning. I'm trying to process what she means.

"No, no, no...come on Hannah. What were you going to say? How can I be prejudiced against them when I've already seen how they behave, talk and dress? I've based my impressions on facts I have *personally* witnessed. And choosing to have nothing to do with them isn't discriminatory. Similar people tend to gravitate together; dissimilar people live and let live. That's Life". I feel vindicated now that I've rebutted Hannah's inferred disapproval, and reward myself with a sip of wine.

Hannah laughs and shakes her head. "Ok Henry. Whatever you say".

Chardonnay brings our tower of food and a forest of condiments on a trolley that looks like a mine cart from the escape scene in 'Indiana Jones and the Temple of Doom'. She wipes two tin plates and cutlery with a long, linen napkin tucked into her belt, and places the burger on a slate between us. Hannah cuts it in half and divides the fries, pickles and battered onion rings into two portions. "This looks delicious, Henry".

"So it should at that price". I smother my share of the burger in mustard, and sprinkle salt and vinegar on the fries, still trying to fathom what Hannah meant, before I attempt a fresh salvo.

"Why am I a "product of my class and upbringing? Just because I'm reserved, and don't appreciate vulgar behaviour when I don't have to, why should that mean I'm prejudiced or discriminatory?" I prod my fork into a mass of shredded pork and stuff it into my mouth. "I don't agree with Vegetarianism, but I have nothing against people who eat bland and innutritious food".

"There you go again".

"What?"

"Basing your responses on little or no knowledge of the subject. Who says that vegetarian food is tasteless and unwholesome? It doesn't matter whether you stereotype others to exercise a self-indulgent desire to vent your opinion, provoke a reaction, be humorous, because you just don't know how to relate to the group you're targeting, or any other reason. If you reinforce a positive or negative stereotype by expressing it to others, it's a pervasive prejudice because it spreads. Your parents probably infected you with their prejudices".

"Bloody hell, Hannah. You sound like a text book!" I chew my food, observing her, considering what she said for a few moments. "And don't bring my parents into it. Of course they didn't!"

"Really? Alright then; let's use that family over there as an example. Can you recall a time as a child when your Mum or Dad said something negative about somebody with a cockney accent and flamboyant clothes?"

My eyes drop to my food. I instantly remember very clearly my father, Basil, describing someone at his place of work, who had irritated him.

"You *can*, can't you? I *know* you, Henry! Come on; what was said? How old were you?"

I can feel the balance of persuasive argument tilting in Hannah's favour. "Twelve", I reply reluctantly; "I heard Dad describe a boss as an "inarticulate barrow-boy"".

"And you remember it straight away, twenty-six years later! I wonder how many times you've defaulted to that judgement, rather than give someone a chance to prove otherwise?"

I can hardly admit that before I met her there were occasions when I was initially attracted to a number of women, but felt peevish when they opened their mouths and spoke! They had sounded like characters from East Enders, glottal-stopping and tee-dropping.

Hannah is warming to the subject, getting into her stride. It's my own fault. I've 'pressed her buttons'. I challenged her to explain, so I must take the flak, because I can't take it back.

Colour is rising in her face. She places her cutlery down, warming to her subject.

"Stereotypes are distorted taxonomies: corrupted sat navs of the sociological landscape. Just as an obsolescent sat nav causes a traveller to become lost, making sweeping, over-simplified, positive or negative generalisations result in a loss of true perspective. This causes people to form false and inaccurate impressions of their targets, who are disadvantaged when they are the brunt of passive or active prejudice".

She picks up her fork and shakes it towards me for emphasis.

"Imagine someone overlooked for a place studying an academic subject at university, because he's from a group wrongly considered to be lazy, or only good at physical activities; or an applicant for a job as a long-distance driver not being offered opportunities because people from his group are perceived to be hard-working, but dangerous liabilities behind the wheel".

"Yes, Hannah, but I still don't see…"

"What? How your little synopsis of 'Del Boy and the Trotters' over there isn't a prime example of prejudice?"

"Ha! That was very good!"

"*No*, Henry! I was being ironic!"

I can hear Chardonnay asking the man in the black suit whether he wants his steak well-done, medium or rare. He replies, "Rare? Nah! I wonnit blue! Just slap its arse and fro it onmee plate!"

I peer at Hannah and suppress a smile, which is not returned.

"What do you think about ginger hair?" she asks me.

"It's fine on a cat."

"Come on. Be honest about what you feel about people with orange-ginger hair? What if *I* was ginger? How would you feel about that?"

I imagine someone pale-skinned, suffering from mood-swings, shying away from sports, the beach, sunshine, certain foods, having fun...who probably isn't top of my list to invite to a dinner party. So I don't answer.

"What you are feeling is *prejudice*, Henry. Yet how many ginger people do you actually *know*? Now imagine that we have a ginger child. How do you feel that there are people who think like you, who will treat our baby differently because of hair colour! *That's* discrimination!"

Hannah has tears in her eyes, and I move around to sit on her bench-seat and hold her. I wonder whether she is getting this upset because of my lack of appreciation or understanding about the effects of prejudice and discrimination, or whether it's because we have not yet been blessed with a child. This occasionally rears its awkward head at the most unexpected times, and it can make both of us rather emotional. Especially me.

"I'm sorry Hannah. I'll think about what you've said, what I say, how I behave; really, I promise I will".

She uses her napkin to carefully dab her tear ducts without smearing her eyeliner. "Oh, Henry. I really hope that you will".

She leans her head on my shoulder. "Look, I know human frailties can be amusing. Impressionists, satirists, comedians: They all make lucrative careers taking the mickey out of people's peculiarities. But in this competitive world, we've become so quick to judge and label others. Why don't we start giving people a chance? If we 'let them in', we'll see strengths that make us realise that stereotypes aren't inviolable. Then those longstanding myths will slowly be undermined, and replaced with fair and balanced facts, so people can be judged and treated according to their true merits. Don't you see? It would create a more harmonious world".

Hannah's lecture is interrupted by the rattle of Chardonnay's mine cart laden with four, griddled, six hundred-gram sirloin steaks and side orders, which the waitress is wheeling to the cockneys' table. A loud cry of "Lubbly jubbly!" and a slow hand-clap echo around the restaurant.

Hannah and I look at each other, and smile. Hunger banished, thirsts quenched, we pay our bill and head towards the exit to take a guided tour of the mine's museum.

Despite making use of our ten percent reduction on the cost of admission to the museum, redeemed on presentation of our restaurant receipt, we baulk at the ticket charge of thirty-six pounds per person. A digital noticeboard outlines the museum's exorbitant pricing strategy, and lays proud claim to the frankly ungenerous reduction of five pounds from the full-ticket-price for old-age pensioners and children. I reflect on whether there is any prejudice or discrimination inherent in their marketing policies, but I don't particularly want to revisit that discussion with Hannah, so I keep my thoughts to myself.

Surprisingly though, there doesn't appear to be a shortage of families willing to pay one hundred and fifty pounds or more for a tour that will probably last no longer than a few hours.

I reluctantly pay seventy-two pounds, before cathartically bombarding the cashier with a full and frank opinion about how ridiculously expensive it is. Handing me the tickets, she explains that if I had pre-booked the tickets on-line, I would have saved fifty per-cent on the cost of both the admission and our food and drink. I'm quietly seething, and Hannah's admonish-ments not to be so tight, and to remember that I'm on holiday, do little to change the fact that I could have saved over *fifty* pounds; this being almost double the cost of admission for two to the Sable Theatre, for the matinée performance of Dirty Rotten Scoundrels.

We each take a plastic miner's helmet that incor-porates over-earphones, and switch them on to begin the tour. The male commentator has a broad Corn-ish accent. I turn to Hannah to make a comment, and she raises a cautionary forefinger. My thoughts remain thoughts. It has taken me precisely ten minutes since promising her to stop making remarks based on com-mon stereotypes, before I was about to do exactly the same thing again. Still, it is her loss: Now she won't see and hear my impression of a one-legged pirate with an eye-patch and a shoulder-mounted parrot.

"Good arrrftnoon an' welcum to Godleven Moine. Move overrr to the doorrr on yourrr rrroight wherrre the tourrrr will starrrrt in the next rrroom, haharrrr!"

The first stage is a snaking route around roped-off displays of hand tools, clothing and equipment, each labelled and numbered for our easy reference, when prompted by our audio-guide to inspect them. The more original and rarer objects are exhibited in locked, reinforced glass cabinets.

Captain Hook introduces us to the science of Geology. He explains the differences between igneous, sedimentary and metamorphic rock, inviting us to hold and inspect physical examples of each. Gradually his commentary narrows to focus on tin, which is mostly produced from cassiterite, an igneous mineral ore.

We move to a video screen which shows the ore being crushed into a powder using nineteenth century rock grinders, before being leached of its impurities. It's heated in a furnace at about two thousand five hundred degrees Fahrenheit with carbon-based materials and limestone, in a process called 'smelting'. This separates the tin, because its greater density means that it drops to the bottom of the furnace. Other metals such as copper, iron and zinc are also abstracted using this method.

We are presented with examples of tin's uses, from centuries ago: containers, and in the production of bronze and pewter. We see how tin is used today: as an electroplated or dipped protective coating for other materials such as steel or copper. Before the introduction of aluminium and other materials common in the manufacture of food containers, tin acted as a rustproofing layer on soldered cans, so acidic food didn't react with the steel. We learn how tin also rustproofs paperclips, hair grips, and safety pins, and even puts the fluoride in toothpaste.

A large pile of rocks have been stacked in the middle of the floor in the next room. We are told it weighs one tonne or one thousand kilograms, and invited to guess how much tin it would produce. Next to it is a bowl of silver plastic coins. There are ten cabinets around the edge of the room, alternating in size. The largest contains a stack of two hundred and twenty, tin ingots arranged like a Jenga tower, and weighing one hundred kilograms. The smallest is a wall-mounted, glass display case, measuring just six inches by six inches, with two, one-gram paperclips mounted on black flocking. Beside each display is a Perspex box with a coin slot. We are challenged to insert a plastic counter to indicate which we think is true.

I choose the stack representing the intermediate option of one hundred and ten ingots weighing fifty kilograms, which would represent a five percent yield. The greater volume of plastic coins in the box suggests I've followed the same collective logic as the majority. I watch Hannah tapping her counter against her lips as she considers each display, before dropping her coin into the box representing the two paperclips.

I laugh and shake my head, and momentarily remove my helmet. "Two paperclips, from all of that?" I ask mockingly, pointing at the massive pile of rubble.

"Oh don't get so competitive" she replies. "It's only a bit of fun!"

"Yes, but that would represent a *miniscule* yield!" Everyone else has chosen, and is looking around for the correct answer. After a few minutes, clearly the time the writers of the tour considered sufficient for the slowest punters to make their choice, the earphones crackle back into life.

"*Rrroight! You wanna know the answerrr? One tonne, or one thousand kilograms of rrrock would give you...*" He leaves an excessive pause worthy of an announcement of the results from a public phone-in for a television singing contest. I'm surprised that there is no irritating cut to a commercial break. He resumes, "*...about two grrrams* *of tin! It's box four: two paperrrclips!"*

Hannah stares at me, suppressing a smile through pursed lips, raising her eyebrows and inclining her head to one side in a manner that tells me that I shouldn't be so arrogant and smug; which is ironic really, because that is just how she looks to me. "Let's move on", I say testily.

The sequence of the tour's information provokes animated conversation. Perfect strangers discuss how labour-intensive it must have been two hundred years ago, digging a deep shaft into a seam, let alone excavating, extricating, grinding and treating all that rock for so little tin, predominantly without automated assistance.

We enter the next room and immediately fall silent. A figure is standing motionless on a raised platform. I have to look twice to check that it is not a replica of the manikin in the restaurant. He is wearing nineteenth century, miner's garb covered in soot, and holding a Davy lamp. Deep creases in his forehead and nasolabial fold show bright white on his coal-black face, as though a sustained, pained expression caused by his exertions underground have protected rivulets of skin from contamination by this pervasive dust. His eyes are cast down unblinkingly at the floor, and his lips are stretched enigmatically over broken and missing teeth. When the room is full, an usher closes the door, the lights dim, and the miner slowly raises his gaze and lamp like an automaton on a predetermined programme.

He inspects us in the dull glow, before gently setting the gas-light on a podium which illuminates his face from beneath his jaw, eerily throwing the majority of his face into shadow. With a scowl he slowly recounts verse in a deep, gruff, Cornish baritone, increasing the tempo and volume to fortissimo with each verse, until slowing down for the last, in pianissimo:

"Each day lowered down the shaft;
Eight more hours of toil and graft.
Pray to God who reigns above
For safe return of those we love.

Armed with pick-axe, hammer, chisel,
Boryer [1], banjo-shovel [2], kibble [3],
Carve out rock, & send up bin to
Whittle down and eke out tin.

Just a hoggan [4] for our crib [5]
Miner's jack [6], no beer to sip;
Please the captain [7], get no spale [8]
Or hefty kick from his hobnail [9].

Roof collapsin', miner's lung [10],
Poison gas, nowhere to run!
Drownin', helpless in flash flood,
Crushed by rock in sea of mud;
Careless dynamite explosion,
Cage [11] cut off, our bodies frozen.

Toilin' in the dark eclipse
Barely lit by flickerin' dips [12];
Dust intrudin' eyes 'n' noses,
In our throats 'n' on our lips.

If you'd like to come and see
Us wallow in our misery,
Step this way and follow me
Underground, to Purgat'ry!

Two children burst into tears as the miner lifts his lamp to illuminate a door that is slowly opening automatically. A loud, piped soundtrack of the lethargic door's painful creaking and miners' anguished toil, make the kids scream with renewed vigour. Their parents scoop them up and hurriedly carry their writhing, wriggling little bodies back through the museum to the gift shop where they can be consoled with sweets.

Hannah looks up and me. "Shall we give it a miss too?"

"Are you kidding? It's just getting interesting!" I pull her into the next room: a pithead featuring a cage above a vertical drop that falls five hundred and thirty metres through the strata. Next to it is the mechanism that lifts kibble buckets of rock from the mine, and a pump that keeps the water-table below the working platforms.

Just when it appears that our contingent has been reduced by half to an elderly couple, Hannah and me, Darren and his family enter the room. We now number eight again. The miner-guide follows them in, and the door closes behind him, again accompanied by the recording of tortured, metallic screeching. He enters the cage, which sways slightly as he does so, and turns to face us.

This room is better illuminated, and I see that he's wearing an incongruous, red, plastic name-badge on his chest, declaring his name to be "Gryffyn". I'm not sure whether it is his Christian or surname. After our small group has absorbed the surroundings and the soundtrack of the miners' exertions is faded out, Gryffyn, or Mr Gryffyn is off again:

Those who want to bear witness

To fear in Earth's darkest abyss
One third mile we'll hurtle down
To hell incarnate, underground!

You see the wheel that pumps out water
Installed after 'nother slaughter:
Fifty-seven desp'rate souls
Drowned & buried in these holes!

Gryffyn points at Hannah.

You! Bring caged canary here,
To warn if lethal gas appears.

He points at me and Darren's family.

You! Those hammers, chisels, picks,
Bundled piles of wooden sticks;
Wedges, drill rods, kindling straw,
Pails of water, strong bucksaw,
Mining kit from days of yore.

Darren is unmoved, and checking his mobile phone messages; Wendy is scrutinising her eye makeup in a small, gaudy, vanity mirror. Their jaws continually churn in unison, mechanically grinding their gum, as though the speed and intensity of mastication is directly proportionate to their ability to concentrate on business and appearance respectively.

Even though neither of them seem interested in the exhibition, Darren must at least be listening to Gryffyn to some extent, because he pushes his teenagers towards the lift with his free hand, without removing his eyes from his screen. This distracts Princess from the game she's playing on her pink iPad. She tuts and whines at him.

"Dad! Dat woz mah best evvar score, you dick-'ead!" Neither of her parents react to her rudeness.

I drag the heavier equipment and deposit them in the caged elevator. Princess tosses in the light sheaf of straw before returning to her game. Her brother makes more effort by bringing the bundles of wood.

We obey Gryffyn's order to enter. Once we're seated, he rings a bell which signals to the wheel-operator to feed us into the darkness. Thankfully we're not 'hurtled into the abyss', but descend in ten-feet stages, reminiscent of a casket being manually lowered into a grave.

Gryffyn doesn't appear to have a poem for the gloom, which is only occasionally disrupted near the top of the shaft by the strobing light shed by Darren's phone and Princess' iPad, and later by the dimly lit platforms passed on our descent to the mining level. I fill the silence by pointing out to Hannah in this intermittent, weak light, the vague outline of adjacent, vertical, wooden ladders that would have been scaled by brave miners if the lift wasn't working.

When we have exhausted discussing what we can see and what we are feeling, we chat about the merits of our pitch at Godleven Caravan & Camping Park, and how it is well-positioned for day-trips to places of interest, particularly in central and west Cornwall, but too far away to explore west Devon.

It takes time getting used to the negative gravity experienced as the cage drops ten feet every five seconds. Inexorably we descend for what feels like half an hour, before arriving with an unedifying jolt at the bottom of the shaft.

I put my arm around Hannah's shoulders to warm her in the chillier, damper air, as we step out of the lift onto the rough-hewn, rock floor. The absence of gantries and viewing platforms I remember from visits to Wookey Hole and Cheddar Gorge suggest that those responsible for 'Customer Experience' at Godleven Mine, intend their visitors to endure the unadulterated, edgy authenticity of a Cornish tin mine, circa 1820.

Gryffyn volunteers the two teenagers to unload all of the equipment from the lift, which they do with surly protests that he is picking on them. He arranges the tools in a crescent shape on the ground in front of him.

Darren's partner is complaining about the damp atmosphere and what it's doing to her hair, and primps her perm in the reflection of her compact. Darren seems confused that he has no phone signal, and is switching his phone off and on again in the hope that this will re-boot it.

The other couple, (whom we learn are called Ken and Irene), Hannah and I are enthusiastically absorbing and commenting on our surroundings, waiting for Gry-ffyn to resume his presentation.

Disappointingly, he resorts to prose instead of verse to explain and demonstrate how stone was cleaved from the rock-face that surrounds us. His accent is no longer a broad Cornish lilt, perhaps betraying the fact that he spent part of his life in the home counties. His character slips again when he dons a pair of twenty-first century eye-protectors. Yet in spite of his change in tone and adherence to health and safety regulations, his delivery still creates a frisson: This was, is, a dangerous environment, and there'll be no play-acting down here. This phase must be taken seriously.

"Ladies and gentlemen. To extract the tin ore, the hard rock had to be broken. Before dynamite was introduced later in the 1870s, the breaking of the rock was done by hand using hammers, chisels, rock wedges and poll picks". He indicates each one with his boot. "It was laborious and time-consuming".

He picks up the hammer and chisel, and rams the latter into a fissure with the former to make a larger crack. He drives metal wedges into the gap, and then a cone-shaped piece of metal in between the wedges. He forces the cone into the rock with a larger sledgehammer. The rock starts to fracture slightly, and when it's clear that he cannot make the gap any larger by this method, he lifts the poll pick and swings it at its crumbling edges.

After twenty strikes, the rock starts to separate into pieces of varying sizes that fall at his feet. He wipes the sweat from his brow with the back of his hand. "This is known as 'gad and feathering'. Who'd like to put on goggles and have a go?"

Darren's partner suddenly screams, making us jump; all except Darren, who keeps grinding his gum, but stops stabbing a fat forefinger at his dead phone's keypad. He turns to observe her down his nose, frowning. "Wossa matta wiv you?" he asks, in irritation rather than concern.

"The fackin roof's leakin'! It juss dripped dan me bra!"

"Surprised you felt it, Wendy, considerin' day iz mosely gel 'n' rubba!" he replies unsympathetically, before nudging and leaning towards me and adding, "Six fairzind quid day coss me...but werf every penny! Knar wotta mean? Heh, heh."

I glance at Wendy who is thrusting a silk handkerchief down her massive, white, lacy brassiere, before hastily averting my gaze. Hannah and I reciprocate raised eyebrows, before I respond to Gryffyn's invitation to excavate some rock.

I make several attempts to hit another chisel and wedge into another fissure, and experience at first-hand just how exhausting the process is. I can't imagine what it would have been like doing this for eight hours a day, every day.

Gryffyn resumes his lesson: "At the beginning of the eighteenth century, many mines were still using a Roman method of breaking rock, by fire-setting." He picks up the dry straw and bundles of stick, and places it next to the rock. He then removes a twizzle-stick, wooden strip and string from his pocket, and demonstrates on a few strands of straw how he would light the kindling and wood-bundle using friction. I'm glad that he's not demonstrating the process fully. Whilst we would be glad of more heat, it was clearly a hazardous technique, with miners risking asphyxiation by smoke or lack of oxygen.

"The fire would be left to burn, so heating and expanding the rock. Once the fire went out, the rock would cool and shrink; but throwing cold water on the rock would help it cool quicker". He kicks the bucket of water at his feet. "The expansion and sudden shrinking of the rock weakens it, and eventually breaks it apart, aided of course by miners wielding hammers."

He bids us to place the mined rock into a kibble bucket. Only Ken, Irene, Hannah and I oblige. Gryffyn tugs on the rope attached to the full bucket, and after a few seconds, we stand back when it rises up the shaft, its smooth sides causing it to bounce off the hard edges of the shaft, rather than get stuck, as it would if designed with a squarer shape.

Gryffyn asks if we have any questions so far. Zack raises his hand. He's unexpectedly earnest. "We saw earlier dat alotta rock produced very lill tin."

"I asked if you had any *questions*," Gryffyn replies drily. "And *that*, my little cockney friend, was a *statement!*"

"Yes, er, ok, I was juss wonderin', 'ow profitable a business woz this, considerin' it took so much rock to produce so lill tin?"

Gryffyn thrusts his hands into his pockets and looks disapprovingly at Darren. "Look, son...", Gryffyn begins.

"It's Zack", replies Zack.

"...This was an industry that thrived for hundreds of years. Mining tin wouldn't have continued if there wasn't any money in it, would it?"

Darren chuckles and shakes his head dismissively, clearly not having listened to or understood his son's question, before turning his attention back to removing, shaking and replacing the battery in his phone.

"What I mean is..." Zack continues.

I notice that Gryffyn is starting to shake. I wonder whether it is a stress reaction, anger or embarrassment that he can't answer Zack's perfectly reasonable query, given the dilemma posed about tin yield in the museum. "I'm moving on now, Rodney Trotter. There's a time-limit for this tour, you know".

Darren clips Zack mockingly on the back of his head, and chuckles. "'e means well, bless 'im", Darren says to Gryffyn.

I shift my weight from foot-to-foot, uncomfortable with the way Gryffyn has spoken to Zack. I look at Hannah who's glaring at Gryffyn. "Hang on, a minute", I say. "Zack makes a valid point. Do you have an answer?"

Gryffyn sneers at me, and through clenched teeth sarcastically says, "Well I would've thought that labour was plentiful and cheaper in those days, wouldn't you?"

He moves back to the arc of equipment laid out on the floor, glancing at me periodically to check that I am not going challenge him again. I decide that this isn't an environment where I want to alienate myself with the person responsible for our care.

Gryffyn continues. "So, moving on…Even earlier, in the seventeenth century, Cornish miners drove boryers into the rock-face with hammers". He picks up a long drill rod and swings in it the direction of my face before placing its tip against another part of the fissure, and striking the other end with a hammer. "The boryer was turned after each hit of the hammer, chipping out a piece of rock. This would eventually create a round hole". He demonstrates the technique with twenty strikes and turns of the drill-bit. He stands back for us to inspect his work. "This is called a 'shot-hole', but is much smaller than would be required. It could take many hours to bore a two-foot hole. The process could be expedited by 'double-handed drilling', where one man held and turned the drill, and two men struck it with hammers". He points the head of the hammer at me. "You…twist it, whilst your wife and I hammer it in".

I oblige, keeping my hands clear of the place where the hammer will fall; but Gryffyn doesn't warn me to remove my hands from the drill-bit when he strikes it with full force. The reverberating metal rod transfers sharp pain through my wrists and forearms. I recoil and clamp my palms under my armpits, waiting for the aching to subside. Hannah abandons her hammer and consoles me, whilst Gryffyn laughs and alone twists and hammers the rod alternately until the hole is slightly bigger.

Gryffyn removes a paper pouch from another pocket, and pours black powder from it into the hole, before stuffing the pouch in too. "Gunpowder was then ignited to blast the rock apart. This stuff is highly volatile", he explains, dropping his chin, smiling sinisterly, surveying us consecutively from beneath hooded eyelids.

He produces feathers from his capacious pocket. "Fire is introduced to the powder by 'rods' of these goose quills. These primitive fuses often fired the charge prematurely, and it wasn't uncommon for miners to be killed using this method. The luckier ones lost their eyes and fingers. It wasn't until 1831 that a safety fuse was patented".

He places the rudimentary fuse into the hole, and tells us to stand back. We look at each other nervously. Surely, he's not going to detonate gun powder with paying visitors present in such a small space.

I raise my hand in objection. "Er, we'll take your word for it Mr. Gryffyn" I say, hoping that the others will support me and express their disapproval. They remain silent, unsure whether he is teasing us, and reluctant to appear foolish.

He steps into my personal space, his purple-veined nose no more than a few inches from my own, and I smell the hint of booze on his breath. I suddenly realise that he's one of those hardened alcoholics who can appear lucid, coherent and sensible, until they start to crave the poison that helps them to function. As they become sober, they conversely start behaving unpredictably or foolishly, as most of us do when we are drunk.

"It's 'Gryffyn', not *Mis*ter Gryffyn: a good, old, Cornish, Christian name. It'll only be a little bang", he says chuckling, before menacingly ordering us to stand back against the furthest wall, which is only ten feet behind us and with nowhere to take cover.

He removes a wadded torchlight from a wall-bracket and takes it over to the shot-hole, where he touches the flame against the rudimentary fuse of goose quills. They start to burn irregularly in fits and starts towards the gunpowder. We huddle even closer together in a scrum, palms pressed over ears, lips stretched over teeth, eyes squeezed shut, hoping that this will in some way mitigate and protect us from the explosion of noise and debris that must only be seconds away.

I wonder whether it would be safer to stand closer to the blast, so projectiles of stone can't gather momentum. Common sense tells me to stay-put, and I stand in front of Hannah protectively as I hear the crunch of stones under Gryffyn's feet as he casually walks back towards us, presumably to take what little shelter that distance and our tight-knit group may provide.

As I continue standing there shielding Hannah, my eyes and ears closed against the imminent explosion, I reflect on my last glance at the burning fuse, and consider its speed of progress as the seconds pass; I'm surprised that the gunpowder has still not ignited. I cautiously open one eye…

"*BANG!*" Gryffyn shouts, his mouth against my ear. I instinctively push him away, and he howls with laughter before swigging from a hip flask.

The paper is still smouldering in the hole. Ken has turned bluish-grey and is clutching his chest, hyperventilating in panic. Irene is offering him soothing words of comfort, loosening his shirt, and urging him to sit down in the dirt against the rock-face and raise his knees. Wendy is panicking, shouting, "Oh mah days!" and running backwards and forwards looking for her escape, and Darren is telling her to "Shut der fackap, will ya? Wuzz only 'is little joke! Carm darn, ya silly care!" Zack starts ladling water from the bucket onto the paper pouch to extinguish the acrid smoke, and his sister is only momentarily distracted from her iPad, on which she is achieving a new and unprecedented score on Candy Crush.

"Not funny!" I say to Gryffyn, who replies that we are over-reacting, because it wasn't gunpowder but ground black pepper that he had poured into the hole. "Take us back to the surface. The show's over!"

"Oh, come on! Can't you lot take a joke?" he asks, waving the hip flask in the direction of the shot-hole, and spilling an arc of brown liquid that I assume is whisky, brandy or rum, perilously close to the torch he has carelessly left burning on the floor.

Hannah is helping Irene with Ken, who appears to have regained control of his breathing, and has returned to a more normal colour. I go to the caged lift and open the door so everyone can take their place.

Eventually Irene, Ken and Darren's family are ready to join us, but Gryffyn decides that he will remain in the mine. He removes a rock that secretes his stash of Famous Grouse, sits down on an upturned kibble bucket, and swigs straight from the bottle.

I close the gate, ring the bell, and press a hidden red button next to it, just in case. Seconds later, we begin our long ascent to the surface in silence.

CHAPTER 11

Saturday, 4.30 pm

Having thoroughly debriefed the day's events while taking the cliff-top path back to the site, Hannah and I are now reclining in our Bailey caravan, with books and mugs of coffee. The grievances we expressed in person to the site's manager about Gryffyn's conduct, were not supported or corroborated by Ken and Irene, nor Darren's family, albeit for slightly different reasons: Ken and Irene didn't want the stress and fuss of it, which is understandable given Ken's near-death experience. In fact, all they wanted to do was get back to their car and find the nearest hospital so he could have a check-up. Darren, on the other hand, silenced his wife's protests, convincing her that Gryffyn was no more than a colourful character who was just having a bit of a laugh, and probably had problems of his own, without making them worse by complaining about him.

The manager listened to us, but did not apologise; probably because he did not want to imply any acceptance of liability for an unsubstantiated and uncorroborated allegation. We hoped that he would at least investigate it, perhaps finding Gryffyn safe but comatose at the bottom of the mine shaft, slurring a Cornish, mining ditty.

"I'm proud of you Henry", Hannah says to me, looking over the top of her novel.

I lay down my Ben Elton, which I have started reading as a replacement for my last book. There was no point persevering with it after Hannah effectively told me how it ends. I return Hannah's scrutinising gaze. "Why is that?"

"You stood up for the little man today, in the face of prejudice and discrimination by that drunken oaf. Not even his own father did that".

I realise that she's talking about Zack, and the way Gryffyn undermined him and disregarded his intelligent question, ridiculing his accent by referring to him as Rodney Trotter. "Yes, but Darren, Wendy and Princess still rather fit the stereotype though, don't they?"

"Don't spoil it, Henry! No, you could have acquiesced like his father did; but you resisted it, and I'm proud of you."

It doesn't matter how much money I spend on buying gifts for Hannah of jewellery, perfume, clothes, flowers, surprise weekends away, or meals in critically acclaimed restaurants; nothing quite makes my heart swell with pride and happiness than receiving her praise and approval when I say or do what she considers to be the 'right thing'.

Honestly, it reminds me of being a little boy again, when I did something routine and mundane that pleased my mother beyond the realms of reasonable hope or expectation. It could have been remembering to put the cap back on the toothpaste; or pulling the toilet's flush handle; or cleaning away soap scum after a bath; or not leaving a damp towel on the floor after a shower. You could have sworn from Mum's effusive praise that I had won a Nobel Peace Prize, or discovered a cure for cancer.

It is, of course, a very clever, female strategy; one that is bound to result in bending mankind to their will; making us more inclined to do what they want us to do, which is probably what we should be doing anyway. It's ingenious, inventive, resourceful. Or is it manipulative?

Well, even if it is, I do enjoy those praising words, or little rewards for good behaviour: The extra pillow under my weary head, or woollen cover when I'm resting on the settee; the extra bottles of real ale I find in the cupboard after her weekly shop; the additional helping of food at mealtimes. They don't happen as often as I would like, which may be an indicator of my own behaviour, but I love them when they do.

We get back to our books. "This one is excellent. I'm getting another one of his when we go into town, cos I've nearly finished it", she says.

"Well don't give away the plot line", I say, not looking up from my own novel. "I'd like to read it after you, if you recommend it".

"Yes, I do. I just wish that the ending wasn't so tragic. I like happy endings".

She's done it again. I drop my book print down on my chest. "Right, well I won't bother now then".

"Why, do you prefer happy endings too?"

I look at Hannah and shake my head. She carries on reading, oblivious to what she's said.

"Hannah. I now know that one of the characters, in all likelihood one of the *main* characters, must have died in tragic circumstances. Knowing that kind of spoils it".

"That's daft", she replies vacantly, still engrossed in the closing chapter. "You didn't know that it was the girl who is killed. It could just as easily have been the..." She stops reading and puts her book down. "Whoops".

I shake my head and get up from the bench seat. "I'm going to empty the waste-water and fill the water butt. What do you fancy for tea?"

"It's a lovely evening. The weather forecaster said

that there's an area of high pressure arriving for the next few days. Let's have a glass of wine outside, and then walk to the pub that's next to that weir".

"Sold! You open the Sancerre, and I'll sort out the waste and water."

––––––––––––––––––––––––

Dragging the wheeled cylinders back to the caravan, my shoulders drop when I see Barry, shirtless and wearing flip-flops and swimming shorts, his huge belly folded over the strained, elasticated waistband. He is tossing rolled up newspaper and pouring charcoal into his drum barbecue, which he has installed on the grass outside his caravan, near to where we have set out our reclining chairs, table and parasol. Hannah places a sweating bottle of wine, two glasses and a sharing-bowl of salty snacks on our table, while I reattach the pipework of the waste and fresh water containers.

"'Ello 'enry" he calls out cheerfully, squeezing barbecue fluid onto the charcoal. "Maureen and me are 'avin' a barbecue!" he tells me, rather pointlessly. "D'you wanna join uz? Plenty to go 'round! Burgers 'n' bangers…salad… the usual!"

Hannah's warm praise for my treatment of Zack is still only half an hour old, so I consider my response carefully before making it. Hannah has now gone inside our van, but the walls are thin, and she'll hear me. I don't want to undo my good work.

But it is still playing on my mind that Maureen and Barry replaced the half a dozen eggs we had given them, which cost us four pounds at Waitrose, with an inferior punnet that cost them less than a pound at the local Happy Bargains supermarket. I've also recently been privy to Barry's unsanitary habits and poor personal hygiene. I dread to think about the quality of their meat, or the prospect of him handling food that I would actually have to put in my mouth. I long to give him short shrift, but I really don't want to blot my copybook with Hannah.

"That's a very generous offer, Barry", I reply; "but Hannah and I shall be going out for dinner this evening".

Barry acknowledges me with a wave as he enters his 'van. I sit down on a sun lounger, and Hannah comes out and joins me. We raise our glasses, toast each other, and sip our Sancerre appreciatively.

Barry re-emerges with a can of Happy Bargains own label, extra-strength lager in one hand, and a plate of burgers and sausages in the other. The burgers are so grey they look as though they've been oxidising in the sun all day. The sausages are unnaturally pink, and appear to have been cut with food colouring. He places the uncovered plate on a shelf next to the open lid of the barbecue, instantly drawing flies to the meat like iron filings to a magnet. Barry either doesn't notice or care, and squirts more lighting fluid onto the coals.

"This is the life, intit campers!" he says. It would have been hard not to find his appreciation of simple pleasures endearing, but he swigs the entire contents of his can in three gulps, and belches so loudly that a murder of crows take flight from nearby trees, startling them so much that they drop their cargo of white and black bombs that noisily land in a running, wet splat over our caravan, car, and Barry's meat.

I take a deep intake of breath, and am rewarded by Hannah smiling at me; she's clearly impressed that I haven't rebuked Barry by expressing my displeasure or disgust. "I'll just go and get a bucket of water and a sponge and sort that out before it hardens", I say, our peaceful drink in the sunshine suddenly delayed by our irritating neighbour.

When I return, Hannah has already finished her first glass of wine. I wonder whether quaffing it so liberally helped her to endure conversation with Barry, whilst I was busy. Just as I'm about to empty the bucket and replace it and the sponge in our caravan's front storage box, I turn to see Barry tossing a lit match onto the coals of his barbecue.

With a loud *"Whoosh!"*, orange and red flames billow out from the drum and engulf Barry for a second or two, before extinguishing themselves with a crackling sizzle. The once-thriving hairs of his eyebrows, eyelashes, facial stubble, chest, stomach, legs and toes are now shrivelled to short, crispy, fuliginous curls.

I launch the bucket of bird-poo-water at Barry, to soak the smouldering embers of hair, before standing transfixed, waiting for some reaction or signal from him to let me know what else he needs. Hannah is jerking her head from Barry to me and back again, not knowing how to respond either.

Barry is standing motionless, staring at the coals which are now burning nicely, sending up wisps of blue smoke into his wide, open eyes. I wonder if the flames got his eyelids too, which may explain why he isn't blinking.

"Er, Barry...are you ok?" I ask, urgently.

Barry slowly nods. His skin is looking pinker and shinier than normal. "Ah think ah'll go 'n' av a nice cold shower," he says flatly.

"Something smells good!" Maureen says as she steps out of their van, taking her iPod earphones out of her ears.

"Umm, that's not the food", I say. "That's Barry. He just set fire to himself. Too much lighter fluid", I explain.

Maureen looks at her husband, who is now turning to a beetroot-red. "Oh mah God!" she exclaims, grabbing a towel and dragging him in the direction of the shower block. "Let's get ya under a cold shower! Ya still cookin'! I can smell it comin' off ya!"

As she leads her stiff-limbed husband away, I sit down with Hannah, and pour her another glass before draining my own. When they are out of earshot, my look of horror, becomes a smile, which transforms into a chuckle, before morphing into a giggle. Soon I am laughing unrestrainedly, tears rolling from my chin, ribs aching.

When I can bear it, I take advantage of the lull in my mirthfulness to squint through blurred eyes at Hannah: She's regarding me with revulsion, which suddenly alternates with short, barking guffaws, as she remains unable to maintain her disgust at my sense of humour, or resist my infectious laughter. The odd contradiction of her behaviour makes me howl and roar anew, forcing the air from my lungs. And when she starts snorting like a pig, my perspiration intermingles with the tears, and I am forced to recall the tragedy of a bereavement just so that I can draw breath again.

Why does unrestrainable hilarity often strike at the most inappropriate times? Perhaps it is the awkwardness of the occasion that triggers a sub-conscious, converse reaction to the circumstances? Or maybe we do it knowingly, rebelling against our innate, repressed Britishness that usually makes so much effort not to offend.

We're furthered sobered by the proximity of crescendoing sirens alternately warbling and chirping, before being silenced abruptly somewhere in the vicinity of the site's reception office. Someone, perhaps Maureen, must have phoned for an ambulance. Why didn't *we* think of that? Guilt sets in. We were too busy laughing.

Surely, he isn't that bad, is he? He was still standing up; he seemed alert; he said he was ok. But that could have been shock, adrenaline triggering his body's response to pain, boosting the output of his heart to increase blood-flow to his muscles.

We consider the time it must have taken for Maureen to escort Barry to the shower block, and shove him under a prolonged flow of cold water to stop him cooking. Why didn't we save precious time by getting him into our caravan and showering him? Or preferably, into his own caravan? They are all equipped with showers these days. But he's obviously not in the best state of health; maybe his heart couldn't stand it. Maybe he's had a heart attack!

"Do you think we should go and offer our support?" I ask Hannah.

"A bit late for that now" she replies accusingly.

"I don't recall you taking charge".

Hannah seems to be reflecting on her own behaviour. At least I threw the bucket of filthy water at him. "He's in the best hands now", she replies. "Maureen will be accompanying him in the ambulance". Hannah again pauses for contemplation. "Perhaps we should just go and check".

Consumed with guilt, we douse their barbecue with water and throw away the contaminated, fly-infested meat, buns and salad.

We slow our pace as we approach the reception office. A solitary ambulance is parked on the shingle driveway, engine running, blue lights strobing, indicating that its crew is dealing with an emergency.

The side door opens, and Maureen emerges,

stooped, tearful. We cautiously approach her.

"How is he?" Hannah asks, placing an arm around her shoulders.

"Barry's got first-degree burns to at least forty percent of 'is body", she replies, suddenly sobbing, and pressing her face against Hannah's chest.

My hand shoots up to cover my mouth to stop me from verbally responding in a way that would unhelpfully reinforce the dreadfulness of the situation, and make Maureen more anxious. Maureen's howling renews with increased intensity, and I realise, too late, that my reaction has had the same effect as a shocked inhalation, or some exclamation of dismay.

Hannah rubs Maureen's lower back, and I notice my wife's sympathetic expression is changing to inquisitiveness. "Maureen, are you sure that they said *first*-degree burns?"

"Yes!" she cries, a gloop of snot trailing from a nostril onto Hannah's top.

"But that's good!"

"Eh?" says Maureen, moving her face away from my wife's breast, stretching the strand of mucus, which detaches from her nose and clings like a question mark to Hannah's shirt.

"Well, maybe not 'good', but it's the most superficial type of burn! I learned it at my 'First Aid at Work' course. Those burns only affect the top layer of skin. He may get a bit of redness, mild pain or swelling, and his skin may peel after a day or two, but he'll heel really quickly".

"He'll peel and heel?"

"Yes, he'll peel and heel!"

"I'd better get back". Maureen turns and hurries back into the ambulance.

"Let us know if we can do anything to help. Anything at all", Hannah offers, as Maureen shuts the door.

As we return to our caravan to change into smarter, light, casual clothes, the warm feeling of redemption is increasingly replaced by a creeping realisation that I may regret Hannah's compassionate offer.

CHAPTER 12

Saturday, 6.05 pm

Hannah and I are riding our bikes through a part of the campsite we have not previously explored. Our destination is a pub next to a weir, which the brewery that owns it has imaginatively named, "The Weir Inn". Passing through the manicured grounds and serried ranks of caravans and camper vans, it is interesting to see what other, like-minded holiday-makers are buying this season.

I often observe couples taking early evening strolls around camping parks. They are obviously not exercising or unwinding in preparation for bed, so much as commenting on who has superior or inferior gear. They seem blissfully unaware that their snide remarks issued from the sides of their mouths about the age of a camper van, or congealed moss embedded in the window seals of a caravan can easily be overheard. Their barely concealed jealousy about the size of an imported Winnebago is carried by the wind like dust in the early evening lull, when noisy children retire for bed, exhausted by the effects of energetic days spent in fresh air.

This evening, Hannah and I find ourselves window-shopping, albeit expressing our opinions more reservedly, drawing each other's attention to some bit of kit with a nod or a grunt.

A brand-new, German, Tabbert Cellini caravan with a full-length, black and cream Isabella awning catch our attention. There does not appear to be anybody in or outside them. Parked next to them is a pristine, black, luxury SUV of the kind driven by Conservatives when new, and by UKIP-voters when sold-on after ten years of ferrying its original keepers around their estates, or their children to public schools and gymkhana events.

Both the car and caravan bear the UK 'cherished transfer' registration number, CAR 93T, which makes me consider the owner's name, surname or business: Carpenter? Would a woodworker be able to afford them? There must be one hundred and twenty thousand pounds' worth of kit standing on that thirty-six square metres of space. There again, the two hundred pounds a plumber recently charged me for his labour alone, just for changing the mixer taps on our bath, may suggest otherwise.

We deviate our route slightly to peer through the expansive front window. A wall-mounted, forty-inch TV is visible adjacent to a designer kitchen of lacquered cream and dark wood-effect that wouldn't look out-of-place in a luxury apartment. We continue, waiting until we are well away from other pitches before commenting on who could afford to spend so much on what is really only a holiday diversion for a few weeks during the year.

Ten minutes later we arrive at the pub. Hannah and I padlock our bikes to the base of a post. Atop the pole is a sign representing an artist's impression of the pub and weir in the nineteenth century, with jolly townsfolk in contemporary garb clinking frothy beers in pewter pint jugs in the foreground.

We hold our breath and slalom around the smokers and vapers to access the front door leading into a beautifully restored space. It is furnished with modern fabrics and colour schemes that do not compromise or detract from its period low-ceilings, oak wall-panelling and beams. The ambience exudes an air of opulence that is slightly undermined by a small but vocal contingent of football-supporters who are still drinking after watching England play football against Denmark, screened live earlier in the afternoon on a ninety-eight-inch screen in the Public Bar.

We notice a sign for the Lounge Bar, and follow its arrow through a door into an oasis of relative calm. Here we shall willingly pay an additional twenty-five percent for our drinks, to enjoy better glassware, more comfortable furniture, and less raucous and boisterous company.

I pay for Hannah's large gin and tonic and my large whiskey and ginger, both of which are freshened by crushed ice and complimenting fruit and fauna: fresh slices of lemon and lime for her, just mint for me. We settle down into plush, wing-backed chairs.

"Well, until now, I can hardly call it 'relaxing'". Hannah's summary is succinct, but accurate.

"What doesn't kill you, makes you stronger", I reply.

"First the mine, then the barbecue. Poor Barry!" she says.

"Serves him right for taking our Burford Browns and replacing them with miniscule battery eggs".

"Well, I don't believe you feel that way anymore. You seem more compassionate in the last twenty-four hours. Ok, so you had a fit of the giggles over Barry's unfortunate accident, but I'm almost as guilty as you are on that score. I'm impressed".

"*Almost* as guilty?" I don't want to admit that my so-called, newfound compassion has been a supreme effort. It has really gone against the grain, so it is important for me to highlight any hypocrisy by Hannah so that my inevitable, future transgressions are more readily forgiven.

"Well, what with Gryffyn and all, it's been a traumatic day. My laughter was a stress-reaction," she adds in mitigation.

We are politely interrupted by a young waitress who introduces herself as Charlotte, who wants to know if we would like to book a table for the 7 pm dinner service in the open-air section of their restaurant, next to the weir. Apparently, Lounge Bar guests are given first refusal of any tables that have not been booked in advance. A quick perusal of the menu and the opportunity to eat al fresco next to running water on a beautiful Saturday evening in late-May is too tempting to refuse. I am surprised that there is availability, and we accept without the need for discussion or procrastination, which may risk losing the table. Charlotte invites us to pre-order our food and drinks.

Always with an eye on the prices, I am astonished by the good value of what is on offer. Hannah and I both choose the same: Newlyn Crab Thermidor, followed by thick sirloin steak with jacket potato and a dressed green salad. We request two large glasses of cold Muscadet with the crab, and a bottle of Merlot with the steak. Total cost: seventy-seven pounds. I can live with that.

Hannah and I are sipping chilled Muscadet, having just devoured our crabs, and sit watching and listening to the water crashing over three tiers of the weir into the pool below. After the froth and frenzy of the day, it's blissful losing ourselves in the white noise of the river's spume and spray.

"I want to try and replicate that at home", Hannah says, glancing at the carapaces we have picked clean.

"Yes, delicious, and according to the menu it was all sourced locally, apart from the calvados and pecorino".

The conversation lulls again, but is not awkward or strained.

Charlotte brings our main course, and pours samples of the Merlot to taste. It is a perfect, room temperature, and heavily laden with tannins: a perfect accompaniment to the sirloin.

"Unless we find somewhere better, let's return for dinner on our last night", she says. I agree wholeheartedly. "What would you like to do tomorrow?" she asks.

I spear a perfectly griddled piece of tender meat and smear some Maille Dijon mustard onto it with my knife. "I checked the forecast again when you were changing your clothes, and it looks like that band of high pressure should stick around for a while. It should be fine; about twenty degrees". There's only one thing I'm particularly keen on visiting during this holiday, and that is the open-air, Sable Theatre to see the play, later in the week. "I'm easy. What do you fancy?"

Hannah redistributes the dressing that has drained to the bottom of the large bowl by tossing the salad with the two wooden spoons provided. "In that case, I'd like to go to St. Michael's Mount".

I enjoy going to places of historical significance, and the Mount has a particularly long and fascinating past. But I don't want to be too positive about her choice; I need to feign a fair degree of indifference, and use it as a bargaining chip to persuade her to accompany me to the Sable Theatre, in which she has shown scant interest. "Yeah, we could do. But it's a smaller version of its counterpart, Mont Saint-Michel in Normandy that we visited last year".

Hannah is frowning, chewing on some jacket potato, regarding me quizzically. I need to be more convincing; to fake more apathy.

"You remember? Access difficulties due to the tides, then steep climbs; and all for what? Loads of Benedictine, religious mumbo-jumbo!" I add.

She maintains her gaze, unblinkingly looking me in the eye, peering into my soul. "You *love* all that history and architecture," she says after a long pause. "You don't fool me, Henry. What's this all about? That bloody trip to that theatre, I suppose! You know that stuff bores me; people pretending to be other people, usually very unrealistically."

Damn! Busted! I need to hold my nerve. "Well, ok, we could go to the Mount; but it's good to experience different things. We did a history trip today, and you want to do another one tomorrow. I think it would be good to indulge ourselves in another form of culture. And the Sable isn't just an 'open-air theatre'. It attracts highly acclaimed acting troupes, and is set on a remote, sandy beach. You get to it via a steep staircase that has been hewn from the cliff above it. All the buildings on the beach have been cleverly formed in concrete-reinforced sand, so that the stage and seating look like they have morphed from the beach itself".

She's still inspecting me. "A theatre on a beach that you can only reach and return from, by scaling a cliff?"

I'm getting excited by the prospect that she is warming to the idea. "Yes!"

"Mmm. And you're worried about access difficulties and steep climbs!"

Don't crack now. I must maintain my resolve, so she'll never be completely sure that I'm tactically bartering…"I'm just suggesting we do something different. Variety is the spice of life, right?"

Still she deploys the cold, hard stare: one of the most powerful weapons in her arsenal. I hold my breath and her gaze, determined not to blink; but tiny pins are pricking my eyes, and it feels as though the seals on my tear ducts are about to fail. And then, just as I start looking like I'm sucking on a lemon, she breaks the deadlock with a simple, "Ok".

I exhale my bated breath. It's settled with a compromise: St Michael's Mount tomorrow, and Hannah will accompany me to the matinée performance on Wednesday, the last day of our holiday before our return home on Thursday. We've just got two other days to plan.

We leave the pub to retrieve our bikes, at 8.30 pm. Both of us are a little tipsy after consuming spirits, and about a bottle and a half of wine. I am unable to process the fact that just my front wheel is attached to the post, so I keep looking around for the rest of my bike.

"Henry, it's no good searching for it. Someone's pinched it. You forgot to lock the frame to the post, too."

"Arsehole!"

"Come on. We'll report it stolen, and get back to the caravan for a coffee".

"Arsehole!"

"It's no use fretting. What's done is done; and it is insured".

"Yes, but the excess is more than the value of the bike. In broad daylight! Well, dusk. Arsehole!"

Hannah produces her mobile phone from her back jeans pocket and dials 101, the non-emergency number for the police. "Hello. I'd like to report my husband's bike stolen from outside The Weir Inn, in Godleven".

Hannah continues to provide a description of my

bike, the material time period when it was stolen, and the fact that there are no known witnesses. She receives a crime reference number and the call-taker tells her that he will be allocating the incident to a local police officer for further investigation. This is surprising given there appear to be few lines of inquiry. An appointment is made for 9 am the following morning with a PC Blinkerton, who will meet us at our caravan on pitch 60.

The unexpected seriousness with which the local constabulary appears to be taking my misfortune does little to lessen my indignance. I unlock and retrieve my front wheel, and follow Hannah forlornly. Every ten feet or so, I cast around in the bushes in the hope that the offender abandoned it rather than risk being caught in possession of 'hot goods'.

"You know you'll never see it again, don't you", she says rhetorically.

I harrumph distractedly, continuing to use my chain lock to scythe aside the long grass to peer along the roadside ditch, all the way back to the campsite.

CHAPTER 13

Sunday 8.30 am

Henry has been very quiet since he became a crime statistic. He's busy outside in the Volvo, looking for the instructions that came with his bike, trying to locate information that will assist PC Blinkerton's investigation.

When I buy new equipment for the kitchen, I always throw away the stuff that comes with it. Not Henry! There is a filing cabinet in our home-study that he has filled with documentation, manuals and receipts for every leisure, audio-visual and electronic gift or purchase he's made; even if the item itself has long since been consigned to the local council's refuse tip. He stores the original packaging in the loft. I've seen them: the box for a fourteen-year-old Moulinex food processor; shaped polystyrene that encased our ten-year-old Breville sandwich toaster; the large twin oven and grill, which was a wedding gift from his great Aunt Beryl five years ago, and was the subject of considerable conjecture when it was delivered, fully gift-wrapped at the hotel wedding reception.

Why on earth does he do this? They are so old, it's not as if he can return them to the shop for an exchange or refund if they develop a fault!

I can hear him now, cursing the fact that the first time he has ever needed a product's specifications, he's left them behind at home. I must remember to remind him that life is too short for this sort of obsessive meticulousness. Perhaps he'll see sense, and I'll be able to reclaim some space in the house.

Anyway, I was telling you about Henry's options for gaining practical work experience, whilst studying for his postgraduate LPC, his next step to qualify as a lawyer. These were an unpaid internship at a prestigious law firm in Bristol, or a modestly paid one at run-down offices in Cardiff.

Well, as I'm sure you guessed, he chose the one in Bristol. He was required to start there on 1st September, which coincided with the first day of my second year as an undergraduate.

I was unsure whether his decision was influenced by a desire to remain in closer proximity to me, or because he felt that future employers would be more impressed if they saw the name 'Uppingham & Snook Advocates' emblazoned all over his curriculum vitae.

Whatever his justification, I was delighted that he was remaining in Bristol. I remember encouraging him to do so, which I accept was rather selfish. But I was acting in the interests of our relationship and our future together. He lapped up my suggestions that he would have a 'foot-in-the-door' that could lead to an offer of permanent, paid employment there, if his placement was successful; and that even if an offer wasn't forthcoming, other prospective employers would be impressed by the enthusiasm and ambition necessary to undertake unpaid work for eight months.

Privately I felt that the smaller, Cardiff firm would have given him broader exposure and responsibility, as well as an income. But I kept this to myself.

It didn't take long before I deeply regretted any influence I may have brought to bear on his choice. Henry swallowed a huge dose of his own medicine from his very first day at U & S. Having always differentiated himself as an upper-middle class man in a middle-class university, he soon realised that he was a fish-out-of-water in a sea where he thought he would swim in harmony with the shoal.

Ninety percent of the lawyers at U & S Advocates were alumni of top public schools and Oxbridge colleges, and all of them had achieved first-class honours degrees in Law. Henry's education at the respectable and highly regarded Bristol Grammar School, and his upper-second from Bristol University became something of an open joke amongst a clique of loud and predominantly male antagonists. They referred to him as a 'pro bono' case: an opportunity for U & S to 'give something back' to the less fortunate. The women acquiesced in this toxic, alpha-male environment, and sided with the dominant personalities. No one wanted a reputation for 'not fitting in'. Henry wasn't immune to the irony of his situation, considering the way in which he had previously treated others.

Amongst the four other interns were two sons of Lords, two daughters of Baronesses, and a minor British royal who was distinctive in being one of the very few members of his family to have achieved academic excellence.

Henry felt miserable and isolated. In fact, the only similarity he held in common with the paid and unpaid, male and female employees at U & S, was being named after a British monarch. The whole firm seemed populated by people called Elizabeth, Eleanor, Victoria, George, Edward, Charles, James, Alfred, Harold, or William.

But there was even divergence to be found in nomenclature, as everyone adapted their Christian names to jaunty, casual monikers, such as Lizzie, Ellie, Tori, Georgie, Charley, Jamie, Freddie, Harry and Billy. How could Henry informalise Henry?

He vaguely remembered a story told to him by

his mother when he was at primary school: In mediaeval times, children's names were shortened and stemmed with the suffix "-kin", meaning "little". So in the Middle Ages, a young Henry became "Henkin", and then "Hankin". This, she explained, is why the shortened version of Henry is "Hank". Well, designating himself as "Henkin" was out of the question, even amongst the plummy, stomach-churningly saccharine females employed there; and he knew what alternative name the domineering males would rhyme with "Hankin"; or "Hank", come to that!

It was too much for Henry to hope that one of his nemeses, whom he had privately named 'Big-headed Eddie', wasn't named after a sovereign with a cool name like Edward, but a naff one, like Edmund or Edgar.

Whilst the rich kids were allocated to the firm's partners to work on high-profile, high-value divorces, company law suits and class actions, Henry was sent to the Criminal Law department. He was briefed on how to represent those who had found themselves arrested and in custody at police stations all over the city. Whilst he was not paid a salary, he was entitled to claim back his taxi fares on production of the receipts.

By the time he received the phone call from an investigating officer or jailer, travelled to the required venue, been admitted through security, read the detainee's custody record and any medical notes, well over an hour would have been consumed. He would often have to wait to receive the official form providing written disclosure of what the investigating officer was prepared to tell him about the case.

Being highly meticulous, Henry always scrupulously went through the motions of asking questions to elicit additional details, which were always denied by the officer with the learnt addendum, "You have been given sufficient information for you to advise your client".

Henry told me that he felt as though the whole bureaucratic process was designed to encourage prisoners to forgo legal representation, just so they could get out of there quicker. The tedium made Henry sink lower in his chair, which gave him the sensation that he was shrinking. He watched as the officer painstakingly wrote down verbatim every question Henry asked, and every word of the officer's rehearsed, stock reply, even though it never changed. The officer was often on over-time; Henry was working for free. Who was the mug?

More than two-and-a-half hours would have typically elapsed since the original call, before Henry could meet his client. Consistently it was a male who was often the worse-for-wear. Despite having received a 'rest period', his dishevelled and malodorous appearance suggested that he had barely slept-off the drink and drugs: chemicals which had contributed to his behaviour, and the reason why he was incarcerated there.

Each time, Henry sat and listened to a prisoner spew out an unlikely version of events that either entirely avoided the focus of the allegation, or consisted of a raft of denials and blame directed at both the alleged victim and the police officer who arrested him. It seemed impossible to Henry, who would request a copy of the detainee's criminal antecedence and sentencing history when he received the disclosure document, that so many victims and police officers could have so misunderstood his client; that CCTV footage misrepresented his actions; that his client's implausible, alternative explanations for the presence of forensic proof, rendered it inconclusive; that the incriminating messages on his client's phone must have been sent by someone else. Henry heard the same fictitious defences replayed so many times by so many different defendants, some of whom would find themselves in custody, several times a month. It was only the times, dates, victims' and witnesses' names, and circumstances that differed.

Henry couldn't believe the idiotic responses these people made when experiencing the kind of normal, every-day pressure that most people take in their stride: The client who was driving his car, when someone cut in front of him in another vehicle, reacted with a torrent of foul-mouthed abuse, which quickly escalated into an attack on the other driver's car, and then on his person. The client who was walking down the street with his girlfriend, when he perceived that another man looked at her "the wrong way"; so he punched him and fractured his jaw; and when he pole-axed face-first onto the pavement and was rendered unconscious and defenceless, thought that it was reasonable to kick and stamp on his chest and head.

Henry had to represent these people, day-in and day-out. Even in the cold light of day, they rarely took responsibility for their actions. They behaved indignantly during the legal consultation, like *they* were the wronged party, and it was everyone else who was at fault. They were completely incapable of accepting that they were the architect of their own misfortunes, and deserved every-thing that the courts were going to throw at them. It was Henry's job, if not to believe them, to place the burden of proof squarely on the shoulders of the police. For there is a rule of criminal law that states the defendant does not have to prove his innocence. It is for the prosecution to prove his guilt beyond all reasonable doubt.

Nevertheless, this work took its toll on Henry. He quickly tired of having to take every case, no matter how he felt about it. A lawyer or legal representative was never allowed to mislead a court. So as long as a client did not compromise Henry by admitting the offence to him, but denying it to the officer, Henry had to take their denials in good faith, and prepare the best defence that Legal Aid could buy...even if none of the money was going to Henry.

Henry was also present to safeguard his client's legal rights when the officer conducted the audio-visually recorded interview. Henry was aware that other representatives saw the interview as their opportunity to intervene on some minor point, to throw the interviewer off-track, or to prompt the defendant to respond in a particular way. Henry was at least admired by most officers for keeping his trap shut, unless the line of questioning became oppressively repetitive. Nevertheless, what should have been a four-hour day, was usually doubled, by the time Henry had prepared summaries for the lawyer who would be defending the case at court.

It was no better for him back at the office, where all of the mundane office work fell to him: tea and coffee-making, photocopying, running paperwork up to the fourth floor. Henry couldn't believe the hours he had spent studying, merely to be the lawyers' lackey. He felt capable of so much more, and resented the other interns telling him in elaborate terms how they had prepared briefs for partners in corporate law, summaries for clients, and materials for court. He knew that you didn't even need to be legally qualified to perform the role of a custody legal advisor. He just wasn't learning anything.

During the Christmas holidays, Henry decided that he was going to resign from his internship at Uppingham & Snook Advocates. He didn't want to completely burn his bridges and lose a good reference for his four months' work; so he explained that he regretted being unable to financially afford dedicating so many hours of the working week to unpaid work, for the remaining four months.

I subsequently overheard him telephoning Wainwright & Associates in Cardiff, who confirmed that they still had a vacancy. Due to his experience at U & S, they were prepared to offer him twenty five percent more than before. I was worried that he was going to accept the position, and was relieved when he ended the call by thanking them, and asking if he could take twenty-four hours to consider their kind offer.

He took me to a pub near to our respective halls of residence that evening, where we discussed the situation over a meal and drinks. Casting his eyes down at his fish and chips, he asked me what I thought he should do. I took his lack of eye contact to mean that he had already made up his mind to move across the Bristol Channel to Cardiff; that he was worried that I would not support his decision. He had already told me that Cardiff University had available accommodation for LPC students, and would recognise the prior, LPC learning he had completed at Bristol. It seemed likely that the money that had already paid to Bristol University for the LPC may be lost. It turned out that his father, Basil, had been sympathetic on that point, and was prepared to bear the additional cost of taking Cardiff's course.

I didn't want Henry to ever have grounds to blame me for a missed opportunity; but the thought of him not being easily accessible to me for the first time in a year made my shoulders, stomach, chest and throat tighten. It was a job to speak without bursting into tears, but I summoned the strength from somewhere. "Henry, you must seize these opportunities with both hands", I told him.

He didn't say anything for a long while. I wondered whether he knew how much I felt about him, but I could not risk saying anything else because I knew my voice would crack.

Another factor that bothered me was our sexual

intimacy; or rather the lack of it. Unlike so many of our peers who seemed to jump into bed given little opportunity or encouragement, we still hadn't made love with each other at that stage in our relationship. Yes, we often slept together, but that is *all* we did: kissed, cuddled with a decent layer of clothes on, and *slept*. What I mean is, I suddenly became consumed by fear that Henry felt our lack of physical intimacy meant that our relationship was not serious or solid enough to warrant inseparability; that this was the beginning of the end.

Finally, Henry spoke. "I just don't think being a lawyer suits me after all", he said.

I wasn't sure that I heard him correctly. I hadn't expected it.

"Up themselves & Snooty Advocates of Bristol', have done me a favour", he continued.

"Why? How?" I stammered.

"By showing me that class and privilege is not necessarily something to be coveted, if it means behaving like an abominable arsehole, merely so you fit in. By showing me that even if you are at the top of the legal pile, you are cashing in on people's misfortune and misery, charging them extortionate fees to sort out their woes. By showing me that whether you are at the top or the bottom, the work is dry and tedious; something that I know Wainwright & Associates of Cardiff would merely confirm, just without the plush, comfortable offices".

I was listening to Henry intently. This, I know, was another seminal moment not just for him, but for us as a couple.

"And that is why I shall be going to the Law Faculty in the morning to request a transfer from my LPC, to do something considerably more worthwhile - a Post Graduate Certificate in Education. I'm going to be an English teacher, and it may surprise you to know that I am not in the least interested in pursuing this in a public or private school, but in the state sector".

I dropped my knife and fork which I had been gripping tightly, and moved round the table to give Henry the biggest hug of his life.

That night, we made love for the first time. Modesty and good taste prevent me from going into details, but at the risk of sounding uncomplicated and shallow, it was bloody marvellous!

CHAPTER 14

Sunday 9.00 am

I've given up searching for the documentation for my bike. PC Blinkerton's police car is meandering its way through the caravans; but as it gets closer, I am baffled to see that no one appears to be driving it. I raise a hand to shield my eyes from the sun, but it makes no difference. The police car is driverless! I've heard about this race to automate professions, but this is surely taking matters a step too far. Surely Robocop doesn't actually exist in coastal Cornwall?

The fully liveried Vauxhall Astra estate rolls to a smooth stop next to our caravan, and a diminutive policeman steps out from behind the wheel. He is no more than five feet tall, aged in his late-twenties, and sporting a full beard and moustache, as is the fashion. He reaches into the car for a folder and his flap cap, which screws onto a completely shaved head.

"Mr Burden, I presume?" he says with a Cornish lilt and a voice that is much deeper than I expected.

"Er, yes".

"You seem surprised to see me. We have a nine o'clock appointment, concerning your stolen bike".

"Er, yes, that's right, er, PC Blinkerton".

"Or is it my size that surprises you?"

"Er, no, um".

"Cos, I get a lot of that".

"Well, erm, may be I was a little taken aback". I stop short of explaining that I was wondering who was driving his car.

PC Blinkerton walks purposefully towards me, one hand clamping a folder under his left arm, whilst the other rests on the top of a bright yellow Taser that is strapped across the front of his black, stab-proof vest. When he is an uncomfortably close, twelve inches away from my chest, he looks up at my face. I look down at his. The sharp angle strains my neck muscles.

"Fortunately, the modern-day Police Service has revoked prejudiced policies that discriminate against those of us who are vertically challenged", he says, looking me in the eye with a deadpan expression.

"Quite right too", I agree, wondering how well he copes with people of the size and temperament I used to legally represent in the custody suites of Bristol's police stations.

"In fact the height restriction for police officers was removed over twenty years ago", he adds, determined to make his point.

"Good", I reply, feeling even more uncomfortable, not just by his inference that I am a prejudiced Neanderthal, but because I am desperate to create more space between us by taking a step backwards.

"Think of all those excellent men and women who would have been prevented from joining the Service and serving their communities, had the powers-that-be not changed Police Regulations".

"Yes, you make your point well, PC Blinkerton".

"I've got one of the highest arrest rates in my division. Fifty-eight, so far this year", he adds, stepping even closer, making me feel as though he is keen to make me his fifty-ninth.

"Bravo, and well done to you! You can surely hold your head up high". I wince at the double-meaning. I'm keen to change the subject. "Shall we go into the caravan? It'll be more comfortable in there." I turn and stop myself from asking him if he can reach the step. "May I offer you a tea or coffee? I think we've got some shortbread some-where". I freeze momentarily. He's obviously sensitive about his height, so I must choose my vocabulary more carefully. Why did I say *short*bread? Why didn't I just say biscuits? He follows me into the van.

"Good morning, madam. Mrs Burden, I pre-sume?"

"Good morning, officer. You presume correctly".

PC Blinkerton smooths down his moustache with a forefinger and thumb, and breaks into a nervous smile. I'm standing right next to him and he's barely disguising the fact that he fancies my wife!

"Now, first I need to check that the call-taker re-corded the circumstances correctly. We don't want this matter going to court, and being embarrassed to find that we've misunderstood some minor detail. Defence solicitors and legal representatives love that. They'll use anything to get their clients off."

"Henry used to be one of those, didn't you Henry?"

PC Blinkerton turns to face me again, and looks me up and down unhurriedly. "Did he indeed", he says with more than a hint of disgust, before turning back to-wards Hannah and smiling. "May I sit down?"

"Oh, yes, sorry, please do," Hannah replies in a slightly confused way that suggests that she thought he was already seated.

"You mentioned this going to court, officer", I say. "Is there any realistic prospect of a conviction and the return of my property, or is the offender still at large?" Christ, another reference to size.

"No, I haven't found him yet. I just want to make sure that my investigation is based on sound foundations, that's all."

"Yes, you don't want to make all the effort and find that you fall short at court." Damn it, I've done it again.

PC Blinkerton runs through the times and precise location where my bike was tethered, telling us that this will assist him when he reviews the pub's CCTV footage. He knows from previous incidents that there is a camera that sweeps a one hundred and eighty-degree arc at the front of the pub.

When I try to tell him that it is a silver, Cannondale Quick CX4, men's hybrid, and describe to him the missing front wheel, its equipment, the after-market, orange handlebar grips and the distinctive scratch on the crossbar, he seems less interested.

"It's most usual for thieves to grind off identification numbers, re-spray the frames, and break them down into their component parts to construct new bikes. This makes identification more difficult", he explains.

"But surely", I begin, drawing on my experience as a legal representative, "many thieves are opportunists, stealing and selling on property quickly for cash to fund their raging drugs habits? Surely, they're not concerned with the rigmarole of disguising their ill-gotten gains. They just want to realise them for drugs as quickly as they possibly can."

PC Blinkerton studies me with apparent distaste. He isn't a man who likes to be contradicted. He asks me curtly for my frame number. I start to explain that I have the details in my filing cabinet at home, but he cuts me short, tutting and exhaling loudly.

"Ninety-eight percent of people who report their

bikes stolen didn't mark them with their postcode, which is visible only under ultra-violent light". He indicates a torch which is also attached to his body armour. "Ninety-five percent are unable to supply the police with the frame number".

"But you said that it's most likely that my bike doesn't even look like my bike by now. What's the use of these deterrents if the frame number's been ground off and the frame resprayed?"

PC Blinkerton replies in an exasperated tone, "You are missing the point if I may be so bold, Mr Burden. A good investigator asks these questions to be armed with as much information about the property as possible; so that when I'm next searching the house of the local bike thief, I'm at least in a position to say that the bike in his shed is *your* bike; to make a case that *he* stole it or is dishonestly handling it, and charge him with the right offence. It would be better if you were able to supply me with better information, that's all". He stops, straightens his back, raises his bushy eyebrows and smiles at Hannah, as if to say, *who is this idiot*? He's flirting with her right in front of me, in our caravan!

My tone is raised, not prepared to be out done. "So there's someone you have in mind then? This local bike thief, who's got it in his shed?"

"I was speaking hypothetically, Mr Burden", he replies slowly, looking at me then back to Hannah and shaking his head at her sympathetically, touching her hand lightly, as though consoling and comforting her for marrying a fool. "No, there are only two viable lines of enquiry as far as I can see: check the CCTV for footage of the theft taking place. If it exists, and I don't recognise him, or her, I'll submit a blown up still photo to the God-leven Herald, appealing to the public for identification.

No CCTV, no detection! Of course, if you'd locked it up in the approved manner, we wouldn't be sitting here now, would we Mr Burden?" Again, he flashes another look of pity at Hannah.

"How can people stoop so *low*? I get a *tiny* bit impatient with this sort of criminality?" I say, now intending to maximise my height-sensitive vocabulary. "It's hard not to become *short*-tempered at this kind of dishonesty, but I should *grow* out of it and stop being so *small*-minded".

PC Blinkerton stops and looks again from Hannah to me and back to Hannah, not quite sure whether he is the butt of a private joke.

"Well", he says, "I'll update you by phone or in person in a few days, to let you know how I'm progressing… or otherwise".

"Yes", I say, through a rictus smile; "a *little* get-together in a few days would be much appreciated. Please do not hesitate to contact me, no matter how *minute, miniature, minuscular, microscopic* or *Lilliputian* your question or news". I extend my hand, and when he shakes it warily, I grip his wrist with my other hand and manoeuvre him towards the door, denying him any further opportunity to paw Hannah.

CHAPTER 15

Sunday 10.00 am

Hannah has made a packed lunch for our daytrip to St Michael's Mount, which she has placed with sealed ice packs in one of our many cool bags. I can see her out of the corner of my eye, her hands on her hips; body language that wills me to put away my iPhone, and get on with the day.

"I just want to check the free ads for any sign of my bike".

"You know what PC Blinkerton said about thieves cannibalising stolen property to avoid detection".

He may be right. I can't yet find any bike of my colour, make and model featured for sale within a thirty-mile radius of Godleven, on any classified advertising website. My instinct is that the thief lives or is visiting locally. I switch off my phone and hide it from view under a pillow. I feel more cautious about safeguarding my property since last night.

Following Hannah out of the caravan, I'm surprised to see what looks like the Michelin Man sitting straight-limbed in a deckchair outside the neighbouring caravan, wrapped from head-to-toe in white bandages.

"Barry! What time did you get back?" I'm trying to maintain as normal a conversation as possible, without referring to his alarming appearance.

"It were late, weren't it Maureen," he replies, tonelessly.

"Aye, it were late".

There is a stunted silence, which I feel obliged to fill. "Oh, we didn't hear you, did we Hannah?"

Hannah shakes her head. The silence is uncomfortable. It is unusual that Barry and Maureen don't want to engage us in conversation, and I wonder whether they bear a grudge for not being more proactive in responding to Barry's burns.

"So, what's the prognosis?" I ask.

"The wha'?" replies Maureen, poker-faced.

"Erm, the diagnosis...I mean, the outlook?"

Maureen surveys the sky, straight-faced. I think she thinks I'm asking her for a weather forecast. Perhaps she is wondering why I'm asking superficial questions, when her husband is shrouded like Tutankhamun.

I persevere. "The burns. Will Barry be ok?"

"Oh, snot juss the burns, 'enry", she replies. "Iss the infection caused by you throwin' watery bird shit over 'im. What was ya thinkin', chuckin' that into open wounds?"

"Ah, um, sorry. I just wanted to stop him from cooking," I reply. "It seemed to be the priority in the, er, heat of the moment. Well, if there's anything we can do", I offer. Only Barry's eyes and lips are visible, and he is surveying me with a hard stare.

As Hannah and I start walking towards our Volvo, Barry pipes up again.

"Where did our meat get to, 'enry?"

I pause for a moment. "Erm, I threw it in the bin, Barry".

"You did wha'?" Barry and Maureen chime, simultaneously, accusatorily.

"I threw it all away. In the bin. Over there." I point to a collection of metal and plastic bins, strategically placed to be accessible to the largest number of caravaners and campers. Their gimlet eyes follow the direction of my finger, and then slowly return to me.

"By the time we got back to the caravan, the meat was spoiled. The flies had been at it, and the crows had crapped all over it. We felt that you wouldn't want it. So I threw it away".

Barry and Maureen turn their faces towards each other, and then back to me, before Barry speaks again. "That were top-drawer Aberdeen Angus burgers and pork sausages, that were 'enry".

"Yes, but..."

"One 'undred percent beef. Ninety-seven percent pork".

"But they would have been inedible, Barry."

"I coulda washed 'em off and cooked 'em".

"Right-o, well I'll get you some replacements then, shall I?" I say, feeling that in the circumstances, this is not a battle worth fighting.

"They was from Marks & Spencer food 'all" Maureen adds.

"Really? Ok, well, I thought I was doing you a favour".

"Twenty quids' worth", adds Barry.

"And that's not including the buns and salad", Maureen says.

I look at Hannah, and she knows that I am struggling to maintain my reserve. I'm sure they think I stole their food and ate it. I recall the cinereous burgers and synthetically coloured sausages, so obviously purchased from their favourite, budget supermarket, Happy Bargains. But without the packaging, there is no way that I'm going to able to prove it. So, I shall have to find a Marks & Spencer food hall and be out-of-pocket to the tune of twenty pounds plus, just for doing them a good deed.

"I'll sort it out", I say as we climb into the Volvo, a little ruse taking shape in my mind. What if I bought food from both M & S and Happy Bargains? Yes, it would be marginally more expensive, but I could swap the labels and keep the superior meat for Hannah and me. I vow that once the perceived debt is repaid, I shall no longer feel it necessary to engage with this couple of freeloaders, or pretend to like them. Seeing as Hannah has witnessed this unreasonable series of events, and my effort to make reparation and exculpate myself from blame, perhaps she will overlook my scam.

Getting into the car, I prioritise the search for the nearest M & S food hall and Happy Bargains supermarket. I buy the food, placing the better-quality purchases into a cool bag with ample ice packs to keep it fresh for six hours. I leave the Happy Bargains food in carrier bags in the boot, where they will sweat all day, unrefrigerated.

Revenge is a dish best served at about seventy degrees Fahrenheit!

What is it, with some people of a certain vintage? Young people don't seem to do it! No matter whether it's a demographic sample of the elderly in a Marks & Spencer food hall, or a Happy Bargains supermarket, they seem totally oblivious to the presence of other shoppers; pushing their trolleys at a snail's pace, and getting in the bloody way! I swear that they've got tiny rear-view mirrors inside their bifocals, watching me approach them from behind, and then stepping into my path at the very last second. And it's no good trying to use my relatively youthful agility to spring a fighter-pilot-like change of direction; they'll deploy their wingman, their infernal trolley, which they'll casually deflect to the left or right to block me as I try to make my advance.

They stop at the displays, bringing their trolleys right up to the shelving units, so I can't see or select what *I* need to buy. I'll ask them to "excuse me", which they either don't hear or choose not to hear; and so I'll try to move their trolley aside to gain access to, say, the various brands of tinned soup. Then they turn nasty. An arthritic claw will shoot onto the trolley's handle, yanking it back into its original, obstructive position. A narrow-eyed glare challenges me not to resist them, or they'll loudly accuse me of attempting to steal their purse or wallet. And so I wait an interminable length of time for them to make their choice, before they hobble off again... not having selected anything.

It's no less frustrating at the till. If they are behind me, then you can bet that they will find strength and flexibility that is incongruent to their age and fragility, to forcefully ram forward the plastic divider I have placed on the conveyor belt to differentiate their shopping from mine. They do this just so they don't have to wait a few seconds for space to become available to load another packet of Werther's Original. And it would be alright if the last item in my row of shopping was something sturdy like a bag of jacket potatoes. But why would I put hardy vegetables last on the conveyor? That is the space reserved for my breakables; the groceries that must sit at the top of my shopping bag, not the bottom: my Burford Browns and multipack of dry snacks, which I shall only know are respectively cracked and turned into fine, powered dust, when I get them home and unpack!

If they are ahead of me at the till, it will become clear that their shopping trip is not to stock up on provisions, but to hold an endless conversation with the cashier about the weather; the news; the cost of living; a TV soap opera; the cashier's children; or their own children and grandchildren whom they never see because they moved away to Uttoxeter.

The process of watching and waiting for them to pay for their goods, is equally exasperating. They don't use bank cards, and would certainly never contemplate making a rapid, contactless payment, because they don't trust new-fangled technology. Given the choice, they would laboriously write out a cheque, but they are being phased out. So it's cash. But it won't be a fan of paper money they will tender for their Horlicks, sweets and cold cuts, but as many jars of loose change that they are able to carry, accumulated since their partner died, several years ago. They'll count it out themselves, because as much as they are prepared to chat to the cashier, they don't trust anybody; and anyway, they like to exercise *some* independence. Just when I feel that the transaction is about to be completed, they'll suddenly remember that they've got a variety of money-off vouchers, which will take an age to locate at the bottom of their wheel-mounted shopping bags, beneath the groceries they have just loaded into them.

If I dare to huff, puff, and show my displeasure by checking my watch, rolling my eyes and tutting, they'll make me feel particularly guilty by loudly thanking the cashier for being so patient and understanding; for taking the time to chat to them, explaining that they would otherwise go from week-to-week without speaking to a soul. Then, all of the women in my own and parallel queues will scowl at me in disgust at my insensitivity.

I return to the car with my shopping from both shops, place the M & S food in a chiller bag, and leave the Happy Bargains fare in their thin, plastic carrier bags. I am in a foul mood, which I must disguise, because I'm trying to show Hannah that I am a changed man; that what she calls my prejudice and discrimination are held in check and are under control.

"What's happened, Henry?" Hannah asks, as I climb into the driver's seat.

"What do you mean?" I reply, forcing my most casual and relaxed smile.

"You came out of both shops with a face like thunder."

There is no fooling Hannah. "I twisted my ankle", I say, coming up with something to which no blame or criticism can be attributed.

"Oh, darling, I'm sorry to hear that… You seem to be walking very well on it".

I decide that if I keep silent and don't respond, I won't put my uninjured foot in it. I reach underneath the steering wheel to turn the keys in the ignition. They are not there. Patting my pockets, I get out to check the shopping in the boot. They are not there either. Just as I start to panic that I have lost them, Hannah raises her hand and lets the keys dangle in front of me. Thinking that she is playing some form of annoying trick, I reach out to take them, but she snatches them away from me. Turning to face her, I see that she is observing me sternly.

"So do you want to tell me what *really* happened in there?" she asks.

"My ankle… I went over on it. Really hurt", I say, like a kid who has been caught lying.

"Henry, please tell me it wasn't another one of your 'shopping-rage' incidents".

I look away and stare at the steering wheel, unable to maintain eye contact.

"What was it *this* time? People eating things before they've paid for them at the till, or you not being able to find what you are looking for?"

"Old people getting in the way", I reply, sulkily.

Hannah exhales deeply. "Oh God, Henry! So we can add ageism to your long list of prejudices, can we?"

"It's just that…"

"No, Henry!"

Hannah is really annoyed. I feel one of her lectures coming.

"Why is it that you never hear a woman being ageist? Ageists always seem to be younger and male. What makes *your* need to shop more important than *theirs*? Why do *they* need to drive during the rush-hour? Why do they need to drive at all, getting in your way and slowing you down? The least they can do is re-organise their schedules, and keep out of the way of young, important, busy and dynamic people like Henry Burden, who are, after all, paying their pensions!"

"Precisely", I say. But I can tell from Hannah's face that she was not agreeing with me, and doesn't find me funny.

"No, Henry! Why should people like you cause the elderly to become less engaged in society, to have less fulfilled lives? Ageism is an incredible, modern phenomenon: Just when the world is beginning to take a stand against other evil prejudices, ageism is increasingly tolerated. It seems to have become 'acceptable'; and that's dangerous, Henry; because if it is not challenged, it flourishes and grows until it leads to discrimination".

My eyes drop lower to my hands in my lap. I should have known better than to respond when Hannah is in full-flow.

"Discrimination means that people are not allowed to sit on buses, or take jobs that are reserved only for men, or vote, or get paid less for the same work. The elderly are not a unique, homogenous group, standing alone as a burden on the rest of society. It is time, before it's too late, for the young to stop seeing them as inconveniences, as barriers to their right to prioritised treatment, for succession for jobs, or other opportunities. The elderly have knowledge borne from experiencing most things. They are a benefit, not a burden, so why do we deny ourselves their contributions? Ageism merely stymies our progress; it certainly doesn't enable it! What of the elderly themselves? If we constantly bypass and ignore them, limit their autonomy, what happens to their health and self-esteem? And to take it a stage further, knowing that we all hope to live long and healthy lives, why do we feed such destructive prejudices? We are effectively destroying our future selves! Henry, the time has come to stop this repetitive cycle, and make a concerted and collective effort to challenge such stupid stereotypes and attitudes".

This is Hannah at her most sanctimonious and idealistic, but I daren't say so. "Is there nothing in this world that irritates *you*, Hannah?" I ask.

"Oh yes...", she says, handing me the keys, "... you!"

CHAPTER 16

Sunday 11.30 am

The twenty-minute drive south to St Michael's Mount at Marazion has given both of us the opportunity to calm down after my sorties to M & S and Happy Bargains, and Hannah's sermon on the evils of ageism. We have found a parking space easily at West End, and pause to contemplate an unencumbered view of the rocky island.

The castle stands about seventy metres above sea level and four hundred metres offshore. It's reached by an ancient, pedestrian causeway constructed of granite setts, which are currently submerged by the tide. According to a chart on display in the car park, it will remain closed until this evening, when the pathway will be revealed by the sea. I have seen some extraordinary photographs of visitors making their pilgrimage to the castle, shortly before low tide and shortly after high tide. In both conditions, a one-inch depth above the paving stones gives the illusion that they are walking on water.

Having taken our picnic from the boot, we walk to the ferry station, and pay for our tickets to cross to the castle's harbour. I stand in-line for the next boat, but Hannah has spotted a resourceful and opportunistic bookseller, who has set up his stall near to the queue and a captive audience. She quickly makes her selection and purchase. Returning to me, she threads her free arm through mine, rests her head on my shoulder, and opens her book.

I stand silently for fifteen minutes taking in this unusual and spectacular land and seascape, allowing Hannah peace to read the introduction uninterrupted. As the next boat approaches, laden with tourists from the island, she tucks in her ticket to mark her place.

"Any good?"

"*Very* good. I like guide books that cut to the chase...don't dress everything up in flowery language".

A boat moors, and once its passengers have disembarked, eight new daytrippers, Hannah and I climb aboard. Once we have settled into our seats, the small inboard motor starts churning the water, propelling us towards the little island's harbour.

"So what have you found out so far?" I ask her.

She snaps the book shut, and enthusiastically summarises the etymology and chronological history of the island and its structures, from the twenty or so pages she has read. I am enjoying listening to her soft, feminine voice and clever précis, which provides a fitting soundtrack to the live experience of the subject:

"St Michael's Mount is built on fifty-seven acres of land, and is one of over forty unbridged, tidal islands accessible on foot from Britain's mainland. Its unpronounceable Cornish name translates as 'hoar rock in woodland', suggesting that it may once have stood in a forest, before being cut off from the mainland by the sea. The remnants of trees have been seen nearby at low tide. The discovery of a flint arrowhead suggests that the island may have been settled thousands of years before Christ, before becoming a tin trading centre before the first century B.C."

"I'm impressed. You should have studied general History".

"That was a bit patronising, Henry. Shall I go on?"

"Sorry. Please, it's fascinating".

"From the eighth to eleventh centuries it may have served as a monastery, before Edward the Confessor gave it to the Benedictine order of Mont Saint-Michel, its larger, French counterpart we visited last year. The oldest buildings on the summit originate from the twelfth century and still exist. Its association with the French version was terminated by its dissolution by Henry V during the war with France.

After that the island served various religious, monastic and territorial purposes. It was the first place from where the invading Spanish Armada was spotted in 1588. It had various owners for the next four hundred years, before it was sold to the St Aubyn family in 1659. The same family own and manage it today, with the National Trust".

I draw her attention to the village at the foot of the mount, next to the harbour. "What about those cottages?"

"Hang on a sec'". She opens the book again and scans the relevant chapter for several moments, before periodically summarising its contents.

"Not much is known before the eighteenth century, but it's thought that there were always fishermen's cottages and monks quarters there...The harbour was improved in 1727, when it became a successful seaport, which would have required a working population, as well as staffing for the castle..." She frowns; "Crikey... Coastal Cornwall suffered loss of life in 1755 when a tsunami a thousand miles away in Lisbon made the sea continually rise and fall two metres for five hours...Ah, here's more about the village...In 1811 there were fifty-three houses and four streets...By 1821, two hundred and twenty one people lived there, and there were three schools, a Wesleyan chapel and three pubs! In 1823, the harbour was enlarged to accommodate five hundred-tonne vessels."

"The village doesn't look that big!"

"Ah, no, well… it says here that the development of nearby Penzance and its harbour in 1852 meant that many of the Mount's buildings were demolished. In 2011, the parish had a population of just thirty-five".

"Anything else in modern times?"

Hannah flicks forward through the guidebook. "It was heavily fortified during the Second World War, and Joachim von Ribbentrop, the Nazi Foreign Minister, possibly ear-marked it as his residence once Germany had conquered Great Britain."

When I turn around in my seat to gaze back at the mainland, my right eye is blinded by a mini Go-Cam. The cuboid camera is being held aloft, betwixt the podgy forefinger and thumb of an overweight man behind me. I squint through my remaining, working eye at my attacker. He has heavily tattooed forearms and is wearing a Leeds United baseball cap and football shirt, Bermuda shorts, and trainers.

"Careful mate!" he says with the trampled vowels of a Yorkshireman, as though it was my fault that he was invading the immediate space behind my right ear, and almost using my shoulder as a tripod to shoot his bloody holiday video.

"What the hell d'you think you're playing at?" I shout, pressing the heel of the palm of my right hand into my bloodshot eyeball, which is leaking a steady stream of tears.

"I were jus' tryin' t' record ya missiz. It were rart interestin' wot she wuz goin' on abart. It'll ger a-bundle on YouTube!"

"You were doing *what*?" I shout, incensed, unadvisedly standing up and upsetting the ballast of this small and unstable craft. I hastily sit down again to lower the centre of gravity, much to the relief of the teenaged captain and the rest of the passengers. "May I suggest you bloody-well ask permission before assuming people *want* to be videoed; let alone broadcast all over the blasted internet!" I am *very* middle-class when I swear, which I think lends a certain gravitas to the cogency of my argument.

Hannah pats my knee and leans in close to my ear. "I don't think he meant any *real* harm. It was an accident", she whispers, so as not to appear disloyal but clearly eager for me to calm down and shut up.

I obey by turning around and facing the front, grinding my teeth in tense, round-shouldered annoyance. But my blood is up, and it's *so* hard to swallow my frustration. I want to humiliate him in front of this boatful of people for his inconsiderateness; for poking me in the eye with his camera. I know I've had the last word, but I want to twist the knife; so I add, loud enough for everyone to hear: "Dull oafs and their social media! So fixated by their child-like compulsion to record and share what they're doing, and too bloody stupid to intelligently engage with their surroundings, or understand and enjoy the experience!"

After a few seconds, the cameraman replies timidly, still holding aloft his camera, with its intermittently flashing red light. "Ah s'pose you want me to stop recordin' then?"

Hannah grabs my wrist to stop me from turning around and throwing his Go-Pro into the sea.

Well, everyone is active on some form of social

media these days aren't they, so Henry's managed to insult everyone on the boat. We're not even half-way across the water yet, so you can imagine how tense it feels on board, in a confined space where there is no chance of escape, and every chance of things turning nasty. I can feel the heat coming off Henry when he spectacularly fails to stifle his simmering rage; although, I know from experience that the worst has passed. Just when I think he's getting better at controlling his emotions, something like this happens. I just wish that he could take a deep breath, and *think* before he speaks or reacts.

Henry likes to take the moral high ground and have the last word. But the irony is that he will be an internet sensation by the end of today, for all of the *wrong* reasons. I can imagine how many 'likes' and 'shares' he'll achieve, once his rant has been uploaded. Instead of limiting his ridicule to the vacuous man behind us, Henry will be televised directly insulting the watching Facebookers, Whatsappers, Tweeters and YouTubers, all of whom enjoy social media, or they wouldn't be on-line streaming it in the first place. It's a lose-lose situation, but he doesn't see it that way. Yet.

Right, where did I get to in the biography of our relationship? Oh, yes. So Henry decided that the Law was not for him, and that he would train to become a teacher in the state school sector. This change of heart was a huge surprise to everyone, not least his father. Basil Burden made it very clear that he and Henry's mother, Susan, had made sacrifices, and spent well over one hundred fifty thousand pounds on Henry's secondary and higher education. I'm not sure what Basil meant by that, other than to infer that Henry's change of career direction was a disappointment to them. Perhaps if Henry had become a barrister, they would have been prouder, and Henry would have been wealthy enough to keep Basil and Susan in their dotage; to repay the debt, as it were.

Maybe I'm being uncharitable. Basil may merely have intended that his investment would result in a lucrative, legal career that would afford Henry and his future family certain benefits and privileges.

The rest of us were surprised because Henry was always so materialistically and socially aspirational; impressed by wealth; admiring those who possessed it; believing that they were in some way superior because of it.

I remember hoping that he wouldn't regret his decision when he inevitably found fault with some aspect of the course or Education Faculty; or later on, if the state system wasn't grand enough for him, or was too regulated by an interfering government. I wondered whether he had sufficient patience to teach complicated concepts to people who couldn't or wouldn't grasp them.

I needn't have worried. Henry's three months at Uppingham & Snook Advocates was seared into his memory forever: He had seen enough to know that he wouldn't be able to break into the aristocratic, elitist clique that prevailed there. He knew he would be at a complete disadvantage when competing with his rivals to progress to the level that paid those higher salaries.

If he chose a more modest, and more typical High Street firm like Wainwright & Associates, it would be the tedium and bureaucracy that would destroy his spirit. Potential salary wasn't a motivator either: He had asked some cheeky questions when deliberating whether to take their offer of a paid internship, establishing that even W & As' fully-fledged solicitors earned about the same as a teacher.

So Henry reckoned that it was more important to be happy, and that he would be happier as a teacher. He reasoned that if he wanted to aspire to bigger and better things in the future, then he could work towards becoming a Head of Department or a Head Teacher. If he wanted to develop his academic portfolio, then he would take a master's degree and then a PhD. Being a teacher didn't mean that he had given up on life; although Basil and Susan weren't convinced.

If ever I doubted our compatibility as a couple, or continued to harbour concerns about his suitability for a career as a teacher, the months that followed laid those misgivings to rest. Apart from the chemistry that made us best friends as well as lovers, and the fact that we couldn't wait to share our experiences, and debrief them in conversations that could last for days, it turned out that we both shared a common interest and need: appreciation of the aesthetics and meanings inherent in the Arts. In my case it was the visual, and in Henry's the literary.

We educated each other respectively, discovering a stimulating new world in museums and galleries, libraries and bookshops. It was his ability to explain, say, imagery or characterisation within the novels he recommended, that made me realise that he *was* capable of patience, and muting his cynicism. There was hope for the longevity of our relationship.

Henry loved the psychology of learning, and applying theoretical concepts to practical, scenarios in the classroom. He was surprisingly avant-garde when it came to overcoming barriers to learning, not necessarily in the physical, environmental sense, but by proactively diagnosing, recognising and overcoming learners' difficulties. His reward was seeing the fruits of his efforts, when a struggling student suddenly experienced the 'light bulb moment' of comprehension or expression.

Yes, Henry was a popular teacher amongst the pupils. His method ensured that the less able achieved standards that would otherwise have been difficult, whilst simultaneously affording unrestrained opportunities for more academically gifted students to thrive and progress.

Henry's own peers osmotically benefited from the measures he introduced, thereby allowing masters of other subjects to enjoy results that may otherwise have been less impressive. Frimlington High School was doing well in the Ofsted league tables, thanks in large measure to Henry Burden, teacher of English.

We are approaching the harbour now, and I am glad to say that sight has almost been restored to my eye. The boat's complement of passengers disembark in silence. I forget to consider the wider effect of my temper on Hannah, but I am relieved that she seems to be taking it well, holding my hand in solidarity. Like with so many emotive occasions, it isn't until afterwards that people consider the collateral damage. It can't be easy having to suffer the embarrassment of my outbursts. I just find it difficult suffering fools gladly.

"Sorry about that", I say sheepishly, when we have walked a distance along the ancient pier, out of earshot of the moron in the football shirt.

"Oh Henry. I'm not going to say it's ok, because it really isn't. I worry about your heart, your nerves; and one of these days someone is going to bop you on the nose!"

We continue towards the tiny village in silence, passing by The Change House, which used to be the island's male-only pub, then The Barge House, and on towards the Ticket Office to pay for admission to the gardens and castle. We note where the blacksmith's forge and sail repair workshops used to be situated, which now accommodate a shop and restaurant respectively.

We then walk around the south side of the village towards another shop, and then the café, which was once the castle's laundry. We enter the gardens where we plan to have our picnic.

"That's a lovely spot, over there", Hannah says, pointing to a shaded area beneath a tree, just beyond the cemetery.

"That's the dead centre of the island", I say, smiling at my own joke. Hannah rolls her eyes.

Having unfurled our woollen picnic blanket, removed our shoes and sat down, I open the cool bag.

"Shit", I say, removing a packet of raw, Marks & Spencer beef burgers.

The fact that I have to carry the cool bag full of meat and freezer packs all day, is a constant reminder to Hannah of my mistake. Whenever she starts giggling spontaneously, I know the cause of her mirth.

We have enjoyed the gardens and its thriving stocks of hardy vegetation on the southern side, nourished by natural, seaweed fertilisers disgorged by the sea. We have inspected one of the island's three, World War 2 Pill Boxes that were manned by the Home Guard, and we have consumed a lunch of Cornish pasties, baked beans and coffee at the café. We have climbed up to the castle, stopping en route at the Victorian dairy and Giant's Well, a freshwater spring that was the island's main source of water before it was connected to the mains in 1936.

Now we are inside the castle: A labyrinth of corridors and staircases rise and fall into rooms and spaces, some of which have an indeterminable intention of purpose. Did the architect design them for some specific function, or did they evolve, arbitrarily over the centuries? It would surely be a draftsman's nightmare to reproduce the floorplans.

The role played by other quarters are easily apparent: open-air terraces that provide visual vantage points of the sea and the mainland; places of worship; a museum that now displays an arsenal of weapons, and which may have served as the original armoury.

The living areas retain a gothic quality that is contemporarily comfortable, as well as acknowledging an historically authentic context: dark wood panelling and ecclesiastically shaped doors and windows; heavy, gilt-framed oil paintings of the castle's great and the good; ornate plaster mouldings, and tasteful, modern carpets that retain and evoke period style.

I want to interrogate every guide who stands like a sentry, guarding the artefacts. I want to read every laminated page of information; every square of explanatory text that sits at the foot of a musket; or next to an original painting; or horse's head that protrudes from a wall like its unseen rider was unable to stop. Not since I surprised the housekeepers with my obsessive interest during a visit to Thomas Hardy's Max Gate in Dorchester (13), have I wanted to immerse myself in the stories that this island has to tell.

So why do the majority of other visitors bumble from room-to-room, bouncing off each other like disoriented bats with faulty sonar in a hay loft, making no comment on the treasures, the breath-taking architecture and views; or worse, loudly reflecting on what they're going to have for dinner; or the length of time left on their parking ticket? They mill about as though they are bored, preferring to say anything or nothing, rather than offer an insightful remark about what surrounds them.

Then there are those with their infernal preoccupation with taking selfies. Some of them even have contraptions which hold their mobile phones at a distance, presumably so they can pretend that they have friends taking pictures of them. Pathetic!

The rest of us, who want to enjoy and commit the experience to memory, rather than record everything in photos we shall either never look at again, or accidentally delete, or lose when we drop our phone down the toilet, have to keep an eye out for them. I'm tired of stopping dead in my tracks, or advancing circuitously and falteringly so that I don't spoil their snap. So now I'm not going to bother looking out for them, or give them the time and space to frame their shot. If I photo-bomb their picture, then I don't care. In fact, I may occupy the best spaces for longer than normal on purpose. Dimwits! I bet my friend from the boat is amongst them, although he appears to be giving me a wide berth since our little disagreement, because I haven't seen him since.

"Henry?"

"Yes, my love?"

"Are you ruminating again?"

"What makes you say that?" It perplexes me how Hannah seems able to read my thoughts.

"Oh, I don't know. Perhaps it's the way you're scowling at those people taking photos of themselves, and generally getting in the way of where you want to stand."

"Well, it *is* irritating, isn't it? They're right in front of that map, which I know they have absolutely no intention of reading".

"Come on, you've exceeded your threshold. And there's the man with the Go-Cam over there. It's time to head back, before anything else happens".

Several years ago, Hannah identified what she calls my "two-hour exposure-to-people threshold". It is based on the premise that even if I actually like someone, and may even have invited them into our home for, say, a dinner party or barbecue, there is just a two-hour window of opportunity before they start to get on my tits.

It's a wonder I am able to function really; but seeing as my lessons last only forty minutes, there is plenty of margin before my pupils begin to irritate me. Lunch hours are, as the words suggest, only sixty minutes long. So the opportunity for my colleagues to provoke my honest and forthright feedback, is negligible.

Occasions that almost always land me in hot water are crowded excursions like this, and plane journeys to any place further than the south of France. The only person I know to be incapable of irritating me, is Hannah.

Back at the car park, I point my electronic key fob at the Volvo. It is then that I see the two-feet tall, deep scratches that occupy the whole of the driver's door panel: A 'W' followed by a pictorially represented anchor. My beloved car! I look around for CCTV cameras, but there are none.

Morosely, I telephone the police to report the fact that I am the victim of a crime. Again.

CHAPTER 17

Sunday 4.30 pm

Back at the campsite I prioritise handing over the Happy Bargains meat to Barry. I wait until he is preoccupied with checking the tyre pressures on his ancient Rover 75, before giving it to him. The distraction means that he doesn't notice that I have re-labelled the packets with M & S stickers. The burgers and sausages look as though they are partially cooked having been locked in the boot of our Volvo all day, unrefrigerated and in a plastic bag. He has left it on the bonnet of his car in the heat of the late afternoon sun, so I can always blame the meat's condition on him, if necessary.

Hannah proposes that after the exertions of the day we have a shower and get ready for a relaxing evening. I suggest we take advantage of the fact that the shower block is unlikely to be busy at this time, and that it would be fun if we could bag the family bathroom and have a sexy shower together. She slaps me on the arm and calls me "saucy". But she doesn't say "no"!

Tucking rolled towels under our arms, in which we have wrapped shampoo, soap, deodorants, and a fresh change of clothing, we walk across the site towards the nearest block.

Ahead I see the silhouettes of the owners of the expensive German caravan we admired on the way to the pub last night. They are sitting outside it on expensive, Lafuma, reclining chairs. As we approach, I realise that I've seen them before.

"You'll never guess who owns that Tabbert Cellini", I say to Hannah, nodding in its direction.

Hannah follows my gaze. "It's Darren and his family! Let's go and say 'hello'".

I groan. "God, do we have to?"

"Come on, they might let us see inside their caravan".

"I can do that on-line, on Tabbert's website".

It's too late. Darren has seen us and is waving, bidding us to go over and join them. He saunters towards me, his gold jewellery jangling, and thrusts out a hand. He's still dressed completely in black, but more casually in Bermuda trousers, V-necked T-shirt and flip-flops. "Iss da geezer an' 'is missiz from da mine!"

I dutifully extend my own hand, and tell them our names. I am surprised by his lack of grip. It's like holding onto a small, cold, lifeless, wet fish. When he releases me, I resist the urge to wipe my palm on the back of my shorts.

Wendy looks up from applying moisturiser to her face. It seems she has either had a bad reaction to a peanut, or she has had her face re-Botoxed since we saw her yesterday. "'ello babes", she says indiscriminately to Hannah, me or both of us, barely looking up from her mirror, and as expressionless as ever.

Darren tells us his name and his family's names, unaware that we have eavesdropped on their conversations on two former occasions, and know them already. Perhaps eavesdropped is not the right word. It would have been impossible not to have heard them in Godleven Tin Mine's restaurant and museum. As Darren makes his rollcall, Wendy gives us an unenthusiastic wave, without looking up from her mirror. Princess is oblivious to everything, lost in her Grime music piped through white earphones, and which I can hear thudding from fifteen feet away. Zack raises his eyes from his biography about one of my favourite authors and poets, Thomas Hardy, and offers us a polite, "Good afternoon".

We stand there, for several, awkward seconds. Do we make conversation by raising the subject of yesterday's incident in the mine? We both recall that they didn't seem to be adversely affected by it, took Gryffyn's behaviour in their stride, and left instead of complaining about him.

For the sake of something to do and filling the void, I point at Zack's book to draw Hannah's attention to it, and we chuckle in appreciation of the fact that a teenager can be on holiday and still find pleasure in school work.

Darren misreads our behaviour entirely, and assumes that we are mocking his son. "Yeah, ah know…'e ain't mine ah don't fink. Product of 'er shaggin' da milkman ah sh'tunt wonda, ain't dat right Wend?" he says, clearly less impressed by his son than we are, and believing that he's showing us solidarity.

"Piss off, Daz" Wendy fires back, still working the cream into her face and throat. "If anyone 'as 'ad an affair, iss you!"

Darren laughs like Sid James, and an embarrassing silence descends again. We shift from foot to foot nervously, Darren looking at us intently, apparently unconcerned that the conversation has shrivelled up and died.

I think I've found safe ground: "Nice bit of kit you've got here", I say genuinely, nodding towards his caravan, awning and SUV.

"Yeah. Top odda range. Can't get betta than ya German, can ya?"

I stop myself from correcting him that his car is now owned by a Chinese company, and assembled in China, India and England. I vaguely recall reading that Isabella awnings are Danish. "Very nice. We were admiring your caravan yesterday. Great build quality and style", I say, which I hope will encourage him to invite us in for a peek. "Have you had it long?"

"Less danna munf. Nearly for'y granz worfa 'van dare", he replies, clearly feeling that he has provided us with the most salient points of interest.

I stretch my neck towards the front window, as though trying to look in, again hoping that this will prompt him. The seconds tick by, but Darren fails to take the initiative. For a man who likes showing off, he's not very quick on the uptake.

"Well, we must be going", I say, as though late for an important engagement, even though we've still got our towels tucked under our arms and we're heading in the direction of the ablutions block.

"I wuz wonderin' wevver yude larkta comfurra barbie tomurra night, say six o'clock", Darren says finally. Wendy stops moisturising and stares at us.

I start umm-ing and ah-ing, caught off-guard by the unexpected invitation. I am trying to communicate to Hannah my inclination to decline it, only by using my eyes and subtle movements of my body, honed over many years of familiarity with each other: Is an evening of painful conversation with people with whom we have little in common worth it, merely to establish what he does for a living, and see inside their caravan?

"We've gotta Weber Genesis 2", Darren says, as though this will influence our decision. He walks over to a massive black and stainless-steel gas barbecue, featuring six gas burners, side tables and a shelf, that wouldn't look out-of-place in a professional kitchen. "Cost twelve 'undred quid and can cook for more than eleven people", he adds proudly. "German again", he adds, patting the lid.

I'm fairly sure that although Weber sounds as though it is German, it is actually American. Again, I don't want to contradict him. "Eleven? Yes, great, we'll look forward to it" Hannah replies.

I am at least relieved that five others will be present to alleviate the pain of making conversation with Darren and Wendy. "Who else is invited?" I ask.

"No one", Darren replies. "It'll just be the six of us".

"Well at least we'll have something different to do to amuse us tomorrow evening…", I say to Hannah as we continue towards the shower and bath block. "…If you count listening to someone showing off their wealth as entertainment".

"Live and let live, Henry. You never know, if you give them a chance, you may actually make some friends".

I drop the conversation just as we enter the block. We have already discussed how we shall enter the family bathroom, which has been reserved exclusively for the use of parents with small children, or disabled people. Seeing as we do not fall under either category, we know that we have no right to wash in there; but it represents an opportunity to enjoy some 'adult time' together without the paranoia of every hip thrust or wriggle being transferred into the fragile floor, ceiling and walls of our caravan, and drawing attention to our activity by loud banging…if you pardon the pun.

Deftly approaching the door of the bathroom, each step along the corridor carefully measured to be silent, we tune in our ears to identify the sound and presence of anyone who may thwart our objective. Should someone appear, then we shall stall for time until they pass, by fabricating some conversation, or pretending to read one of the notices pinned to the wall, about the times when the block will be closed for cleaning.

I have previously developed a convincing hobble when using the more generous accommodation provided in such places. But it is no good doing that here at the campsite, because if I am spotted entering or exiting the hallowed bathroom, I would have to sustain a limp indefinitely to keep up appearances.

Just as I extend my hand to open the door to the capacious bathroom, the gents' washroom door opens. Trevor the campsite manager is standing there in his trademark, khaki micro-shorts and T-shirt, one hand on his hip and the other holding the door open for me. My hand hovers momentarily over the bathroom's door handle, before I raise it in an exaggerated curve to rake my fingers through my hair. Hannah sniggers at my unconvincing attempt to mislead him about our intentions.

"I hope you weren't going to use *that* bathroom", he says testily.

"Of course we weren't", I reply indignantly, injecting as much sense of being wrongly accused and deeply offended into my denial as I am able to muster. I give him a cold, hard stare until he stands aside to let me into the room of tiny shower cubicles with their cold, wet, flapping, plastic curtains.

Hannah turns around and heads towards the ladies' washroom.

We feel like naughty schoolchildren, caught smoking behind the bike sheds.

CHAPTER 18

Sunday 6 pm

I am sitting outside the caravan with Hannah, sipping a cold Chardonnay from a frosted wine glass. But even the refreshing citrus notes of the wine, the fresh air and warm sunshine of an early summer are doing little to lighten my mood. Hannah and I enjoy a full and active love life, and there is nothing more torturous than the enforced abnegation of an opportunity to scratch an itch!

Hannah knows the cause of my irritation, and she sympathises to a large extent. But as always, she is the voice of reason, encouraging me to consider things from Trevor's point of view.

"He couldn't let us wander in there right in front of him. There are rules, he is the manager, and so he has to enforce them".

I make a sound that means that some rules are there to be broken.

"Well, you wouldn't feel that way if you were a father of a toddler that you needed to bathe and get ready for bed".

"No, but I'm not though, am I?" I reply, a little too quickly, before realising that my petulant retort could be construed as a reference to our childlessness. Hannah goes quiet. "I'm sorry; I didn't mean…"

"It's ok", she says, resting her hand on mine. She grins cheekily. "You know, if you're still up for it, and you don't drink too much of that wine, we could…"

Barry and Maureen noisily exit their caravan.

"What, and be overheard by Tweedledum and Tweedledumber over there? I don't think so. It would put me off. It wouldn't so much be a case of brewer's droop, as Brummie droop".

After a short pause, Hannah slowly traces a shape on the back of my hand with a beautifully manicured fingernail. "Well," she begins, seductively, "we are surrounded by fields; and the sand dunes are only through that gate".

To be seen wandering off into the sand-dunes at 6.15 on a Sunday evening, holding my wife's hand and clutching our picnic blanket and a toilet roll would probably make our intentions a little too obvious. It would also push the boundaries of discretion and taste beyond the realms of acceptability; so I have packed the items required for a modicum of comfort into a rucksack, together with a couple of wine glasses and what remains of the bottle of Chardonnay.

When we reach the edge of the dunes, I place my arm around her shoulder, pull her gently towards me and kiss the top of her head. We survey the dunescape to identify a place in a cleft deep enough to avoid any passing voyeur, and far enough away from the established paths to avoid an embarrassing encounter with a dog-walker, or come to that, an inquisitive dog. I think I have seen a likely spot, and scan around for prying eyes before taking Hannah's hand again and leading her there.

We are giggling like teenagers as we stretch out the blanket at the bottom of a gully that is deeper than I had imagined, and surrounded by dense, thorny, yellow-flowered gorse. We sit down, and I pour two glasses of wine.

Chivalry and respect for Hannah prevents me from elaborating on the wonderful hour that followed, spoiled only when I encountered nature more closely than I wished. Lying naked next to Hannah, the act we had just enjoyed rendering my synapses sensitive to the slightest shift of seagrass, I sensed it before I felt it strike.

People say that snakes bite only in self-defence, when disturbed, trodden on, or otherwise provoked. Well, I don't know what level of provocation I could possibly have offered the snake, which is already slithering back into the undergrowth, after sinking its fangs in my upper, inner thigh. It must have missed my scrotum and left bollock by less than half a centimetre.

"What's the matter?" Hannah asks, starting when she hears me shout in pain and shock.

"A snake bit me!" I shout, pointing in the direction in which it escaped. I can no longer see it. "About two and a half feet long, brownish, with a darker zig-zag pattern", I add, thinking that the description will be useful if I suddenly pass out, its venom coursing my veins.

"My God, you're joking, right?"

"I wish I was. Have you got your mobile?"

Hannah fishes her phone from the rucksack.

"Phone 999 and ask for an ambulance. Tell them it's a snake-bite, where we are, my sex, age, and that I am conscious at the moment. Give them the description of the snake", I say, remembering the key actions required in a medical emergency from the lesson I give to my pupils. I cannot believe that this is actually happening for real.

Hannah phones, explains what has happened and gives our location in the dunes about three hundred metres north of the Godleven Caravan & Camping Park.

She confirms she will stay on the line to give updates and receive instructions, when suddenly the battery discharges and the line goes dead. "We forgot to re-charge it. They said it sounds like an adder which is venomous; because of where we are, they're alerting the Coastguard too", she tells me, tossing the phone back into the bag.

"Did they say what we should do?" I ask anxiously.

"No. The phone died before they could. Should I try to suck out the poison?" she asks earnestly.

Despite the panic which is starting to set in, I imagine us being found naked in the dunes, with Hannah's mouth clamped to my groin. "No", I reply. "I seem to remember that's a fallacy. It's not possible to suck it out quickly enough, and it spreads the venom quicker".

"Oh God. Just keep as still and calm as you can. Should I go for help?" she offers.

I envisage Barry and Maureen, Trevor or Darren coming to my assistance and bursting into fits of laughter. "On no account leave me!" I shout, more emphatically than I intended. "The emergency services should be on their way".

Hannah is cradling me in her arms, and stroking my face. "You had better put your clothes back on", I say.

Fifteen minutes later I hear thudding rotor blades getting louder from the south, and wailing ambulance sirens from the east. The emergency services must have notified Trevor, because it's not long before Hannah tells me she can see him bouncing over the dunes with a delegation of groundskeepers on quadbikes, and a trailer. I imagine that if the helicopter isn't required, and the ambulance doesn't have the ground clearance or traction to venture onto the sand, I'll be transferred from the dunes by Trevor and his staff. Oh, the humiliation!

The helicopter hovers at about one hundred feet above us, beating the dunes and billowing clouds of choking sand. Its crew pinpoints my precise location and signals it to three paramedics on the ground. Thankfully the chopper then moves away and lands on the beach, presumably to await further instructions for my evacuation to the nearest Accident and Emergency Department.

As my wound is assessed and treated by the paramedics, I hear one of them commenting that "quite a crowd is forming", a short distance away on the beach. I convince myself that our burrow is providing sufficient cover from exposure, so I have no further cause for embarrassment. For the time-being.

Having three people focusing their attention on my groin is not helped by the fact that they medical professionals. I try to take my mind off it by talking to Hannah, who is supporting my head. "Not quite what we had in mind, is it love?"

She smiles, kisses my forehead, and combs my hair with her fingernails.

The paramedic who seems to be in charge introduces himself to us as Steve. He is the one asking the questions: "Apart from two, in-line puncture marks from the snake's fangs, there is only a little reddening around the bite. How are you feeling?"

I intend my reply to lighten the mood, but what comes out of my mouth resembles extreme sarcasm. "Oh, never felt better in my life. Having a whale of a time".

"There's no need to be like that, sir. We're trying to help, to establish your symptoms. Do you feel nauseous?"

"Yes. Not sure if it's from the snake bite, or having three men prodding and staring at my ball-sack; but 'nauseous' is apposite. 'Anxious', too".

"What about pain? Localised to the bite? Transferred elsewhere?"

"Bite feels sore and tender, not painful", I reply, echoing the clipped phrases of my rescuer.

"Breathing ok, at the moment?"

At the moment? The implication of the addendum and his professional sternness shock me into cooperation, of dropping the wisecracks. "Yes".

"Open your mouth wide".

I comply long enough for him to inspect inside it.

"Vomited?" he asks, casting his eyes around the sandy floor for evidence.

"No."

"Always conscious and lucid since the bite?" This question is aimed at Hannah, who nods vigorously.

"Dry bite inconclusive", Steve says to the others. "It can take two or more hours for venom to circulate and produce symptoms or anaphylaxis. Temperature raised but not high. B.P. and heartbeat currently regular and normal in the circumstances. Some swelling and redness around the bite. No signs of swelling to the lips, tongue, gums or throat. Skin not sweaty, cold or clammy to the touch." He produces a blister pack and removes two white tablets.

"What are they?" I ask. "Anti-venom?"

"No", he replies. "Paracetamol".

Steve disappeared for about ten minutes, but he has returned. He announces that he has phoned a doctor back at the hospital, and a decision has been made to transfer me to the Accident and Emergency Unit in Addleton. The staff there will be far better equipped to keep me under observation and subject me to stringent blood tests and assessments, than the paramedics on a sand dune on a remote beach in Godleven.

I am still lying in the hollow with my head on Hannah's lap. A metallic mylar blanket provided by one of the other paramedics covers my torso, and a wad of toilet tissue is wrapped around my cock and balls. The latter is necessary, so Steve tells me, to maintain access and keep observation on the bite.

I feel that I am ticking the check boxes in terms of my lucidity, coherence and consciousness, as I am continually bombarding Steve with questions; so many in fact that he's not entirely sure that I haven't entered some state of panicked delirium. I have learned that if the snake injected its venom into my bloodstream, it can take more than three weeks to recover; for some it's even longer than that. It is imperative that if I need antivenom, then its early administration can reduce the time required for recovery from pain and swelling.

I dread the answer to my next question. "How long will I be kept in hospital under observation?"

"Well, that all depends. Usually, a full prognosis takes up to twenty-four hours, but there's no guarantee that it won't take longer".

I look up into Hannah's eyes, "I'm sorry I've ruined the holiday".

She smiles and shakes her head. "Don't be so silly".

Trevor suddenly breaches the rim of the sandy crater, and announces that they are ready.

"Ready for what?" I ask, irked not to have been included in discussions, considering my integral involvement in the drama.

Steve steps forward. "We need to transfer you to the helicopter or ambulance without you moving too much. We can't justify winching you into the helicopter, especially with all this sand, and the ambulance isn't a four-wheel-drive. So we'll have to load you into a trailer drawn by a quad-bike. The stretcher will be too heavy for it, so we'll have to ditch that for the time-being. Seeing as the helicopter is on the beach and available, and has to fly back to base at Addleton anyway, we'll take you in that, which will free up the ambulance for the next emergency".

I have to say that I am incredibly impressed by their efficiency. I'm even overwhelmed by Trevor's new-found willingness to be helpful, rather than an obstructive pain in the neck. It's not as if he is being so co-operative because the accident is his fault, or even happened on his campsite. There is no liability on his part.

A folding, light-weight stretcher is brought from the ambulance, and the campsite's groundsmen and paramedics lift me onto it and strap me down. They carry me over to a quadbike which is attached to an Erdé trailer, which is clearly not long enough for the task of carrying my six feet one-inch frame across the dunes and onto the beach. My head is propped up by our picnic blanket against the metal rim at the tow bar end, but my legs and feet are overhanging the rear. Another mylar blanket is used to cover my gift-wrapped nether regions.

I spoke too soon about Trevor. Despite Steve's instructions to him to make slow progress across the dunes, the uneven ground tosses me several inches into the air, causing me to knock my skull repeatedly against the sides of the trailer. I end up receiving cuts and bruises that require treatment before I can be loaded into the helicopter.

A line of people has formed a safe distance from the helicopter, although I suspect they are oglers rather than well-wishers. Barry and Maureen are amongst them, but they don't return my feeble wave. I wonder if it's because they've worked out my ruse with the meat that they conned me into buying for them.

After a series of electrical clicks, the helicopter's engine starts, and the rotor blades start fanning. Hannah climbs in ahead of me, to be strapped in and have headphones placed on her head. The blades are spinning quicker, causing the lower mylar blanket to flap furiously, before taking off like a demented albatross. I am aware of a series of camera flashes from Maureen and Barry's direction, immediately before the toilet tissue follows the blanket into space, and my pork sausage and sprouts are exposed to the elements.

The paramedics cannot hear what I am shouting over the noise of the engine, and are clearly wondering why I am clutching my nut-sack in both hands, and turning my knees inwards to protect my modesty. I look like a schoolboy who desperately needs to pee. Realisation finally dawns, and one of them unclips a replacement thermal blanket from inside the chopper, and wraps it around me to restore my dignity. They hoist me inside on the stretcher, which is lashed to a shelf in front of Hannah. A forth paramedic I have not seen before, who is wearing a jumpsuit and a helmet with integrated earphones and a boom-mic, is sitting on a jump seat next to me.

Suddenly, thankfully, I feel the positive g-force as we are hauled into the air for pre-flight checks, and then southeast to Addleton, just as the sun slips beneath the horizon through the starboard window.

We landed at the hospital in Addleton at 9.30 pm, after a short hop lasting less than ten minutes. The calm and assured efficiency of the medical staff continued: My arrival was expected, my bed was waiting, and potential treatments were prepared.

Despite my insistence that Hannah should immediately check-in to a local hotel and get some rest, she insisted on waiting for me to undergo additional checks, and for a fuller diagnosis to be pronounced. She was also able to borrow a phone charger from one of the nurses, to top up her battery.

It was just after 11 pm when the doctor, Dr Jackson, told us she was almost certain it had been a "dry bite", because she could find no trace of any venom in my system. The snake was positively identified as an adder, based on my description of it and the bite pattern.

I am curious to know how many adder bites she has dealt with, and am surprised when she tells me that she has not personally dealt with any. In fact, there are only about one hundred adder bites reported annually in the UK, with only fourteen recorded deaths since 1876. It is unusual to be bitten in May, as such incidents usually occur during the warmer months. She suggests that the unseasonably warm weather may have had something to do with it.

My small wound has been sterilised, washed and dressed, and I have received a tetanus booster injection. She is keeping me in overnight to "be on the safe side".

Having convinced Hannah that there is no need for her to spend an uncomfortable night on the chair at my side, she finds the number of the nearest Superior Lodge and books a one night's stay, and orders a taxi.

Kissing Hannah goodnight, I watch her leave the ward, reflecting not on the shock and embarrassment caused by the snake bite, and the inconvenience to our holiday, but on the wonderful hour I spent in the dunes with her; behaving like we were fifteen years younger, without a care in the world.

Whether it is the medication intensifying my emotions, or the strength of my feelings for Hannah, I recall quotes from the nineteenth century, French dramatist, poet and novelist, Alfred de Musset: *I don't know where my road is going, but I know that I walk better when I hold your hand.*

With a smile on my face, and feeling like the luckiest man alive, I drift into a deep and impenetrable sleep. *Life is a deep sleep, of which love is the dream.*

CHAPTER 19

Monday 7 am

A nurse called Barbara who is working the 8 pm to 8 am shift gently wakes me, and tells me that my breakfast is ready and not to let it get cold. Hannah phoned at about 2 am to see how I was doing, and Barbara told her I was fast asleep. The doctors do their rounds between 7 and 8 am, so she told Hannah not to visit until 8.30 am, when my ward exercises an open visiting hours policy for friends and relatives until 10 pm, unless an extension is agreed on a case-by-case basis.

As much as I would like to see her, I hope that Hannah got as good a night's sleep as I did, has a lie-in, and eats a proper breakfast. Unless she found something to snack on, the only food and drink to have passed her lips since our adventure in the dunes, was a cup of tea and a biscuit at about 10 o'clock last night.

Tucking in to my two rashers of bacon, chipolata, scrambled egg, grilled tomato, baked beans and round of buttered bread, I survey the men in the three beds opposite me, and the two to my left. All of them appear to be in a far worse condition than I am, which makes me feel a little bit guilty. Two of them are grey, and look like heart patients. Another two are in various plaster casts. I suspect they are road traffic collision victims. The last one has got a consumptive cough that rattles so badly it sounds like fragments of his lungs are being wrenched loose, and jettisoned into the handkerchief which he constantly holds to his mouth.

Of my five room-mates, one of the heart patients and one of the crash victims has dropped straight back to sleep having been woken by Barbara. Their stentorian snoring reverberates like a kango. How on earth did I manage to sleep so well in here, with the racket those three are making? It must surely have been a combination of the intensity of yesterday's experience, the drugs, and the long lull afterwards whilst being treated. Relief at Dr Jackson's last prognosis must also have played its part.

I wonder if the two snorers are going to sleep through breakfast. Perhaps I could have their bacon and eggs? My emphysemic friend doesn't appear hungry either; but I've ruled out asking him if I can have his – there is every chance that his convulsive coughing has caused collateral contamination. I consider asking Barbara if I can have the others' untouched food, or just helping myself, before feeling guilty again and putting the thought to one side.

So, what next? Shall I go to the TV room and watch the news? I try to recall whether Dr Jackson said anything last night about moving around. I haven't been to the toilet since I was given a bed pan just before I fell asleep last night. Am I allowed to walk to the toilet and exercise my legs? I lean forwards to try to see if Barbara is outside in the ward. I can't see her. I don't think this warrants an emergency, so I resist the temptation to press my nurse-call button.

I wonder what my wound feels like to touch. Poking out my tongue in concentration, I reach my right hand down under the bed covers, down my abdomen, past my old boy, and pull my gonads over towards my right leg. I suddenly notice that the snoring, heart attack patient opposite me has woken up, and is eyeing me with suspicion. "It's not what it looks like", I say, before gingerly touching the dressing at the top of my inside left leg. I exhale loudly with relief, when I discover it is not as swollen or sore as I feared, which causes the heart patient to call me "Disgusting", before rolling over onto his side, and pulling his duvet up to his chin, presumably so that he cannot see or hear me.

God, I'm bored. It's still only 7.20 am: There's over an hour before Hannah arrives, when hopefully the doctor will have decided that I can leave. I reach over to my bedside table, pick up the remote-control unit, and start pressing buttons. I am able to reconfigure my mattress in a number of different positions. I must get Hannah and me one of these! Except this particular model makes quite an annoying, electrical whirring noise.

After a couple of minutes of playing with the bed, Barbara appears and removes the control unit from my hands, replacing it onto the bedside table. I think I've annoyed her. In fact, I think I've annoyed everyone, including those who were asleep, because she is now going round the other beds, cancelling their call buttons that they have clearly pressed to complain about me.

Unfortunately, she confiscated the remote control before I had a chance to return the mattress to a normal, comfortable position. Perhaps she did it on purpose, to teach me a lesson. The back rest is now far too far forward, and the area that supports my legs is too raised. I feel like I am being held in a 'crunchie' exercise position, with my nose only a few inches from the dressing next to my testicles. Thankfully, I can just about reach the reset button, and I slowly unfurl.

Barbara returns. "Do you have your own wash kit?" she asks.

"Er, no. I came in as an emergency".

"I'll get you one. It will be good exercise for you to go to the washroom and freshen up: out of the door and to your right. I'll get you some paracetamol, too". She's obviously occupying me to stop me from making any more mischief. I search for yesterday's clothes in the little cupboard in my bedside table. My wallet is there, but my clothes are not. My deck shoes are under my bed, so I put them on.

I am now walking from my dormitory and into the ward, passing predominantly female nurses who are working at a large work station, or scurrying around, going about their duties. I am wearing a thigh-length nightshirt provided by the hospital, and I am very aware that someone appears to have put it on me back-to-front. I know this because there is an almighty draught around my naked buttocks. Never mind, I'll sort it out in the bathroom. I continue, holding the towel provided by Barbara, against my backside.

Inside the bathroom, I am reminded of the space that I was forced to forego at the campsite's washing block. I lay out the tiny bottle of complementary shampoo, a little square of soap, single-use razor blade, towel and comb onto a shelf. Having removed the thin, cotton gown, I take care to mix hot and cold water to my preferred temperature, and turn the selector dial on the shower head until I find the blast setting that will massage my scalp, neck, shoulders and back.

Fifteen minutes later I am about to leave the bathroom, shaved, showered and completely refreshed. However, I cannot fathom what is wrong with this blasted hospital gown. I'm now wearing it with the opening at the front, but it won't close. There is at least a three-inch gap when I try to draw the two sides together.

If it was not for careful positioning of the towel provided, I would either have to walk back to the dormitory with my meat-and-two-veg hanging out, or with a hand clamped over them: Enduring such humiliation twice within a twelve-hour period really would be too much.

I walk into the dormitory, just as a porter is leaving with a trolley with newspapers on it. I retrieve my wallet, and buy an Addleton Echo, mainly for the 'What's on in Cornwall' section.

Barbara comes over with some messages. The first: Dr Jackson has decided that the diagnosis has not changed since last night, and I can be discharged. She recommends a course of Paracetamol and to exercise my leg. She will write to my GP to advise him of what has happened, and to see me in a fortnight's time. I must seek medical assistance if there are any developments or causes for concern. The second: Hannah has just phoned to say she intended to take my clothes to a laundrette this morning, but it doesn't open until 9 am. She is going to wait until the shops open, also at 9 am, when she will buy me some new ones. It'll be quicker than waiting for my old ones to go through a wash-and-dry cycle.

Glancing at the clock, I note that I have just over an hour to kill before Hannah arrives. I settle down to read the latest tales of violence and tragedy that have taken place in Cornwall since yesterday's edition.

CHAPTER 20

Five minutes' later

Well, I didn't expect that! Plastered all over the front page under a bold headline is a picture of me, lying in an Erdé trailer that is not long enough, my legs bare, and my pork and beans wrapped in white, toilet tissue. My facial expression betrays my discomfort, which is not due to the effects of the snake bite, but the fact that the wind from the helicopter's spinning rotor blades has just whipped off the mylar blanket that was keeping me decent. My hands are outstretched towards Hannah. I look like a baby in a nappy, crying for his mother.

"SNAKE BITES DURING SAND SEX!"

How tabloid newspaper editors love alliteration. I feverishly start reading the one-page spread...no, hang on a minute! It's a *two*-page spread! In fact, there is even more to be found in the comments section, where a snake bite specialist gives advice to those who fall victim to an agitated adder. God, I'm doing it now.

Didn't Dr Jackson tell me that there have only been fourteen fatalities in the UK in about one hundred and fifty years? That represents less than one tenth of a fatality every year! It's incredibly rare, so why does the media love to whip up public fear and frenzy? It's not as though it is ever a slow news day, what with all the reports of stabbings, glassings, domestic murder and outrageous social injustices; and having listened to the local bulletins on my car radio on the way back from St Michael's

Mount, you don't have to look outside Cornwall to find them, either.

It says, "*A couple known only as Henry and Hannah, are visiting Cornwall on a caravanning holiday during this week's half-term schools' break. At about 6.30 last night they were making love in the sand dunes at Godleven, when a venomous snake bit Henry's penis...*"

Oh my God! They know our Christian names! It won't be long before they know our surnames, where we're staying, and where we're from! Christ! This could get back to my school! I'll never live it down! My heart is racing, breath quickening, and perspiration is dripping from my forehead, down my cheeks and from my chin onto the page.

I look up. My other room-mates are all reading the same newspaper, and clearly cannot decide whether to carry on reading or look at me, comparing my face with the one in the picture. So they do both, in a succession of double-takes. At least the heart attack patient opposite is now offering me a comprehending smile, now that he knows my earlier fumbling was not motivated by an uncontrollable urge to practice self-abuse in a dormitory full of other men.

"*Although Hannah is not thought to have been bitten, at least not by the snake, both were airlifted to Addleton General Hospital, where Henry's condition is believed to be serious but stable*". Oh, so the editor enjoys alliteration, sensationalist inaccuracy *and* making jokes at other people's expense. "*We hope to bring you more on this story later today*".

Christ! I reach over and press the nurse-call button maniacally. Why will no one respond? I glance at the clock radio: It's 7.55 am – shift handover time. They're busy, and they know that whatever is my crisis, it will not be a medical emergency now that the doctor has given me the 'all-clear'. They probably think I've been messing about with the bed controls again and have got myself stuck. But I could be calling on behalf of one of the others! Why won't someone *come*?

"*Yes*, Mr Burden?" a nurse asks testily, as she approaches me. I haven't seen her before. She must be starting her day shift. Her name badge says that she is a staff nurse called Matilda.

"Have you seen this, Matilda?" I say, raising the front page of the newspaper towards her.

She smiles, "Yes, I read it on the bus on the way in. I understand that you are feeling much better now and that you will be leaving as soon as your wife gets here with your clothes".

"How do they know so much about me?"

Matilda's smile evaporates. "I hope you're not suggesting that anyone from this hospital leaked your personal information", she says, cancelling the call button which is still flashing red on my bedside table.

"No, well, I..."

"Because we take our responsibilities over privacy and data protection *very* seriously". She tucks in my bedclothes with some vigour, which has the effect of lashing me down on the mattress.

"But how do they know our names?"

"I only read it briefly, but I recall that only your Christian names were mentioned. Should anyone from here be so unprofessional as to disclose information illegally to the press, then why not give them more? Your surnames, the town where you live, your ages? If I was you, Mr Burden, I would look elsewhere for your suspect".

Of course! Trevor! But isn't he privy to the same

sort of information from the campsite booking sheet? No, it's someone else...

I know! Who took that photo? Who only knows our Christian names; the fact that we are caravanning, but not where we are from? Barry and Maureen! Bastards!

I didn't sleep at all well last night. Although the prognosis before I left the hospital was good, I lay awake worrying about Henry. At least I was reassured at 2 am when I phoned and spoke to a helpful Staff Nurse, who said that he was sleeping soundly. I've just heard that he is fit to be discharged.

I am sitting alone in the hotel's restaurant having some breakfast and waiting for the shops to open so I can buy Henry some fresh, replacement clothing. I'll get some for me too. I have just picked up a local newspaper, after my attention was drawn to its headline. It can't have happened to *more* than one person, can it? Snake bites aren't at all common; Dr Jackson told us so, last night.

My fear is confirmed: It's all about Henry. He's not going to be at all happy about this, so I'm going to keep it from him, if I can. I bet it was that horrible couple in the caravan next door to ours who leaked the story: Barry and Maureen. I saw them snapping away just before Henry was loaded into the helicopter. Fancy catching someone when they're at their most vulnerable, for the sake of a news story. I wonder if they were paid, or whether they just did it for their five minutes of fame. Or maybe they did it because of what Henry did to their food. I am very disappointed with Henry about that. It was very childish.

Anyway, I know precisely how Henry will react if he finds out about this article, and suspects that it was them.

I was telling you about Henry's success as a teacher.

197

Well, his excellent work record and reputation are such that the Head Teacher and the Board of Governors support his application to become Head of English. He is also completing his master's degree in Education, with a view to progressing to a PhD in Managing Learning Difficulties afterwards. So, the ambition that we always knew was there has finally shown itself. Who knows? It may lead to a career in higher education, or perhaps a school headship.

Anyway, these latest developments, the snake bite and newspaper article, are classic bad-timing for Henry's career, if the circumstances reach Frimlington High School. Henry's colleagues and employers will surely do more than laugh about it if it becomes known, but not publicly known. But if it spreads to the ears of pupils' parents, then I can imagine the indignation, the outcry! As if they never did anything similar!

It seems people are more finickity these days about the extra-curricular behaviour of its educators, than they are about their politicians. It's not as if Henry has done anything bad or immoral – he was merely making love to me, his lawful, wedded wife, discretely, but in the open air; just like men and women have done for millennia. No one would have known had it not been for that bloody snake, and probably Barry and Maureen.

Poor, dear Henry. I hope it won't be another case of one step forward and two steps back.

CHAPTER 21

Monday, 10 am

Hannah was going to keep the newspaper article a secret from me. I was initially upset about that. We have always promised *never* to keep secrets from each other, *ever*, under *any* circumstances. But she was worried that it would spoil my holiday even more, if I found out.

Whilst I was waiting for Hannah, I thought about the consequences, in this internet age, of my misfortune reaching my school, one hundred and seventy miles away. But when all is said and done, people can think what they like; no one knows for sure what Hannah and I were doing in those dunes. Who is to say we weren't merely taking an early evening stroll down to the beach with a bottle of wine, when I brushed past a bush and disturbed a snake that was asleep in it? Far-fetched? Maybe. But no one can prove otherwise. Certainly not my pupils' parents or the Head Teacher at my school.

So, we've decided to put the whole regrettable incident behind us. Que sera, sera. Today's news is tomorrow's fish and chips wrapping paper. Seeing as we are already here in Addleton, we shall spend the day exploring it. We've heard a lot about its history as a sea-port and smugglers' paradise, and it will be interesting to soak up a bit of its culture. We shall return to the campsite later on by train and taxi.

We remember that we have been invited to a barbecue with Darren and his family at 6 pm tonight. I still feel very negative about that, but Hannah urges me that experiences are what you make them, and it will be sensible to keep Barry and Maureen out of our sight for a while. I know that Hannah is keen to keep them out of my reach, too.

Matilda advised us which bus to take from the bus stop outside the hospital's main entrance, and we have arrived in the High Street. I must say that my first impressions of Addleton are not what I expected. I'm sure I read somewhere that it is a town bursting with Celtic culture and outstanding natural beauty. The reality is that it has seen better times.

It's not just the graffiti scrawled over the metal shutters that shield the ground floor windows and doors of the majority of shops; it's the fact that the only ones that appear to be open and trading are the betting shops, pound shops, charity shops, and fast food outlets.

There is an absence of private cars, too. In fact the only vehicles that pass us are mopeds delivering food, workers' vans, lorries and buses. There is a stationary taxi waiting at a rank nearby, but it seems to have little prospect of a customer. I note that it is a maroon, 1987 Ford Sierra 2-litre GL. Its lacquer is peeling off the paint on the bonnet, like it's been in the sun too long without lotion. Blue smoke is billowing from the exhaust. You used to see these cars all the time thirty years ago, but now they are incredibly rare. I hope that it's more mechanically sound than its appearance suggests.

Having Googled the Tourist Information Office at the hospital, I check for number 254. We are standing outside 228, and the numbers descend by two for each building, in the direction of the harbour; so we start walking along the cracked and litter-strewn pavement.

Having found and entered the tourist office, we

approach the desk and speak with an enthusiastic young man, who seems only too willing to help us. It may be because we are the only customers there. The speed with which he slams a computing magazine in a drawer suggests that we are the first people to speak to him for a while.

"We've found ourselves in Addleton, and we'd like to make the most of it. What do you recommend?" Hannah says.

He introduces himself as Doug, and shakes both of our hands eagerly. "Well, you've made a great choice!" he replies, without any discernible trace of sarcasm. "I was born and raised in Addleton, and it's richly steeped in history!"

I look at Hannah. The only evidence of heritage I've seen so far is the Ford Sierra. "Do you have a map? Maybe a list of the 'must sees'?" I ask, wanting to move things along a little.

"I can do better than that!" he says, standing up straighter, and adjusting his tie. It's a slow day today, and my apprentice is due to come in at 11 o'clock for her four hours of work experience; so I could show you around for a couple of hours if you like? It would only be a modest fee; shall we say thirty pounds?"

Again, I look at Hannah, before looking back at Doug. "If she is your apprentice, shouldn't you be here to guide her? Show her the ropes?"

"Oh, no!" Doug replies. "She's been here for several months now, and she knows what she's doing. She does the admin. In any case, I'll be back later for her last two hours, to make sure she hasn't burned the place down".

I can't imagine how much administration is required in a place like this that could possibly occupy one hour, let alone four. Thirty pounds seems reasonable enough though, for two hours of live commentary from someone who has lived here for all of his twenty-five or so years, and presumably knows his subject matter inside out.

So it has been settled. Three, waxy, newly issued ten-pound notes have changed hands, and we shall return in forty-five minutes for our personal, guided tour of Addleton.

In the absence of a Costa or a Starbucks, we have found a greasy spoon café a short distance away that will serve us two milky coffees and some Happy Bargains digestive biscuits. The tables are stained with ketchup, and the chairs with tea. Well, at least I hope they are, and not anything more 'bodily'.

"Do you think this is a mistake?" I ask Hannah. "The guided tour, I mean, not this shit-hole of a café". Unfortunately I have said this loud enough for the proprietor to hear, and he scowls at me. Fortunately, Hannah doesn't see that I have offended him, so I am saved from her castigation.

"Well, think of it as an adventure. What's the alternative? By the time we get back to the campsite and have lunch, it'll be too late to go anywhere else. We'd just sit around reading for the rest of the day, until it's time to go to Darren's.

"OK. What would you like to do tomorrow?" I say, open to the prospect of reading my Ben Elton novel in the shade cast by our caravan, with all the comforts of food and drink just a few feet away.

"The Ecological Charity Project is on our list".

I stop myself from correcting her. The Ecological Charity Project is on *her* list, but I need to assuage my guilt and make amends for the last fifteen and a half hours. "Great!", I say, with feigned enthusiasm.

_____

"Right, health and safety first!", Doug says exuber-antly. "Do you both have sunscreen and sunglasses?"

"No", I reply bluntly.

"Oh, right, ok then."

There must have been something about my tone which causes him place to one side what looks like a pre-prepared disclaimer that he intended us to sign. Some-one in a think-tank has obviously required this council-subsidised agency to promote awareness of skin cancer, to indemnify themselves against the risk of us contract-ing it during our two-hour tour. The UK really is becom-ing more of a nanny state.

"We'll be heading towards the harbour, with its Georgian terraces, artistic quarter and gardens."

I glance at Hannah and we raise our eyebrows. My earlier negativity about the prospect of Doug's tour of Addleton is another example of me pre-judging a person and place. It sounds as though I was too hasty. Things are looking up. Well, everything except the gardens.

Doug shuts the front door to the tourist office, and we start walking down the hill towards the harbour.

"Before we begin, just a brief toponomy: You may have wondered about the name 'Addleton'. The suffix 'ton' is, as I'm sure you already know, signifies a town or settlement. 'Addle' is a Cornish word for something that is ruined or rotten. You may have heard of 'addled eggs'".

So I was right after all: Addleton is a rotten town.

Doug is glancing at me warily, as though reading my thoughts. "Pirates and smugglers played an import-ant role in our history. Well, it's generally considered it was *their* salacious behaviour that resulted in those of moral rectitude from neighbouring communities naming it a 'town of rotten people'".

"So, it's not the town that is rotten, just it's people", I say, which earns me a jab in the ribs from Hannah's elbow.

Doug ignores me and continues. "Back in the 1500s, during Henry VIII's and Elizabeth I's reigns, English privateers operated off the coast of England. They were paid to prey on vessels belonging to enemy states, such as Spain. They were considered to be local or national heroes, not villains. But when James I succeeded Elizabeth, improved relations with Spain meant that English naval forces were decreased. Many sailors were redundant, and tempted to use their seafaring skills as smugglers. Smuggled tea bought in Europe was a sixth of the price paid in Britain, and brandy from France was a fifth. Other earners were rum, gin and tobacco. Ships returning from the far east heaved-to offshore, selling their consignments of bone china, pepper, silk and cotton, free-of-tax to local smugglers. Smugglers were seen as opportunists, even if they resorted to violence. They operated on a grand and organised scale, assisted by whole communities who stood to gain from their activities. These blurred lines of moral acceptability even existed for pirates: seaborne robbers, who often resorted to kidnap and murder. When communities stood to gain from the availability of cheap goods, such practices were tolerated".

"Was the coast not policed?" Hannah asks.

"Not very effectively", Doug replies. "Being so far from London, foreign powers were not interested in Cornwall as a strategic point of invasion, so the reduced navy was deployed elsewhere. There were few revenue men to patrol a long and largely uninhabited coastline, and those there were risked their ships being hijacked, together with any confiscated contraband. Geography played another part: Cornwall is near the mouth of the English Channel, and had many hundreds of unfortified, coastal havens in which to hide; Addleton being one of them".

We have arrived at the harbour, which is situated at the bottom of a U-shaped bay, an enclosure which affords privacy from viewpoints from the west and east, beyond the straights of the U. Doug points out to sea towards the tops of the U.

"You can see that the oldest buildings are situated at the sides of the natural harbour. Once the pirates' or smugglers' vessels first passed land on their starboard and portside, no one could see what they did; unless, of course, the spy was in the town. But that was unlikely. Addleton was a place populated with folk who were either related to the crooks or turned a blind eye, guarding their privacy ruthlessly, and never welcoming strangers who could be revenue men or informers."

"Cornwall's own little 'no-go' area", I say.

"Precisely. Other nations' pirates operated in these waters, too. Barbary Pirates from North Africa, or 'Turks' as they were called, commandeered English ships and sailors. They even made land invasions, conducting raids on coastal villages. None of them managed to land near Addleton though. They were always repelled. The fierce reputation of Addletonians quickly spread, and the Turks soon gave up trying".

We are now walking to the left straight of the U. A narrow road separates the harbourside from a terrace of tiny fishermen's cottages. But these houses are not like the pretty, well-maintained homes I have seen in other historic, port towns; where oak front doors, freshly painted in a timelessly tasteful mushroom, olive green or light grey, reflect the diminutive stature of their seventeenth or eighteenth century occupants; where doorknockers have been replaced by substitutes with maritime themes: a mermaid, dolphin or whale; where those entrances are decorated with hanging baskets and jardinières overflowing with a blaze of colourful, fragrant flowers.

Blowing around in the sea breeze outside Addleton's harbourside cottages are cigarette butts and last night's fast food cartons. Pavements are peppered with splodges of chewing gum, ground flat into the tarmac. Door and window frames are neglected, and have dry, flaking paint. Filthy, yellowed panes are not adorned with smart shutters or swag-tails, but dismally draped in stained offcuts of mismatched materials stapled to the ceiling and coving. Weeds tumble out of the guttering, irrigating colonies of black, bronchitis-inducing mould.

The harbour features a depressing lack of ocean-going vessels. Apart from algae-covered dinghies, just two rusting fishing trawlers are secured by chains to large, metal, horn cleats that are periodically mounted along a dockside with capacity for thirty more. Coils of frayed ropes discoloured by ultra-violet light, and torn, tangled netting lie on the decks, undisturbed for months, maybe years.

My attention is drawn to the opposite, parallel side of the harbour. A youth wearing grey tracksuit bottoms and jacket, the hood of which is drawn up and around his face in spite of the warm weather, is riding a bike: a silver, men's hybrid. It looks like a Cannondale Quick CX4. *Just. Like. Mine.*

"Oi, you!" I break into a run. "Stop! I want a word!"

He is about two hundred feet away, but turns towards me. It is only his general gait and bearing that makes me suspect he is young and male. The hood is hiding too much of his face to identify his skin colour. He sits up in the saddle, *my* saddle, arrogantly raising his right middle finger, before riding away. There is no hope of catching him. "Hannah, did you see?"

Hannah looks less than impressed. "Someone on a silver bike? Yes."

"It was *my* bike. I'm sure of it!"

She gets out her mobile phone. "I'll phone PC Blinkerton, shall I?" she says, with mock urgency.

"Yes! Yes! White male, aged seventeen to twenty, I should imagine; grey tracksuit bottoms and hooded top, on *my* bike!". I look at my watch, "11.30 am". "On…" I look at Doug, "Doug, what road is he on?"

Doug is as anxious as I am. "Harbourside West Road".

I look at Hannah, "Got that?" She's not making any attempt at dialling a number.

"Henry. Even if PC Blinkerton is in the slightest bit interested in helping you after the stupid and immature way you kept alluding to his stature, I don't think he'd transmit an 'all-points bulletin' based on *that* information, if I'm being brutally honest".

"*Wouldn't act*?" I ask exasperatedly. "This is *hot intel*! The thief is riding my bike, right now, and heading towards…Doug, where is he heading towards?"

"The Sandcroft Estate".

"The Sandcr…Oh, give me the phone". Hannah hands me her phone and I dial the on-duty mobile number from the business card PC Blinkerton gave to Hannah, (yes, to Hannah, not to me, the actual victim in this case), which she entered into her phone's contacts folder. The officer answers after three rings that feel like thirty.

"PC Blinkerton, Henry Burden. We met yesterday morning at Godleven caravan site, about my stolen bike".

"Ah, yes, Mr Burden. How *is* your snake bite?", he asks casually. I can hear laughter in the background.

"Never mind about that. I've just seen the thief on my bike".

"I see. Can you see him now?" he replies.

I am frustrated by the lackadaisical response to my appeal for urgent action. "Er, no, but I know where he is heading".

"I see".

My God. How on earth did he manage to make fifty-eight arrests so far this year? I can see him in my mind's eye, removing a pocket book from his shirt and a pencil from behind his ear, then pensively licking the tip. "Well, don't you want the details, so that you lot can intercept him?"

"Go ahead with the location, time you saw him, description, and direction of travel, Mr Burden".

"White male, aged seventeen to twenty, grey tracksuit bottoms and hooded top worn up, Harbourside West Road in Addleton, heading towards the Sandcroft Estate. No more than one and a half minutes' ago". I wait for a response. The seconds tick by. "PC Blinkerton? Are you still there?"

"Yes, yes, I'm still here. He was on a bike, you say?"

"Yes! *My* bike!"

"Did he know you'd seen him?"

"Yes, I called out to him to stop".

"I see. What did he do?"

"He gave me the 'bird' and rode off in the opposite direction".

"I see. Did you consider following him discretely and calling us, before scaring him off?"

"No! He was too far away!"

"I see. How far away?"

"Oh, about two hundred feet."

"I see. And how long was he in your view?"

"I'd say, er, eight seconds".

"I see. So how did you positively confirm it was your bike?"

"What?"

"He was two hundred feet away, and only in sight for eight seconds. How could you see the 'Cannondale Quick CX4' stickers, the distinctive scratch on the cross-bar, or the replaced front wheel?"

"Umm".

"I see. And what about your unusual, orange, handlebar grips?"

"Errr..."

"I see."

"Would you recognise his face if you saw him again?"

"I didn't see his face".

"I see. So how can you estimate his age?"

"Look, this is all beside the point. It's *my* bike. The frame, colour, size, his reaction...I just *know* it is. We're wasting valuable time!"

There is a ten-second pause at the end of the line, during which I hear the plodding, slow-tapping of keys on a computer keyboard. Then dead air.

"PC Blinkerton? Are you still there?"

The line crackles. "I've just created an incident log for Addleton officers to try and find him".

I look at my watch. Four minutes have passed since I saw him. Traveling at a conservative ten miles per hour, he could have travelled two-thirds of a mile by now. Even if the officers take just another five minutes to respond and get to the search area, he will almost have covered another mile. God, this is bloody frustrating.

"Mr Burden, I'll call you back later with an update".

"Ok, thank you".

The call is terminated.

Doug changes the subject by leading us beyond the row of run-down cottages to a man-made pier built on rocks. Extending fifty metres into the English Channel and slightly curved, it resembles a crooked finger. At the end of the pier and looking out to sea, he tells us the tale of the 'Grand Voyager', a ship with ninety-eight canons on three decks.

Laden with five tonnes of gold and three hundred and ninety-three souls on its way from Lisbon to Portsmouth, it sank without a trace in 1781. As far as anyone knows it remains lost, in spite of technological advances in seabed exploration and mapping. Somewhere between where we are standing and northern France, in an area that is believed to measure ten thousand square miles, remains a cache of sunken treasure estimated to be worth one hundred and sixty million pounds. It's the stuff of legends and dreams.

Doug explains how the weight of its cargo and bad weather must have played their parts in the ship's fate; but it is also possible that a chemical reaction occurred due to the proximity of copper and iron used in the ship's construction: two metals that are electrochemically different. Their combination, and the fact that seawater would have acted as an electrolyte to create a galvanic cell, resulted in massively precipitated corrosion to the iron. The wooden ship would have literally fallen apart and sunk.

Wandering back along the pier, Doug tells us how

speculative divers from all over the world are drawn to these waters to explore, but choose not to stay locally. They prefer the campsites, hotels and B & Bs at Porthleven, a little further along the coast, depriving Addleton of a much-needed source of income and employment that the tourism trade brings.

I feel a little sorry for Doug, who is clearly an educated and articulate man, proud of his town, and who fears how long his office will remain funded. I suggest that we buy him a fish and chip lunch, and sit on the quay to eat it.

On the opposite quay, Harbour Road West, and situated where I would expect to see a smart, Michelin-starred fish restaurant, is a fish and chip shop; or, judging by its dilapidated sign, a "F SH A D HI H ". My prime suspect for the theft of the missing letters would be someone with the surname of Coppins. We walk towards the lower curve of the U, and up the right-hand straight. I am constantly alert to the presence of police cars, but there are none.

———————————————

"I don't mean to be rude, Doug...", I say, dangling my legs over the harbour wall, and almost placing my wrapped food down on a helical dog turd that resembles a Cumberland sausage. I suggest we move a little further down the quay.

"You were just about to be rude to Doug," Hannah prompts, after we have found a sweeter-smelling place to sit. "So don't!" She glares at me.

"Well, not rude..." I say, undeterred. "It's just...I was wondering...what is your background?"

"A degree in History at Exeter, so I could remain fairly close to my parents; then a post grad in Tourism. It's essential that I remain in Addleton now that my father has passed away. Mum is elderly. I'm her carer".

Sometimes I am bursting to make my point, no matter how much my inner voice, or Hannah, tell me that it is better left unsaid. It's like when you are talking to someone who has snot hanging out of a nostril. You are desperate to tell them about it so they can clear it away; so you don't have to look at it, or worry that it will suddenly detach during a bout of laughter or sudden exertion, and re-attach itself to your face, or land in your food.

There is a pause. Hannah is half-heartedly nibbling on a chip, looking at me sideways with a slight frown, telepathically imploring me to discontinue whatever advice I am about to impart, or line of conversation I am intent on initiating.

I press on. It needs to be said. "I'm sure you already know that there would be far greater job prospects in other towns, if you were able to convince your mother to move with you. What I want to say is: If you weren't tied to your career in tourism, the way you deliver your subject would make you a superb History teacher. As a teacher myself, I would be happy to talk this through with you, if you were interested."

Hannah looks away from me now, and is chewing normally, apparently satisfied that I haven't 'dropped an almighty bollock'.

"Thank you", Doug says simply. "Thank you very much".

I smile at him and nod. Opening my fish and chip wrapper, I gaze down at the greasy, front-page-spread, featuring a photograph of me on a stretcher, my cock and balls wrapped in Andrex. Today's newspapers aren't tomorrow's fish and chip wrapping paper, after all. They are today's.

Having consumed my soggy, battered fish and chips, (the shop claimed it was fresh cod, but it tasted like a poor quality, frozen coley), I hear Hannah's phone ringing. She checks the screen, and hands it to me.

"Hi PC Blinkerton. You have some news?"

"My colleagues in Addleton stopped the boy. He is sixteen years old".

"Excellent! With the bike?"

"With *a* bike".

"Cannondale CX4?"

"No, a Giant. Purchased last month by his father. Till receipt checked and verified".

"That doesn't prove that he wasn't on *my* bike when I saw him."

"No, we're fairly certain that the bike you saw him riding was the one they stopped him on – a silver, gents' hybrid Giant Escape...very similar in appearance to the Cannondale, especially at such a distance".

"But I don't understand. His reaction. The bike. Why wasn't he at school? He must have been up to no good!"

"He is an apprentice electrician who was on his way to work, when 'some nutter', his words Mr Burden, not mine, shouted at him to stop for no apparent reason. He admits that he gave the nutter short shrift, and made off into the nearby estate. There's no evidence of any wrong-doing here, Mr Burden. My colleagues in Addleton send their regards".

"Oh, ok, why is that?"

"They've picked up formal complaints from father and son, who are alleging a wrongful stop and search".

"Ah, I apologise".

"Oh, it won't go anywhere. They responded in good faith. It wasn't their fault they were acting on grounds that were entirely false and the figment of an over-active imagination."

PC Blinkerton terminates the call.

Turning to Hannah, I ask her whether she heard the conversation.

"I got the gist", she says sombrely.

"I'm guilty of prejudiced stereotyping again, aren't I?"

She doesn't need to answer. Her upside-down smile and raised eyebrows say it all.

The remaining hour is proving to be a culturally authentic reflection of modern-day Addleton. Sadly, like so many other deprived towns and cities of its kind, it is remarkable only in terms of what it lacks, not by what exists.

The 'artistic quarter' is not a vibrant place enlivened by acrobats; or featuring coffee-shops where an itinerant troupe of actors may present a one-act play; or where poets perform readings of their work; or musicians give impromptu renditions on violin, guitar or piano. It is a narrow and tatty street that is permanently cast in shadow, situated between the harbour and the town's 'Pleasure Gardens'.

This self-proclaimed area of creativity and imagination only seems to offer tattoo and body-piercing parlours, shops selling vaping products, discordant music CDs, tie-dye clothing, sessions of self-indulgent, meditative navel-gazing, incense, jossticks, and 'alternative tobacco'. There are far too many galleries displaying 'edgy street art' that graphically depict only violence, drug abuse and sexual aggression, all of which are hard-core and deeply disturbing.

The keepers of every establishment we enter look pale, malnourished, zoned-out, ill. Our attempts to make polite conversation are met with mono-syllabic, unintelligible grunts; or silence and vacant stares, as though *we* are the weirdos.

Addleton has neither a museum, nor a theatre, nor a concert hall. Live entertainment is limited to local bands who occasionally play on a Friday or Saturday night in the town centre's shabby pubs, where the five pounds entry fee will also buy you a pint and a burger. Times, dates and venues are advertised on cheaply reproduced A4 flyers that are glued to any vertical, flat surface. Many of them remain, years after the event, faded and flapping on bus shelters, boarded-up shop-fronts, and overflowing dustbins.

There is one church in this soulless place, used as a permanent soup-kitchen and place of shelter for the homeless and dispossessed, rather than of worship. Some may say that the function in which it used is more worthwhile than the one for which it was intended.

In spite of Doug's enthusiastic positivity, I personally find little basis on which to commend or recommend Addleton. I am sure that Hannah would argue that to say so would show that I am unacceptably prejudiced and discriminatory; but that assertion does not bear close scrutiny. My judgement on Addleton cannot be a form of prejudice, because it is based on actual, concurrent, direct experience; and if it is accepted that this is not prejudice, can discrimination exist? For there to be discrimination, someone has to be discriminated against. If I express my unprejudiced observations and opinions to third parties, and as a consequence of my critique they choose not to visit Addleton, then it is the people of Addleton who suffer. But we have already established that it isn't me who is discriminating against them. It can only be the third parties who are guilty of prejudice and discrimination towards Addletonians, for basing their decision not to go there on someone else's experience.

I want to disagree with Doug, to criticise this place, to encourage him to escape from it before it drags him down too. But I don't. I know that would be tactless and rude. I meekly follow him towards the Gardens, and I let Hannah do all the talking, nodding, laughing; ingenuously approving everything Doug says and shows us.

Being adjacent to the deeply coved harbour, and surrounded by protective hills to the north, west and east, Addleton enjoys a sheltered location. As one of the most southerly regions of the British Isles, its temperate climate promotes proliferation of colourful flora and fauna, palm trees and other exotic, sub-tropical vegetation, from early spring until late in the autumn. So, in spite of my usual apathy and ennui towards horticulture, the Pleasure Gardens is the one place where I expect to be impressed.

As we approach, I can see that the rectangular Gardens were once surrounded by a six-feet tall, iron, perimeter railing with fleurs-de-lys heads, and matching entrance and exit gates on its north and south sides respectively. They were painted dark green, a conservative shade that perfectly complimented the predominant colour of the Gardens within. Now, the original paint shows through beneath a gaudy, cracked and flaking orange. Whole sections of the boundary are missing, probably stolen when the price of scrap metal escalated in the early 2000s, and were never replaced by the local council. Those that remain are bent inwards and overgrown with voracious, Japanese knotweed, victims of attempted theft or mindless vandalism, and a council that has given up.

A children's play area is the focal point inside the Gardens, constructed of moulded plastic in primary colours. The swings' seats are missing, their chains hanging pointlessly from their beams. The underside of a stainless-steel slide has been stabbed by a knife, creating craters of razor-sharp metal that will flay open the skin of an unsuspecting child. There is the familiar sight of litter swirling in mini-vortices on gum-speckled tarmac, around the heavier detritus of crushed beer cans, soiled nappies and used syringes.

But yes, amongst all of this, there is a palm tree or two, and the bougainvillea bushes that have not been torn from their roots by morons with nothing better to do, are flourishing in this unseasonably warm, late spring.

By 12.50 pm, and having seen all that there is to see, we thread our way back to the High Street. We sidestep the vagrants who have awoken and emerged from hidden voids in refuse areas behind shops and under staircases in multi-storey car parks. They are now lying down on pavements with pleading, letters of anguish held beneath cups, begging for small change. I suspect any donation will mainly be spent on drink and drugs rather than food, so I avoid eye contact and ignore them.

An overweight, teenaged mother pushes her baby around the discount shops in a pram, complaining about the cost of living. But she is still able to afford the tattoos on her arms, shoulders, legs and ankles, proudly displayed in skimpy and unflattering clothing. She is smoking a cigarette, so she appears to have enough money to buy a packet of fags: the price of which is equivalent to two kilograms of chicken fillets, or two weeks' worth of fresh fruit and vegetables that would nourish her child.

Arriving back at the Tourist Information Office, we thank Doug; I tip him another ten pounds and jot down my telephone number, in case he wants to discuss entering the teaching profession.

Hannah asks him the way to the railway station. There isn't one. Buses operate a service via Helston, but it will take nine changes to return to Godleven.

Our eyes drift towards the ancient Ford Sierra taxi, which is still waiting at the rank.

———————————————

Negotiations over the fare to return us to Godleven started at one hundred pounds. The driver, Terry, argued that it was a one-hour journey that would take him away from his regular customers for a couple of hours. It wasn't until Hannah highlighted the fact that we had seen him waiting at the rank four hours' ago, and it appeared that his car hadn't moved, that he finally relented, and the price started to drop.

After five minutes of haggling like a shopper and a trader in a souk, we agree on seventy pounds, which he insists Hannah pays him up-front. We could *buy* his jalopy for about the same, and then we would not have to endure his overwhelming body odour.

Hannah climbs in and sits on the rear bench seat behind Terry. I shuffle in next to her. Before he engages first gear, he performs a double-take at me in his rear-view mirror, before glancing down at the front passenger seat squab, and then at my groin. It is most unnerving, but I suspect what is coming.

"'ere, ain't you that bloke from the 'paper?"

"No, I think you're mistaken".

He continues to glance at the front seat squab, where I instinctively know that his newspaper lies, before he inspects my face again in his rear-view mirror. I gaze out of the window.

Terry over-revs the engine and grinds the 'stick into first gear with a failing clutch, sending a jolt through the car's aged chassis as it reluctantly engages. We jerkily set off, making us resemble clubbers nodding the beat of a fast time-signature.

"Well, you and 'er don't 'alf look like the ones on the front page of today's Addleton Echo", he persists accusingly, talking as though Hannah is not present, clearly irritated by her powers of negotiation over the fare.

I ignore him.

"Very unusual to be bitten by an adder", he continues.

I'm still ignoring him.

"Especially there!" He glances back at my groin again, and nearly rear-ends the bus that has stopped in front of us.

"Look, let's change the subject, or, even better, sit in silence. My wife and I really want to return to Godleven...in one piece". I don't know how much more of this innuendo I can take. We are not even near the town where I was bitten, so I imagine the story has been regurgitated by every newspaper in Cornwall. I am going to have to endure this wherever I go, for the next two days.

"'ave you 'eard what the government has done today?" he asks Hannah, realising that he isn't going to get very far with me, and prepared to give her another chance if it means that he can speak.

Hannah takes advantage of the closed question. "No", she says emphatically.

I reach out to hold her left hand, which is resting on the seat between us. She quickly draws it away as though she has been scalded, and places it on her lap. I leave my hand on the seat, shut my eyes and pretend to sleep, wondering about the cause and significance of her sudden coldness.

CHAPTER 22

<u>Monday, 1.20 pm</u>

Sitting here in the back of this awful taxi, I am pleased that Henry has rationalised the possibility that the circumstances of his snake bite may reach unsympathetic ears at Frimlington High School. It's so unlike him not to worry about anything that he cannot control.

However I am appalled by his complete lack of emotional intelligence. He is completely oblivious to the fact that he leaks his prejudices without even opening his mouth. He was clearly fascinated by the smugglers and pirates who founded Addleton, the legend of the ship-wreck and lost treasure; but everything else made him curl his top lip in contempt. He made his abhorrence at the town's poverty and decline perfectly clear.

I hope Doug didn't notice Henry's disapproving shakes of the head in the 'artistic quarter', which betrayed his value-laden, superior, middle-class attitudes that suppose anything divergent from his own tastes or perspectives are far less worthwhile or valid.

I gave him fair warning when I realised that he was about to patronise Doug's career as a tourism guide, and I told him to stop. He completely ignored me. The arrogance! Oh, I'm sure that he'd argue he was being complimentary about Doug's ability to communicate information effectively; but his implication that Doug could do so much better by moving away from the town in which he was raised and clearly loves, to seek a more secure and rewarding future elsewhere by becoming a teacher, was deeply embarrassing. Who on earth does Henry think he is?

Then he offered himself as Doug's personal career advisor, not registering that Doug's thanks were borne from politeness, not interest. Much later, when we parted company, Henry actually foisted his phone number on Doug, when he *still* hadn't demonstrated any interest in a career change!

Don't get me started on the fact that Henry bought Doug lunch, as though he was too impoverished to buy his own. Then there was the excessive tip of ten pounds, which was given like a charity donation, rather than appreciation for the tour.

You may say that I am being harsh on Henry. You may feel that Henry's career demonstrates incredible interpersonal skill, in terms of his adeptness to educate others for their own and society's benefit. But Henry doesn't do it for them. He does it for him. He is completely self-indulgent. It is the intellectual process of teaching that motivates Henry. It is the victory of leading the horse to water and making it drink, that excites him; but only provided that it is done *his* way, on his *own* terms, and according to *his* values. Why else did Henry suggest that Doug became a teacher in a different town, rather than in one where its youth desperately needs more first-rate educators?

Henry believes that the world is always out-of-step with Henry, and never the other way around. I thought he was improving, but he is not. He is getting worse. The hubris that brought us together is the wedge that drives us apart, and he just doesn't see it.

CHAPTER 23

Monday, 4.30 pm

Hannah has sent me to Coventry. I use this idiom in its figurative sense. She has not literally required me to travel up the M5 motorway to the West Midlands. She didn't speak to me during the journey back to Godleven, or for the last two hours spent at our caravan. The only response I have received is a tut followed by a loud exhalation when I asked her what is wrong. Otherwise, she has not acknowledged my presence at all. I feel invisible and inaudible. Persona non grata.

There are several explanations about the origins of the phrase, 'sent to Coventry'. I think the most likely version is that during the English Civil War in the 1640s, Royalist troops captured in Birmingham were taken to the Parliamentary stronghold in Coventry, where they received something of a frosty reception. I can empathise with the Royalists' feelings entirely.

So whilst I sit in the sunshine trying to read my book, distracted from doing so by my inability to fathom why I am in the doghouse, Hannah occupies herself with a series of chores or errands; anything, it seems, to avoid sitting next to me, or explaining what has upset her, to put me out of my misery.

Having tried to read the same sentence five times, I place my book to one side, and enter the caravan to retrieve my iPhone from its secure spot under a pillow. I Google "used, men's, silver Cannondale for sale in Cornwall", and spend several minutes scrolling through various online marketplaces.

"Eureka!" I shout, triumphantly holding my phone aloft. Hannah is not sharing my excitement, and carries on removing a couple of dehydrated and dead flies from a window-sill, before spraying it with disinfectant. "My bike! I've found my bike!" I show her the screen, which shows my Cannondale with the aftermarket, orange handlebar grips I fitted to make it more visible to traffic ahead of me. She can't resist a quick glance.

"Looks like it, yes", she says, with no hint of emotion.

I read the advert aloud. "Men's hybrid Cannondale in silver. Excellent condition. Small scratch on cross-bar. One hundred pounds. *One hundred pounds*? I paid five hundred for that, just last summer!"

"Well, it is stolen and second-hand", Hannah says. "The thief can't show any proof of purchase to a buyer, and will want to get rid of it very quickly."

I reflect on the fact that Hannah is now talking to me; not in particularly affectionate terms, but it's a start. I'm going to have to move fast if I am to retrieve my bike. The phone number provided is a mobile, probably a 'burner' phone, a disposable 'pay-as-you-go' that isn't tied to a contract that can identify its owner. Only the post-code is given, no full address. I open a new search tab, and enter it into an online address finder: *Gower Street, Godleven, Cornwall.* A gazetteer search shows that it is within a couple of miles of The Weir Inn where it was taken! I dial PC Blinkerton's mobile.

"Yes, Mr Burden? I'm about to book off duty", he replies ponderously.

"I've found my bike!"

"Again."

"I really have this time! Well, not exactly found it, but…"

"Can this wait until the morning, Mr Burden? My son's sports day starts in about thirty minutes, and I am keen not to miss it again this year".

"It's advertised for sale…on 'Second Lives'… orange handlebar grips, scratch on the cross-bar shown in a photo, replaced front wheel…one hundred pounds… sale reference 76944…somewhere in Gower Street in Godleven…That's just around the corner from your police station, isn't it?"

PC Blinkerton sighs. "I'll ask a colleague on the late shift to look into it, Mr Burden. But I can tell you now that there are at least fifty terraced houses on each side of Gower Street. If the thief hasn't made any attempt to disguise your bike, he or she will not disclose their address, which would risk being challenged by the owner or police. There will be various tests and checks to overcome first, an alternative place to meet…"

"Will your colleague do it tonight?"

"If things are as you say, then he'll submit an online expression of interest, and see what comes back. We do this *our* way, Mr Burden. I strongly advise that you do not take matters into your own hands, as there would be a degree of risk to your personal safety. I'll phone you in the morning". The line goes dead.

"So, are you going to tell me what's up with you now?" That sounded rather more impertinent than I had intended.

"What do *you* think is wrong?" Hannah replies, arms folded tightly in front of her.

"I know that the last twenty-four hours haven't been great; you know, last night, and the tour of Addle-

225

ton today; but I promise I'll make it up to you."

"Henry, it's got nothing to do with the last twenty-four hours. Everything that happened in the dunes was unfortunate and regrettable...just bad luck. Addleton was fine. It was interesting to see another side of Cornwall".

"Not *everything* that happened in the dunes was unfortunate and regrettable", I say, attempting to lighten the atmosphere with suggestive humour. Hannah doesn't respond. "So what is it then?"

After a long pause, Hannah sits close to me with a doleful expression, and holds my hand: a combination of movements that make me feel as though I don't want to hear her answer. Then she gives it. "It's just that sometimes I wonder whether we are growing apart."

We are growing apart. With that completely unexpected and unforeseen lightening bolt, my heart misses a beat, my throat and chest tighten, my tears well up, and I am unable to speak for fear of squeaking and sobbing like a little girl. I really hadn't seen that coming. Not at all.

After listening in silence for half an hour to Hannah's innumerable examples of how I have irritated her lately, I suggest that it is best if I go and tell Darren that we are unable to attend his barbecue this evening. Hannah disagrees.

"Stop catastrophising, Henry! I'm not saying it's *over*. I just feel that you are becoming a little bit too self-absorbed! Everything seems to be on *your* terms, and I want you to be aware of your blind-spots. I don't know... we were more accepting of each other's idiosyncrasies when we were younger, but we mature...*I've* matured. I see things differently now. You just don't seem to accept that there are two sides to every coin. Nothing is black and white. There are shades of grey. There is always room to compromise. My life doesn't have to be lived according to the edicts of Henry! I thought you were changing, but you're not. People never really change. Not at our age. We've occasionally discussed your funny ways, and I thought that you had taken some of my comments on board, but you *always* revert to type. Your pomposity, intensity, negative view of the world, of people; none of it can be making you happy. It's certainly not making *me* happy. Sometimes I find myself sliding down the same spiral of gloomy pessimism and despair, and I *hate* myself for it".

There are so many contradictions for me to process: She's *not saying it's over*, but I am *pompous, negative, intense, self-absorbed, unable to change*. I'm *making her so unhappy* that she *hates* herself. I've heard *when* and *why* she feels the way she does, and a little bit of the *how long* she has felt this way, and *what* she feels. I know that I should now focus on what *I* must do, and *how* I must do it, to make things right; but I am so overwhelmed by the fear of losing her, that I can't think of anything other than desperately seeking her reassurance that we shall survive this. "Hannah, I *have* to know that it will all be alright in the end".

"There you go again, Henry! It's all about what *you* need! I can't give you a guarantee, because I *just don't know!*"

"Sorry."

"Don't apologise, just think about things from other people's perspectives."

"Why do you want to go to Darren's barbecue? Why is that a good idea after this row?"

"It's not a row, Henry. It's a conversation that you don't want to have. There is a difference!"

"OK, well why would we be in the mood to socialise, when we feel so low?"

"You tell me, Henry".

I know it would be a good idea to come up with the right answer at this point, so I decide to go and fetch some fresh water and spend time on my own thinking about it.

———————————

Having returned to the caravan with a full Aquaroll, I lightly knock on the door of the caravan and enter. Hannah is making a cup of tea.

"I think I've worked out why we should go to Darren's this evening", I say, feeling like a little schoolboy who has come down from his bedroom after being asked by his parents to consider why it wasn't a good idea to position a dart board on the wall adjacent to the urn containing his grandmother's ashes.

"And?" Hannah replies, her back towards me, not raising her eyes from warming the teapot with a splash of hot water from the kettle.

"You are not averse to their charms, and you would quite like to have a change of scenery, as well as see inside their caravan" I begin tentatively. Hannah is now adding water to two tea bags and swirling the teapot. She hasn't corrected me or raised her voice again, so I continue. "You would like me to come along too, because it would be odd if I didn't, and it would show you that I was able to do something I didn't really want to do, because I am not selfish and self-absorbed".

Hannah places the pot down on a counter to let the tea stew awhile, turns around, and kisses me on the cheek.

CHAPTER 24

Monday, 6 pm

I am a little embarrassed by the two, cheap bunches of yellow roses I purchased from a supermarket fuel station. They are intended as a gift for Darren and Wendy, for inviting us to their barbecue.

Earlier, returning to Godleven from Addleton, the smell of petrol inside Terry's Ford Sierra taxi suggested a serious leak somewhere between the tank and the engine. This was further confirmed by the fuel gauge that indicated fuel consumption equal to that of a battleship. I wasn't hugely keen on the idea of stopping to increase the payload of petrol, but at least it gave me the opportunity to buy Darren and Wendy this token of our appreciation. In spite of the inherent danger of ignition and a fiery death, the added bonus of the renewed intensity of fumes also masked Terry's acrid armpits.

I am constantly reminding myself that I must be on best behaviour, not just tonight, but forever. It is clear that Hannah has developed serious misgivings about our long-term future. The more I ruminate about it, the more occasions I remember when her acquiescent laughter at my obtuse observations and acerbic asides gave way to gentle challenges, before moving along a scale of resistance that ended, tonight, in outright objection that fell short of an ultimatum.

My short-term objective for the evening is to be completely charming; to accept the hospitality of our hosts graciously, and to resist the urge to remorselessly take the piss out of them afterwards. Hannah's unexpected 'shot across the bows' means that I cannot express negative thoughts or feelings to her anymore. But it doesn't stop me from thinking or feeling them, does it?

We are now approaching their caravan. The first test is not reacting to Darren's appearance. I can see him barbecuing two-inch thick, sirloin steaks. It's not going to be easy. He is wearing a full-length, dazzling white apron, with his forename monogrammed in gold thread on his left breast, and a toque blanche on his head. A spatula in one hand and tongs in the other, he resembles a lost Executive Chef from a Michelin-starred, London restaurant. He looks utterly ridiculous.

"Good evening, Darren", I say effusively, raising my hand by way of greeting. "You look fantastic!"

He waves back with his spatula, just as Wendy emerges from the Tabbert Cellini, her facial features as expressionless, shiny and solidified as always. She is wearing a shear, white, halter neck top over a white lace bra that lifts and presents her formidable, false breasts, as though for inspection and approval. Below a flat, hard, bronzed midriff is a white micro-skirt, that ends about four inches above the knees of her flawless, smooth, caramel legs. Unwisely, she is wearing six-inch white heels, which bury themselves into the grass, causing her to blurt out an unladylike, "Oh, fuck", before kicking them off and greeting us barefooted.

She is vaping on a white and gold vaporiser, and exhales a cloud so thick that we actually lose sight of her face for a second or two. Leaning forward at the waist, she welcomes Hannah and then me with a 'mwooah' on each cheek, administered at a distance of several inches; presumably because the Botox means she has lost all sensation in her lips, and she actually thinks she is making contact. It's still close enough to smell her breath: a cheap, sweet, pick 'n' mix odour from her vape.

Wendy accepts my wilting roses without feeling the necessity to feign gratitude, or bothering with any of the usual obligatory motions of courtesy and social propriety: sniffing them, exclaiming how beautiful they are, or insisting that she must immediately put them in a vase of water so that we can all enjoy them. She tosses them down onto a folding table, where the petals promptly detach, and litter the ground like at an ecologically considerate wedding. Wendy pulls us by our hands into the awning which has been prettily decorated with spirals of white fairy lights.

"Cummun sedan. Dissiz Princess, an' datz Zack, mar stepkidz", she says, indicating the familiar teenagers who are sitting at a dinner table dressed in a white lace cloth, gold plated cutlery, and ornate chinaware. Zack offers me his standard wave, still reading his Hardy biography, but having made considerably more progress, judging by the reduced thickness of the remaining, unread pages.

Princess is eyeing me with suspicion. "Dad said you wuz shaggin' inder doons, an got bit onya cock by an adda. Dat right?" These are the first words she has ever uttered to us.

"Shut it, ya lil gobshite", Wendy snaps, taking a step towards her and raising her hand as if to slap her. "Sixteen yiz old, an finks she nose zit awl. We told ya notta talk a bear tit!"

"Yeah, right. Don't kid yasself, Wendy. I 'eard you an' Dad 'avin' a right ole larf dis mornin wen you wuz readin da paypar".

I clear my throat. "Well, don't believe everything

you read", I say as jovially as I am able; "it was much more innocent than how it was reported".

Hannah comes to my rescue, and calls outside to Darren. "Hey, those steaks smell delicious!"

"Fanks, 'annah. Wend! Av you offered ar guests a fackin drink yet?"

"Nar! Gissa charnce! I bin introducin ya kidz, ain't I. Wot you avin den?"

Having asked for a glass of white wine, Wendy explains at length how she only stocks Champagne, because ordinary wine makes her come out in hives. I doubt that the varietal Pinot Noir, Pinot Meunier or Chardonnay grapes, often used in the production of Champagne, present much hypoallergenic difference to any other vin blanc. It's probably Wendy's ruse to get Darren to buy her a more expensive and flamboyant alternative; but I keep that to myself. I am on my best behaviour, and I have vowed not to be argumentative, contentious or 'clever', ever again. Well, not when Hannah is around.

Soon, all six of us are sitting around the dining table, all with full Champagne flutes in hand. Darren is positioned at the head at one end, insisting that I sit at the opposite end. It appears there is no place for feminism in his household. Wendy is on his right, with Hannah on my right. Princess is next to him on his left, and Zack is next to me on my left. We are waiting for the steaks to rest.

Having completed the fundamentals of establishing that we are from Dorset, and they are from Essex, it is not long before we have consumed two bottles of Moët et Chandon.

"We lavvabitter Mowette, dunt we Daz? Can't stand dat Pommery...sairns lark apple juice. An' dat Lorent-Perryay sairns lark fizzy water, duntitdoe Daz?".

I nod solemnly with pursed lips, hating myself for agreeing with her stupidity. *She doesn't buy some of the finest Champagne brands in the world, because she thinks they sound like soft drinks!*

Darren has now directed Zack to fetch another two bottles of Moët every time a bottle is emptied. Zack dutifully obeys, opening and nestling them in a ten-litre, brushed-gold ice bucket, which Darren has territorially placed next to his seat. It is also Zack's job to ensure that our glasses are never empty. My lips are beginning to feel number than Wendy's.

"So how are things in the car trade, Darren?" There is a lull in the conversation.

"Er, dunno. Why d'you ask, 'enry?"

I point to the registration number on his SUV: CAR 93T.

Wendy starts cackling loudly, spilling her Champagne down her cleavage, causing her to scream and giggle uncontrollably. Whatever I have said, whatever error I have made, shouldn't warrant such a reaction. She's obviously pissed already.

Princess looks at me and shouts, "Derrrr!", accompanied by the gormless, open-mouthed gurning favoured by teenagers when mocking the perceived stupidity of an adult.

"Nah, nah, nah, mate. I ain't inda motor trade. Carpets, mate, carpets!" He sits back in his seat, straightens his back and raises his glass to his lips. "I own summada biggiss carpet ware arses inda sarfeast! Turned over furry million quid larse year."

"I apologise. Congratulations", I say, raising my glass.

"Employ two 'undred staff in fyfe premises. Snot

wotizwuz, bus snot too bad". He nods at Wendy. "Keeps 'er in false tits an' Botox doe!"

Wendy giggles and jiggles her shoulders to make her falsies wiggle. But they remain completely motionless like two, over-inflated footballs in a hernia truss.

"You shoulda seenum before! Flatter than Norfolk day wuz, wuntday Wend? An' I treated er to a new nose, dint I Wend?"

Wendy smiles and turns towards Hannah and me, raising her chin so that we have to look up her nose.

"See dat? When I first met 'er, she 'ad a massif 'ooter wiv a fackin great lump onder endovit. Looked larka fackin peanut! Must've bin lark peerin' darnda barrel atda front sight ova rifle!"

"Strue, 'annah, strue! Ar looked lark Burt Bacharach!"

"Cyrano de Bergerac", I correct her.

"Yeah, 'im too!" she adds. My ears twitch reflexively as though the fleshy, helical rims and lobes are trying to fold themselves into the auditory canals, to protect my eardrums from her shrill, cawing laughter.

Darren resumes the narrative. "When ah paid for 'er cleft lip operation, wot wuz botched when she wuz a kid, da surgeon adta take da skin graft from 'er backside..."

I know what joke is coming.

"...So when I kiss her, arm really kissin' 'er arse!"

Hannah and I smile politely, and wait for Darren and Wendy to stop choking on their Champagne, so hysterical is their laughter. Princess is looking at the ceiling of the gazebo, her hands tightly gripping her cutlery. She has clearly heard this many times before.

As our hosts' laughter abates, the conversation lulls again. It's too early to talk about his caravan, with a view to getting a peak inside. Dinner must almost be ready.

"Zack, dishartda grub", Darren commands, waving a hand in the direction of buttered jacket potatoes wrapped in foil, two large bowls of dressed salad, and the plate of steaks.

"Wotjootoodooden?" Darren asks Hannah and me, sounding as though the Champers is taking its effect on him too.

"Henry teaches English and Law, and I work in sales", Hannah replies modestly.

"My wife does a little bit more than that", I add proudly. "She is the southern, area sales manager for a pharmaceutical company". I lean back in my chair so Zack can place a jacket potato and steak onto my plate with tongs. I look at Darren, Wendy, and Princess in succession for a response; for them to engage in a topic that doesn't revolve around them.

Darren is nodding blankly, Wendy is picking her teeth, and Princess is yawning loudly. Zack is looking at Hannah and me nervously as though he wants to respond, but doesn't. Tumbleweed bounces figuratively across the divide; a gulf not only literally afforded by the table, but the disparities in virtually every defining quality that make people who they are.

Again, Hannah comes to the rescue, bringing the chatter back into the 'safe' zone. "And what do you do, Wendy?"

"Ah manidge a bootician spa in Romford", she replies self-importantly.

"Fack off Wend!" Darren replies. "You 'elp ya mate airt wance a week so as she can go screwin' her 'usband's boss at Sarfend!"

"Yeah, an' when she duz, ah look arfta everyfink,

which is wot makes meedar manidge jar".

"These steaks really are delicious!" I say, remembering Hannah's other, earlier success, changing the subject by complimenting the food.

"Fanks", Darren replies, chewing his own steak with an open mouth. "Argentinian Picanhas. Furry quid a kilo. Best *you'll* evar eat".

Again, silence. I really didn't appreciate the emphasis placed on 'you'll'. Every other conversation seems to return to what something cost. I turn to Zack. "I noticed that you're reading a biography on Thomas Hardy. I'm a big fan of Hardy".

Zack looks at his father before replying, as though for permission to speak. "We're doin' 'is novels for English A' level," he replies nervously.

"Which ones?"

"I've chosen Tess of da d'Urbervilles, Far fromda Maddin' Craird, da Mayor of Casterbridge, Jude der Obscure, Return of da Native, an' Underder Greenwood Tree, for me ten farzind-word projict".

"Excellent! What is the title of your project?" Zack's eyes drop down towards his food, and he starts playing with his salad with his fork. I sense that he is not used to talking about his work in front of his ignorant family.

"I haven't decided yet, but I wanna consider 'ardy's portrayal of women..." he says falteringly, looking at me with an expression that tells me that he is waiting for the mockery to start.

Darren loads a forkful of steak, salad and potato into his mouth, making a smacking sound as he chews, while staring vacuously at his son. Wendy is preoccupied, stretching her blouse away from her breasts in an attempt to air and dry the spilled Champagne. Princess dramatically drops her forehead down onto the edge of the table, to draw attention to the fact that she is *so bored* that she has lost the will to live. But she has done so with rather more gusto than she intended, and is now vigorously rubbing the area between her eyebrows.

"Go on", I say encouragingly.

"Well...'s interestin' 'ow 'ardy bucks der trend of Victorian culture an' society. He allows women to exist inder same way as men, rather dan be subjugated by men. Women work outside as well as inside der home; dey travel alone an' wivart chaperones; dey succeed; dey initiate relationships, an'...". Zack is squirming in his seat.

"Go on Zack, this is *fantastic* observation!"

"...Well, he offers as much detail abart women as uvva contemporary authors give men; 'ardy's women are allaird ta explore dare sexuality. Dey ain't paragons of virtue by Victorians' standards, but are imperfect an' unconventional in an imperfect world, which is only imperfect cos it's controlled by men. 'ardy's women are *real*".

I sit back in my chair and look at Hannah, who returns my look and smiles. Expecting to see some form of positive impression on his family, I look anticipatively at Darren and Wendy.

"Wotda fack you torkin abart?" Wendy asks him.

"You ain't gunner sell many carpets wiv dat loader ole bollux", Darren says, laughing.

Princess slumps in her chair, her arms dropping straight down by her sides, her chin on her chest, and her tongue lolling out as though she has now *actually* died of boredom.

Zack's eyes well with tears; he drops his knife and fork onto his plate of unfinished food, throws down his napkin, and walks briskly away from us in the direction of the beach. I stand up, preparing to follow him, but I am vetoed by Darren.

"Nah, 'enry. Le' 'im gah. 'e needs ta learn dat eel be joinin' me inda carpet bizniss in a year, not gallivantin' offta ooniversi'ee wiv all iz soft mates".

This is the biggest test of my vow not to say what I am thinking and feeling. I glance at Hannah for some sign of clemency; that she'll let me speak my mind, and offer Zack a line of defence in his absence. She almost imperceptibly shakes her head, enough to let me know that I must not interfere in this toxic family's affairs, or act as the rescuer in their tawdry drama triangle.

Darren resumes, regaling us with a tale about Wendy's vaginoplasty.

"Ah spent four grand gettin' 'er flaps reduced. Day looked lark a badly made ham sandwich before, dintday Wend?"

"Yeah, daydiddoedintdaydoe Daz!" she agrees.

"Wiv alder meat 'anging airt", Darren adds, in case we couldn't already visualise her pre-op appearance.

No matter how fine the Champagne and food, I lay down my knife and fork, and dab my lips with my napkin. I have lost my appetite. I want to leave.

Hannah and I are back at our own caravan within two hours. We were saved the pain of enduring any more of this hospitality, because of the sudden and rapid onset of Wendy's inebriation. I estimate she personally consumed two of the six bottles of Moët et Chandon that Zack kindly opened, chilled and poured for us.

When she crudely announced that she was "going for a slash", (her words, not mine), she pushed back against her chair to rise from the table; but the back legs got caught in the patterned gaps in the interlocking, rubber mats that formed the floor beneath the awning and dining table, sending her tumbling backwards. Her knees whiplashed, kicking forward her still-bare toes against the underside of the table, making the plates and Champagne flutes jump and spill. The slapstick fall and accompanying 'CRACK!' that signalled her toes fracturing, affected Wendy to the extent that she did not know whether to laugh or to cry. So she did both, the exertion and anaesthetising effect of the alcohol causing her to simultaneously fart loudly and wet herself comprehensively.

So we still haven't seen the inside of their Tabbert Cellini, and I accept that now, we probably never shall; but at least I have acquitted myself well with Hannah. I have not said or done anything to incur her disapproval or criticism. My copybook remains unblotted.

I suggest to Hannah that it will help us to digest the heavy meal if we stroll down to the beach to watch the sun setting. Hannah says she feels too tired to do anything other than collapse in a chair and watch something intellectually undemanding on the TV. I don't force the issue; it will give me an opportunity to find Zack, check he is ok, and offer him some sound and supportive advice.

I don't have to look for very long. He is standing on the shoreline, throwing into the water the odd stone washed up onto the sandy beach. I approach from an oblique angle and cough to signal my presence, so that I don't startle him. He turns, sees it's me, and resumes his pebble-skimming in reflective silence.

"You ok?" I ask.

"Izzit wrong to 'ate ya parents?"

That's a tough one in Zack's case. I decline a direct answer. "I think your Dad wants you to join him in the family business; but it's got be about what *you* want, too. Have you tried discussing it with him? To perhaps broach a compromise?"

"'e won't listen. Twas a struggle persuadin' 'im t'let me do me A' levels, an' not join da business when I finished me GCSEs a year ago. I would've bin jus' sixteen! Still a kid! Day are *so* fick, day embarrass me."

"Well, I expect it's difficult for them to understand, if they don't possess your academic skills", I begin, diplomatically. "Your Dad's strengths lie in commerce, which may take a different kind of intellect. Judging by his wealth, he's very successful at it."

Zack snorts, derisively. "'e inherited da business from 'is farva, an' 'e is running it inta da grairnd. You should see da profitability charts. Day are down furry-two percent since 'e took ova".

I'm beginning to feel as though Zack is taking me into more of his confidence than is right and proper. "Well, I don't know about that Zack; but I'll offer you one word of advice, if you're interested...just between you and me, though. I don't want to be accused of interfering". I let the seconds tick by. I don't want to be pushy either.

"Go on den", he replies eventually.

"When are you eighteen?"

"Next February".

"Well then; you'll be an adult in the eyes of the Law in just eight months' time, and legally able to make your own decisions. Why not take things in bite-sized chunks, rather than becoming overwhelmed by the whole dilemma? You know he supports you in taking your A' levels, which means your immediate future for the next twelve months is already planned. If he won't support your applications for a place at a university at the end of this year, then the worse-case scenario is that you'll need to apply *next* year. You'll be eighteen. No one will be able to stop you. Why not explore loans and scholarships in the meantime, in case he won't fund you? No one can make you do what you don't want to do, Zack. Life is too short not to be happy".

"Yeah? Well, one day eel find art dat I'm gay an' all". Zack carries on throwing the stones into the sea.

I smile and pat him supportively on the shoulder, and walk away to find a place out-of-sight. I shall wait, check the messages on my phone, wait for the sun to set, and watch to make sure that he returns to the safety of his caravan in due course. I don't know him or his temperament. I am worried that he might do something daft, like walk off when soon there will be no natural or artificial light; or heaven forbid, do anything worse.

I am relieved when he wends his way back towards the caravan park after about half an hour.

I return to Hannah after the sun has dipped below the horizon. She is fast asleep, so I spend the rest of the evening reading.

Only I am not really reading. I am staring at the pages so intently that the words are completely out-of-focus. Although I have been bursting to talk about it, I have succeeded in not initiating any discussion about the barbecue, or Darren and his family. I am paranoid that Hannah will interpret any comment as mockery or negativity, which she will use to question our mutual compatibility. Again.

Yet I am also surprised that she hasn't made any remark either, considering how outrageous it all was. Perhaps she is testing my resolve to be more accepting of others, by seeing if I will revert to type. Even though only a few hours have passed since she challenged me so unequivocally and unambiguously about my attitude, I am beginning to worry how long I can maintain the pretence.

If she really is so intent on forcing me to self-censure my values and cynical views about an increasingly mad world and the ridiculous people in it, how in God's name can I reasonably excise or suppress facets of my personality that are so innate and instinctive? It is *she* who has changed. I am essentially the same person I was when she met me.

CHAPTER 25

Tuesday, 8 am

"You went and spoke to Zack last night, didn't you?" Hannah says accusingly, as soon as our alarm sounds.

I am groggy. It took me ages to fall asleep last night, my mind in overdrive, and now I am finding it difficult to wake. I don't realise that my lassitude and slowness to reply make me seem guilty, which of course, I am, by Hannah's standard.

"I knew it! You just can't mind your own business, can you? You always have to offer an opinion and get involved. Why can't you live-and-let-live?"

"Er, because I felt a duty to offer some advice to a troubled young man who is desperately unhappy", I reply croakily. "Is that so wrong?"

"So you're telling me that it wasn't just a little bit motivated by your constant need to air your uninvited views, or control and influence the situation, even when it has nothing to do with you?"

"Hannah, that's not fair. You praised me for speaking up for him at the mine. What is the difference between then and now?"

She thumps the duvet back with her fists, and stomps off into the caravan's tiny shower room to wash and dress.

Lying on my back and gazing at the ceiling, I reflect on the prospect of spending today with Hannah, when she is in such a bad mood. I can't, I won't disclose to her the confidences Zack entrusted to me last night. *Oh God*. Didn't I promise Hannah we would visit the Ecological Charity Project? I close my eyes, hoping that it will shut off my thoughts, too. It doesn't.

As I lie there feeling hard done by, a wave of self-righteous indignance gradually washes over me: Each to their own, but I am in no mood to spend a day being lectured by a bunch of tree-huggers about how organisms relate to each other and their physical surroundings; or be made to feel guilty about my lack of awareness of the natural environment; or be told how every aspect of my selfish and inconsiderate life fails to support biodiversity and conservation. Perhaps this is the perfect opportunity for Hannah and me to spend a little time apart: She can take the Volvo to the Ecological Charity Project, and I can spend some time on the beach, reading my book. Who knows? Perhaps my absence will make her heart grow fonder.

I suggest it to her as soon as she gets out of the shower. She doesn't object. In fact, she appears quite relieved.

———————————————

We haven't driven the Volvo since it was graffitied in such crude and personally offensive terms in the car park at Marazion. Since then, I have parked it with the driver's side facing a bush so that no one can see it, and we can't be reminded of it. It's going to cost hundreds of pounds to re-spray the door.

I really don't know who would have done this to us, or, more likely, to me. My only suspect is the man with the Go-Cam, whom I challenged on the boat over to the island; but that is illogical. He would have to have seen me in the Volvo *before* we met on the boat, in order to draw any connection between the car and me. He was still on the island when we left, so it is unlikely that he travelled back across the water to the car park just to damage my car, and returned to the island again afterwards. No, it's a complete mystery to me.

I consider how to mask the offensive scratching, so that neither of us suffer the embarrassment of driving the car with it on display. Should I use a plastic sheet wedged into the gap between the electric driver's side window and the door card, or smear the whole door in paint-stripper? A sheet will flap in the car's slipstream, so I choose the latter, and set about taking the paint back to the metal. It will have to be completely re-sprayed, anyway.

By 10 am, Hannah has made herself a packed lunch to take to the Project, and left me to my own devices. She bade me farewell and wished me a pleasant day, but only as afterthoughts.

Rather than reflect on her rapidly cooled attitude towards me, which continues in spite of my concerted efforts to do the right thing, I keep occupied by refilling our fresh water drum, and draining the grey-waste container.

I am now completing the worst job in caravanning: emptying the chemical toilet. This involves heaving a plastic tank, brimming with Hannah's and my bodily waste, down to the campsite's cesspit. We normally average two days before this task needs doing. But I hate this chore so much, that I usually procrastinate until the third day, by which time the tank is absolutely brimming, and much heavier to carry. Hannah manages to get out of doing it, because she says she can't lift it.

The process of opening the container and pouring the foul-smelling slurry into the tiny hole that leads to the underground cesspool, is an art in itself. I have learned from bitter experience that it is advisable to safely place to one side the two plastic attachments which must be removed from the tank before its grisly contents can be poured out. The alternative is to risk dropping them into the cesspit. This leads to two options, both of which are awful, but for very different reasons: rolling up a sleeve and thrusting your hand down the hole to locate them in strangers' excreta; or, because the two parts can't be purchased and replaced separately, buying a complete, brand new unit for about one hundred pounds.

So here I am, trying to keep my nose as far away from the 'action' as possible; not easy when you are holding twenty-five litres of wee and poo at arm's length, and generally aiming for a hole that is three inches in diameter. Yes, I am liberally spattering my legs and feet, like a music-lover at a predictably muddy, English, open-air rock festival. But at least this technique reduces the risk of what I call 'facial splash-back'.

I mitigate the risk to my clothing by exercising some contingency planning: No matter whether it is sunny and dry, or wet, windy and cold, I always wear my rubber flip-flops and short trousers, and follow this unpleasant task with a thorough wash in the adjacent shower block. Taking every feature of this ritual into account, it's a five-minute job that takes me thirty.

The dirty deed done, I wander down to the beach. An inflatable chair, towel, sun lotion, my phone, book, and a bottle of mineral water are all I need to sustain me until 1 pm, when I intend to walk to a nearby pub for a pint of best bitter and a stilton-and-cheddar ploughman's lunch.

I emerge from the dreaded dunes onto the vast expanse of sand, and walk some distance along the back of the beach, away from established paths. Choosing a sheltered spot in front of a hillock of sand, but far enough away from the grasses and heathers that secrete those infernal adders, I inflate my chair, and place everything within easy reach of it.

It is already 11 am, but I have the place to myself. Occasionally people walk along the beach, to or from the direction of Godleven Mine, but they are a couple of hundred yards away from me, at the water's edge. I can't even hear their chatter; just the soporific white noise of the wind passing through the grasses, and waves lapping on the shore.

I sit under a cloudless sky, my sports watch indicating a balmy 21°C. Lathered in factor 50, sipping my water and reading my book, I am forcing myself to do something that I am so very rarely able to do: put aside my worries; in this case, about my marriage.

Not even ten minutes pass, when I am aware of a couple approaching. They have any number of routes they can take along the beach, but the one they have chosen is a beeline directly towards me. I am astonished when they stop, just ten feet away from me, and start spreading out their rug, picnic and collapsible chairs.

Why do people do this? They have literally acres of sand in which to choose a place where we may *all* enjoy the peace and tranquillity of our surroundings; of not having to engage in conversation with any other human being. Yet, there they are, nodding in acknowledgement of me, giving their greetings and waiting for me to reciprocate, no doubt so that they can engage me in some banal conversation about how deserted the beach is, how clement the weather, how they hope it will last, or some other tedious bollocks, when all I want to

247

do is enjoy some isolation where I can't upset anybody, nobody can upset me, and I can read my bloody book!

It's a false presumption that a solitary person must feel lonely and in need of company, safety, or kinship. Why doesn't it occur to these space-invaders that I am enjoying the isolation of being in a spot that is unoccupied by any living or mechanical thing; the very quality which drew *them* there too!

So I *do* respond: I stretch my lips over my bared teeth and scowl, which doesn't have the preferred effect of making them hastily move further away, like to Devon; but at least it ensures that they shut-the-fuck-up and leave me alone.

This kind of behaviour reminds me of when we bought our Volvo. Proud of its unblemished paintwork, I drove it from the franchised, Volvo dealership to a supermarket, carefully parking it in the furthest reaches of a huge and expansive car park, in an area where there was no other vehicle. The space I occupied was the furthest from the shop's main entrance door, and being 1 pm on a Wednesday afternoon, it was not a period of peak demand. For all of these reasons, there was the lowest possible risk of anyone parking within one hundred feet of our brand-new Volvo.

So you can imagine my irritation when I returned to my car with my shopping, that in spite of the tens of other spaces much closer to the store, some idiot not only decided to park right next to our car, but so close to it that I had to use my front passenger door to access my driving seat.

To make my feelings even clearer to the people next to me on the sand, I huffily collect my things and walk away from them, before re-establishing myself a hundred feet further along the beach.

After half an hour, I am bored. I have finished my book, and I forgot to bring another one down to the beach. There is one, intermittent signal bar on my phone, and the internet is not working reliably. I can't even read my emails or the national news, without receiving an 'internet lost' message half-way through.

I look at the sea, and wonder whether I should take my first dip of the year. I reason that there are more cons than pros; the fact that it is probably freezing cold being the clincher. So I pick up my phone and start walking around, holding it aloft, changing the angle of it, and squinting at the screen that appears to have turned black in the sunlight, to see if my contortions have made a difference to the signal strength.

It starts ringing unexpectedly, so I answer it, holding my position like a living statue, in case the call drops out.

"Hello, Henry Burden".

"Mr Burden, PC Blinkerton here with an update".

"Ah, yes, good. If I lose you, please call back. I'm in a poor signal area".

"Ok, well I'll make it brief. We've got the CCTV from the pub. It shows a person with a male's gait, but whose face is totally obscured by a hoody, and the back of a blue Vauxhall Corsa. It's a 2000 to 2006 model, which in all likelihood belongs to the thief; but only a partial registration number is visible. We're working on variations of it to identify a local keeper, but so far, no dice".

"I see", I reply. "Have you checked to see if there's one like that parked in Gower Street?"

"Yes, we have; and no, there isn't".

"That's a pity".

"My colleague from the late shift sent a text enquiry to the seller of your bike on 'Second Lives' last night, and a meeting's arranged at 1 pm. One of our colleagues from a neighbouring district will be coming over in plain clothes shortly – he is less likely to be recognised as a police officer if our thief is local to Godleven".

"That's excellent! Where is the meeting taking place?"

"Locally, but I'm not going to disclose precisely where, Mr Burden. Just leave it to us, please. There is no need for you to be involved. We already have enough information to positively identify your bike, and as I've told you before, there are risks involved. We'll contact you later if the operation is successful, because we'll need you to make a formal statement of loss and identification, if we're able to recover your property".

"Oh...ok".

PC Blinkerton terminates the call.

If the operation is successful...*if* we're able to recover your property. I am impressed by the planning, but there were considerable expressions of doubt and negativity about the prospect of successfully nabbing the culprit and recovering my bike.

I reflect on the limited information disclosed to me... The thief lives in Gower Street: possible. The thief owns or has access to a blue Vauxhall Corsa: probable. The thief is male: confirmed. An undercover police officer is meeting the thief at a local but undisclosed location at 1 pm today: confirmed.

I check my watch: 11.41 am. With Hannah away for at least another few hours, and with little else to occupy me, I decide that the police need a helping hand. It may not be with their blessing, but I can't sit around doing nothing. I would never forgive myself if the thief got away and I hadn't lifted a finger to help. Another pair of eyes and ears can't do any harm. I know how to be discrete.

I am going to 'play detective', and make sure that this 'sting' is a success. I have much less information and resources than the police, so I am going to base my starting point on some bold assumptions.

Having returned to the caravan, I am selecting the dullest and most unimaginative clothing in the wardrobe. This exercise is really quite easy, because this fairly describes all of the clothes I own. The idea is to blend in, rather than stand out.

I follow my phone's sat nav directions to Gower Street, arriving there at 12.35 pm. Standing in a telephone kiosk at the end of the road, I can observe the whole length of it. I should be able to see the comings and goings of every pedestrian and vehicle from here. Assuming the rendezvous is somewhere in the town centre, and that the thief will be cycling there, *on my bike*, he will have to leave his house between now and 12.50 pm, to comfortably make the meeting with the police officer at 1 pm.

I am in the kiosk for at least five minutes before I realise that there is no payphone. It has been vandalised or removed by the telephone company, probably the latter, seeing as even five-year-olds own mobile phones these days. The kiosk must have been left here for the convenience of passing drunks, judging by the smell inside it, which is making my eyes water. It's also proving useful as advertising space for ladies of dubious morals: their business cards are covering an entire wall.

Realising that anyone local to this street probably realises that there is no phone in here, and may wonder why a man is standing inside it for so long without relieving himself, I leave and saunter aimlessly up Gower Street. It's not ideal, and it risks contact with my subject, but there is no other suitable cover; no plate glass window where I may turn my back on my quarry and obtain a reflected view; no deviated building-line to make use of; no O.P. (14) where I may view proceedings and remain completely covert. By learning how to evade Travis Grausam and his gang back at Frimlington High School, I have picked up a little surveillance lingo, as well as some of their techniques.

It takes me another five minutes to saunter the length of Gower Street, casually turning around occasionally to check on any activity behind me: There is none; not even an elderly person popping out to the local shops to irritate other shoppers.

I check my watch: 12.45 pm. It takes an additional three minutes to return along the same road at a faster pace. I must hurry if I am going to get to the town centre on foot in time to position myself somewhere along the main drag, a vantage point from which I am more likely to see my bike being ridden.

I arrive in the High Street at 12.58 pm, struggling for breath, folded over double with my hands on my knees. I had to run to get here for 1 pm. Seeing a bench outside a newsagent, I sit down. Suddenly being at rest seems to transmit a signal to my pores, which open and bleed perspiration, soaking my shirt in seconds. What was I thinking? It was all such a long shot. Too little information to work on. Too many assumptions made. Too much ground to cover.

My phone rings. I can see from the display that it is PC Blinkerton.

"Yes, PC Blinkerton?"

"You didn't by any chance stake-out Gower Street within the last half an hour, did you?"

"Er..."

"Yes, we thought so".

I can hear groaning in the background.

"Our switchboard received an anonymous message from a male at 12.39. I'll read it to you: *'Tell the man hiding in the telephone kiosk in Gower Street he's been spotted. You'll never see the Cannondale again. The 1 pm meeting is cancelled'*. I'm afraid, Mr Burden, that you have, as we say in the trade, 'blown out' the operation; and with it any chance we had of recovering your bike and prosecuting the offender. The investigation will now be closed. Enjoy the rest of your holiday. Good day to you."

PC Blinkerton terminates the call.

I find a café, order an iced Mocha, and press the cold glass to my forehead, hoping that it will not only cool me down, but reduce the aching thud that is pulsing audibly between my temples. I replay the message relayed by PC Blinkerton over and over in my head: A male phoned the emergency services' switchboard, and said, *"Tell the man hiding in the telephone kiosk in Gower Street he's been spotted. You'll never see the Cannondale again. The 1 pm meeting is cancelled"*.

There is something not quite right about this message. I sip my drink and close my eyes, assimilating the information, phrase by phrase. Clearly, we can now confirm that the thief or handler has close associations with Gower Street. But he phoned the police and *said*. It wasn't a written message in a text or email; it was *spoken* by the maker, and a communication he intended for the *police*. It was committed to paper, or more likely typed into a computer log by the person receiving it: someone who works remotely in a regional call centre, receives hundreds of calls a day, and can have little or no notion about the details and circumstances of the events to which those messages relate. *"Tell the man...You'll never see the Cannondale again."*

It is safe to assume that the caller is the thief, or otherwise the handler of my stolen property. He must surely have thought that the man in the kiosk was a bungling undercover officer. So why didn't he refer to that fact? My experience of schoolkids is that they revel in making of the most of it when teachers make a mistake. I am sure that the dynamic between criminals and police officers as equivalent figures of authority, is fairly similar. So why didn't he rub the officers' faces in it? Why didn't he say, *"Tell the useless copper hiding in the telephone kiosk in Gower Street he's been spotted"*? Because he knew that the man in the kiosk wasn't a police officer? But how would he know that?

"You'll never see the Cannondale again". That seems pretty straight forward. Or is it? Doesn't this phrase suggest that the *police* will never see the Cannondale again? But the police have never seen my Cannondale, other than in a photograph in the on-line advert. No, this suggests that the *man in the kiosk* will never see the Cannondale again. And I am the man who was in the kiosk. I am the owner of the Cannondale. I have ridden my bike on many occasions. I am the only one in this scenario, other than the thief or handler, to have physically *seen* it before.

So could this be a case of the call-taker wrongly punctuating his or her written record of the message, or of slightly mis-representing it? Should it have been interpreted differently? If so, how could it have been originally spoken?

"Tell the man hiding in the telephone kiosk in Gower Street: You've been spotted. You'll never see your Cannondale again. (And for the police officers), the 1 pm meeting is cancelled".

My eyes narrow, as I zone in on the implications of this possibility. Does the thief or handler know that I am the owner? And if so, how?

I've returned to Gower Street and surrounding roads, looking for a blue Vauxhall Corsa. PC Blinkerton told me that it was a 2000-2006 model, in blue, and that he had only a partial registration number. Only the back of the car featured in the video footage. I have Googled that model range, and I know what I'm looking for. Unfortunately he didn't mention what shade of blue.

You don't notice how many blue Corsas there are, until you start looking for them. There still isn't a blue one in Gower Street, but I have found four parked in an adjacent road, all which are in various conditions of appearance and maintenance. I peer into each of them, looking for any indication of use by someone concerned in the unlawful appropriation of bikes: a reclined rear seat to make the boot's load bay bigger; a broken bicycle lock; some bolt-croppers; tell-tale scratches on the top of the rear bumper where bikes have been loaded in and out of the hatch-backed tailgate. Nothing.

I wish I could see the CCTV footage for evidence of a uniquely positioned, self-adhesive GB badge or missing trim; anything that might help me to identify the thief's car. The police should be doing this, not me, but I can't very well phone the officer up and ask now. He'll know that I'm still 'playing detective', and I already know how he feels about that.

Having used my phone to surreptitiously video

the backs of the four cars and their registration numbers as I walk past them, I slowly walk back to the campsite via a supermarket, to stock up on some essentials.

CHAPTER 26

Tuesday, 3.55 pm

I have truly relaxed today. Not once have I had to listen to Henry's gripes and groans, or fear avoidable conflict with someone who has upset him. The Ecological Charity Project taught me a little about alternative energy sources; how to live more sustainably so that I can reduce our negative impacts on the environment; and how gardening can be therapy for stresses experienced at work... and living with Henry.

My positive and happy disposition was short-lived. When I returned to the campsite, both of our caravan's tyres were flat. This meant that without the extra few inches of height when they are properly inflated, the caravan was now jacked up on its corner-steadies, suspended in mid-air. I couldn't see any sign of puncturing or damage to the rims when I spun the wheels full-circle, which meant that someone had deliberately let the air out of the tyres.

When I went inside to fill the kettle, there was a distinctive smell of urine coming from the tap, which supplies water via a pump from the drum which Henry keeps replenished. When I decanted a sample into a glass, I detected a distinct yellow tinge to it, too. Unless there was a dog on site with an opposable thumb to remove the drum's cap, and a particularly good aim, I can think of no other explanation for this other than someone playing a rather disgusting prank on us.

The final insult is the fact that someone drew in indelible marker pen all over the back of one of Henry's shirts, which I washed earlier and hung on our portable washing line to dry.

The last time I saw Henry, he told me that he was going to spend the morning on the beach, before walking to a pub further along the bay to have lunch. I wonder what he really did. Whom has he upset?

I've knocked on Barry and Maureen's door, to ask whether they've seen anyone acting suspiciously around our caravan. Part of me wondered whether they were the culprits, getting more revenge for the trick Henry played on them with the meat. They said they'd been there all day, but shrugged their shoulders and denied seeing or hearing anything untoward. I have to say that they seemed genuine.

Then I considered it possible that Darren had found out about Henry's unacceptable interference in their family affairs, by advising Zack on how to manipulate his father into letting him go to university. So I made tentative enquiries there, too; but it quickly became clear that Zack hadn't breathed a word to his father about his chat with Henry on the beach last night. My conversation with Darren mainly revolved around Wendy's monstrous hangover and her fractured toes. She still hasn't surfaced, and has been in bed all day.

So the only remaining explanation is that Henry has done or said something to upset someone in my absence, and revenge has been taken again.

I re-inflated the tyres, cleaned out the water butt, flushed through the caravan's plumbing several times with hot water and disinfectant, and threw Henry's ruined shirt into the recycling bin.

I'm about to phone Henry, but I can see him coming now, and I note that he's not coming from the direction of the beach or the pub.

I am just arriving back at the caravan, and I can see Hannah. She is wearing her Marigolds, and she seems to be in a foul mood. I'd hoped that time apart from me would do her some good, but it doesn't appear to have made much difference.

"How was the trip to the gardens?" I ask jovially.

"Never mind about that. What have you been up to?"

"What do you mean?"

"Can you explain to me why our caravan's water system was filled with urine, the tyres were deflated, and someone has drawn a massive, spurting cock and balls in intricate detail on the back of your linen shirt which was drying on the line? They were all waiting for me when I returned, forty or so minutes ago."

Now, I know she won't approve of my activities this afternoon, especially if I tell her how I interfered and fouled up PC Blinkerton's efforts to catch the bicycle thief; and I am fairly sure that she will not be interested in my theory that the thief may know who I am. So I stick to the true and unassailable facts.

"I went to the beach, and instead of having lunch at a pub nearby, I went for a coffee in town, then did a bit of shopping". I hold up the shopping bags as visual evidence.

Hannah regards me with suspicion. "Well, *some-one* is upset with you. And before you suggest it, it's not Barry and Maureen, or Darren and Wendy, because I've spoken with them".

I have to admit that I am at a loss to know who could be targeting us. I may have upset a few people lately, but Hannah has identified the only ones resident at the campsite, who know and may have access to our caravan. I am beginning to wonder how much bad luck one person can have, which increases my suspicion that there are more sinister forces at work. Perhaps I should take Hannah into my confidence...well, partly.

"The police failed to catch the thief today", I begin.

"Don't change the subject, Henry! I want to know, who did this to our caravan? Whom have you upset today?"

"No one! Hannah, please hear me out. I wonder whether these latest incidents at the caravan could be linked to the bike theft. If so, could they all be linked to the damage to our car?"

"What?" she says in disbelief.

"It's something PC Blinkerton said to me today. Something that could suggest that the bike thief knows who I am".

"Is that what PC Blinkerton thinks?"

"Er, no. He doesn't know about the other incidents yet, and I haven't shared my theory with anyone".

"Oh, for God's sake, Henry. You are being paranoid again. These incidents are not linked to a bogeyman with a grudge who is out to get you. The solution is simple: You keep upsetting people, and they retaliate".

"I know it looks that way, but listen: We thought the theft of my bike was opportunistic, because of the ineffective way I locked it to the post. But what if it wasn't? What if it was targeted? Who damaged the car, and why? It couldn't have been the man with the Go-Cam, and we weren't involved in any road-rage incidents before we parked at Marazion; we didn't nab the parking space from someone who had been waiting ahead of us; and you yourself said you're satisfied it wasn't Barry or Maureen, or Darren and Wendy who did those things to our caravan; so who was it?"

"Oh, and I suppose the police officers in the Jaguar

on the motorway were fakes, put up to it by someone who hired a lookalike Prime Minister to sit in the back! Come on, Henry! Accept the obvious! You annoy everyone with whom you come into contact, and they have taken umbrage!"

"No, no, I accept that the motorway incident is unrelated, but you have to admit that there have been a series of unprovoked incidents...what about the boy racer who refused to move out of the way after we collected the caravan from storage? That's another one!"

"Come on! I grant you that wasn't your fault; it was just a bit of mindless road-rage...could have happened to anyone. We were just in the wrong place at the wrong time".

I decide to express what has been on my mind: "It wouldn't surprise me if it was Travis Grausam and his gang stalking me. You know, the kids from my school. They're old enough to drive now, and there is a certain adolescent childishness to the pranks, wouldn't you say? And if they're resourceful enough to know that we're here, they may have worked out where we live. What have they done to our house?"

Whether it's the look on Hannah's face or my intuition that I've gone too far, I don't have long to wait for Hannah's response to my theory.

"I've had enough of your paranoia!" She stretches the Marigold gloves' rubber fingers to loosen them, peels them off, and throws them at me. "I'm going for a shower, and then to The Weir Inn for something to eat. You can suit yourself and eat what's in the fridge." She grabs her wash-kit, and stalks off to the shower block.

I sit down on a deck chair, which promptly collapses, leaving me tangled up inside it on the gravel. Someone has removed the screws that hold the squab to the backrest.

After Hannah leaves for the pub alone and on foot, I spend an hour or so checking the suspension and braking mechanisms on the car and caravan for any sign of tampering. I am happy to find nothing is amiss.

I again try to fathom why these things keep happening to me, increasingly convinced that I am being targeted by someone who is going to a lot of effort to ruin my holiday. What is their motive or reward? Without any pursuable leads at the car park in Marazion, or here at the caravan site, I am completely reliant on PC Blinkerton telling me as much as he can about the Corsa featured in the CCTV footage from The Weir Inn; or even better, sending me the video link or a stills photo, so that I can compare it with the ones parked near to Gower Street, which I videoed. I just don't think I'll get much of a positive response from him, after I messed up their operation.

I feel hurt by Hannah's refusal to consider my point-of-view, so I opt not to join her at the pub to wave an olive branch. I try to occupy myself with my new book, but I feel that I may be on to something that cannot be left unchecked. It isn't just the fact that my bike is still out there, tantalisingly nearby, recoverable but still missing; it is the nagging suspicion that one person cannot be subjected to so much misfortune in such a short period of time. There has to be more to it. There must be an explanation.

My mind is set. PC Blinkerton probably isn't even on duty now, considering he started work this morning; so I shall carefully compose an email to him, attaching to it my video of the four Vauxhall Corsas. I'll apologise for my interference and earlier indiscretion, thank him for his hard work, and ask him to compare my footage with the one he recovered from The Weir Inn. Who knows? Something may come of it, and the police are still the ones best placed and equipped to progress it. Once the email has been sent, I shall concentrate on raising my spirits by thinking about the promised visit to the theatre tomorrow.

It's 7 pm. Hannah has been gone for two hours, and she still hasn't returned. I phone her briefly to check she's ok: There's a lot of laughter in the background. She explains that she's participating in a pub quiz in a team that has called itself 'The Chameless Sheats', presumably because they are taking it in turns to disappear into the toilets to Google the answers. I suppose it's more original than 'The Cupid Stunts'. She says she'll be 'late', but doesn't specify a time.

After all the excitement of the day, and not an insignificant amount of energy expended by running and walking, I set up the spare bed. I need undisturbed sleep, and I have no idea when Hannah will return. Tonight will be the first time in five years that I can remember not sleeping in the same bed as my wife.

Within minutes I fall into a deep and fitful sleep, during which everyone featuring in my nightmares is out to get me.

CHAPTER 27

Wednesday, 7 am

Anyone who has been caravanning in the rain knows that there are aspects that make it worse than camping in a tent in the rain. I appreciate that a caravan is generally more water-tight and less draughty, but the sound of even the lightest shower on a fibreglass roof is far more intrusive than on canvas. A tent's material absorbs the rain as well as its timbre. When it lands on a plastic roof, it sounds like you are trapped inside a drum. You tune your ear into it eventually, but the constant pitter-patter takes a while to transpose from sleep-disturbing irritation to sleep-inducing white noise.

Yes, it's raining. Heavily. And it's woken me an hour earlier than planned. Today is the last, full day of our stay in Cornwall; the day earmarked for our visit to the Sable Theatre and an open-air performance of Dirty Rotten Scoundrels; a place and a comedy I have been wanting to see for months.

So, I lie awake, taking stock of the holiday: My wife is making it increasingly clear that she is sick of the sight of me; an unknown stalker is damaging everything I own, playing tricks, or stealing from me; everybody I meet doesn't like me, with the possible exception of Zack; and now I may have to watch the play not only alone, but under an umbrella, dressed in an oilskin coat. I feel miserable, anxious, and I need a vacation. I Google the Sable Theatre:

"Due to the forecast of storms and gale-force winds, this afternoon's performance of Dirty Rotten Scoundrels is cancelled. Please keep checking the website for further updates".

Well, at least Hannah will be pleased. She didn't want to go there anyway. I lethargically sit on the edge of my bed, and peer down the galley to the end bedroom. Hannah has left the door ajar, and I can see her tangled in the duvet on the divan, fast asleep. I don't know what time she got in last night, and I cast my eyes around me for a note. There is none.

Pouring out some porridge, mixing the dusty flakes with milk, I place the bowl into the microwave for one and a half minutes. I remove it before the ping that indicates it has cooked, so that I don't wake Hannah. Stirring it and waiting for it to cool, I check my emails on my tablet.

There are two: one from my headmaster, sent to me last night that will probably be about the staff meeting that I have to attend on Thursday. The most recent is from PC Blinkerton, who has just replied to last night's message, and must be on the early shift again. He acknowledges my information, and says he will look into it. At least the case has been re-opened. I don't want to complicate matters, but he needs to know about the other incidents that make me wonder whether they are all linked. I start typing, choosing my words carefully.

Having sent the message to PC Blinkerton, I open the email from my headmaster:

Dear Henry,
*   I am so sorry, and I must say a little concerned to hear on the Frimlington grapevine, about the circum-*

stances surrounding the unfortunate snake-bite you sustained during your half-term holiday in Cornwall. There is also talk about your involvement in a very heated confrontation on a boat to St Michael's Mount. Both stories are "trending", whatever that means.

Perhaps we could put aside some time after the staff meeting this coming Thursday to discuss these matters, and decide how we shall handle the inevitable fall-out amongst parents and pupils?

Please don't let this necessarily spoil your holiday.

Kind regards,
Mr M. J. Baxter M.A. Hons, PGCE
Headmaster, Frimlington High School

Great. Bloody internet!

When Hannah wakes just before 9 am, I feel it is time for a frank conversation.

"Did you have a nice time last night?", I ask, hoping that she replies in the negative, and is glad to be back in my company.

"Yes, wonderful thank you; met some lovely people, but drank a little too much Prosecco. I vomited this morning for the first time in a long time".

I don't like to think of Hannah getting into that kind of a state without me there to look after her. I wonder whom she spent the evening with, whether they were male or female, and how she made it back to the caravan; but I don't want to risk my questions sounding like an interrogation motivated by jealousy and paranoia, and setting her off against me again. "Hannah, we're going to be ok, aren't we?"

I don't like the pause that she leaves, whilst plodding heavy-footed into the main compartment of the caravan to sit next to me on my unmade bed.

"Henry, you know how much I love you. You just need to start thinking about what you say and how you say it. You're alienating yourself from everybody. Don't be so quick to make judgements, and if you really can't help it, then just don't impose your opinions or feelings on others; including me. Stop over-thinking everything. Just relax!"

"Ok, I'll try...The weather forecast is terrible and the performance at the Sable Theatre has been cancelled".

"Well, are there any other places you'd like to visit or things you'd like to do? Or do you want to head back a day early?"

I explain that whilst there are a host of museums and art galleries we haven't yet seen, it may not be fun visiting them in torrential rain. My real reason is that I am worried about leaving the caravan unattended whilst the culprit remains unidentified. I agree that in the circumstances, it might be sensible to return home; provided that we're not curtailing the holiday if there is anything else Hannah particularly wants to do.

Hannah squeezes my hand, smiles and shakes her head. "We'll take our time packing everything away, and aim to depart after lunch. It'll take longer in the rain. We sort things out properly on our driveway. I'm sure Mrs Cavil and her cronies can cope with our 'ugly encumbrance' being outside our house for an hour or so, whilst we de-kit".

So it is settled. Our six-night holiday to Cornwall has just been reduced to five. We get dressed and start stowing everything in boxes.

I have wandered over to the warden's office to advise Trevor that we are departing a day early. There is a queue of three people in front of me; Darren is at its head. It appears he is doing the opposite to us, extending their stay until Sunday, because of a forecast of improved weather from Thursday.

"So, yeah, wossya availability to stay 'til Sundee?".

"Camper?" asks Trevor.

Darren asks the question again, giving his stereotyped impression of an effeminate man, with speech and mannerisms that bear a striking resemblance to Trevor himself. I cringe with embarrassment. It's not the sort of humour that goes down well these days.

Trevor peers up at him above half-rimmed reading spectacles, and asks Darren crisply, "To camp?"

"Sorry mate!" Darren drops his voice to base baritone. "We'd larkta extend til Sundee". He laughs at his own, 1970s humour, fittingly with his trademark, Sid James chortle.

Trevor sighs loudly, his hands clamped onto his hips in starchy indignation.

"Are you camping in a tent, or staying in a caravan or motorhome?" he enunciates clearly, through a forced smile and bared teeth.

"Oh, I see. Sorry. Caravan, mate, caravan!"

Darren pays the balance of seventy-five pounds, which he hands over in cash from his gold money clip, produced from his trouser pocket with a flourish.

Watching and listening to Darren's behaviour towards Trevor, I reflect on Hannah's repeated advice to mind my own business; to avoid expressing uninvited opinions when I don't agree with what I see or hear. But what about her encouragement to ruthlessly challenge prejudice and discrimination? Isn't she contradicting herself? What about the standards my parents passed on to me, which I, in turn, cascade to my students: strategies and principles for saying the right thing according to your own beliefs, even if it means failure, or adverse, personal repercussions: Learning from your mistakes and re-evaluating your views accordingly; robustly recovering from failures, and persevering in the face of difficulty; making your own luck. Words and expressions of intent are important, but people are judged by their *actions*.

How should *I* react? I could bow my head, cover my face with a hand, or turn away in the hope that Darren won't notice me. He'll be out of my life for good in less than a minute; two minutes at the most. I'll never have to see or speak to him again. Conflict will have been averted. Would Hannah be proud or ashamed of me if she was here? Hannah is not here.

Darren is now walking towards me and the exit. When I focus on his face, I recognise facial features inherited by his intelligent, brilliant son, Zack. The boy whose life Darren seems intent on ruining. There is no doubt in my mind how I shall respond.

"Allo 'enry, me ole san! Ah just booked up til Sundee wiv Trevor da camp, Camp Commandant!" he says, loud enough for Trevor to hear.

"Oh", I reply. "We're off in an hour or so. Important meeting on Thursday, and the weather today...well, you know".

"Important meetin'? Ah fort you said you wuz a teacher?" Again, the Carry-On cackle.

My heart is thumping, blood rising, fists clenching, teeth grinding. I focus on Darren's smug, pug face, as a fighter acquires his target before throwing a punch.

But I am not going to hit Darren. I am not a violent man, but nor am I a cowardly one. I am going to call him out for publicly humiliating his wife and his son, and now Trevor. I am going to force him to reflect on his swaggering braggadocio. The skill will be communicating in simple terms this ignorant moron will understand.

"Darren, I hate the word 'homophobic', don't you?"

"Wot jew mean, 'enry?"

"'Homus' means 'man'; 'phobia' means 'fear'. You're not afraid of mankind, of Trevor. Or are you?"

"Course not".

"Your innuendo...the suggestive conversation just now. What do you call that?"

"I wuz 'avin' a laugh!"

"Did you hear anyone laughing? Other than yourself?"

This seems to have confused Darren. His eyes are narrowing, chin raised, lips pursed like a monkey's, as his feeble brain attempts to decipher alliance or criticism, gravity or humour.

"I ain't 'omophobic", he exclaims defensively.

"Well, if we can agree that you're not homophobic because you're not afraid of mankind, and that humiliating others is a weak man's imitation of strength, then it must naturally follow that you are a feeble-minded twat".

The others in the queue draw sharp intakes of breath, before sniggering. Darren is lost for words. My blood is up, so I continue.

"And as for the wealth you so enjoy flaunting? Yes, I confess that I am a little envious. But real wealth is measured by knowing the extent of your ignorance, and recognising how much you'd be worth if you lost all of your money; and on both scores, Darren, you are the poorest pauper of all".

"Yeah? You really fink you know everyfink, duntcha? Proper lill know-it-all!"

"Darren, 'the only true wisdom is in knowing you know nothing'."[15]

Darren then does what Hannah always told me someone would do, sooner or later. He punches me on the nose.

As I lie on the Lino, wondering whether Darren will follow with a kick to my ribs, I foolishly offer him another quote: "'A man should be able to hear, and to bear, the worst that could be said of him'."[16]

Trevor ejects Darren from the office before he renders me unconscious or kills me, and then helps me to my feet. I dab my bloody nose with a handkerchief, and those who are ahead of me in the queue usher me to the front. Trevor cancels my booking, refunds me twenty-five pounds for that evening's pitch, in glorious contravention of the policy he dictated verbatim to me fewer than five days' ago, and insists on giving me a free voucher for a week's holiday next year. He appreciates my stand against Darren, and allows me to wait in a back room until I stop bleeding.

I merely did the right thing, but I can't face explaining to Hannah what happened. I am sure that I can concoct some plausible explanation, if she notices my sore nose.

––––––––––––––––––––

Hannah has made considerable progress packing during the twenty-five or so minutes I have been at the site office, so all that is left for me to do is detach the water, electrical and gas equipment, stow it, raise the corner steadies and attach the caravan to the Volvo.

I am sitting in the driving seat and Hannah is standing behind the caravan, calling out instructions to me to depress the brake pedal and switch various lights on and off, so that she can check everything is working correctly. Once this is completed, she sits next to me.

My phone rings. I have synchronised it with the car's Bluetooth to enable me to use it hands-free. Pressing a button on the steering wheel to take the call, PC Blinkerton's voice is amplified through the Bowers and Wilkins speakers, loud and clear.

"Mr Burden? It's PC Blinkerton".

"Good afternoon, officer".

"I have some news for you".

"Please, go on".

"Do you want the good or the bad?"

CHAPTER 28

Wednesday, 6.55 pm

Well, who would have thought it? I must say that the police did a marvellous job in identifying the offender; and Henry also gets credit for securing the evidence that led to the arrest for theft of his bike, and criminal damage to our car and caravan.

I know that Henry is trying to modify his obsessive, opinionated and judgemental behaviour; but is he ever going to change enough to make life with him tolerable? It really can be rather stressful at times. He has just returned from the campsite office with a red and swollen nose. He says it's the onset of a cold, but I wouldn't be surprised if Trevor finally had enough, and bopped him. I always warned Henry it would happen one day.

Henry's reformation of character is all the more essential now that we're going to have another little person to consider. Yes, the vomiting this morning was not a consequence of Prosecco in the pub. I didn't drink any, because I am pregnant! The results from the five tester kits I bought last night at Happy Bargains, show that the news isn't the only thing Henry and I made in the dunes.

I haven't told Henry yet, because I am undecided whether having a baby is the right thing to do at the moment, considering our relationship seems to be going through a difficult period. I guess that I've got a few months to make that call. I know I can't keep it from Henry for that long. I plan to tell him very soon. He has a right to know, and be a part of this life-changing, life-giving decision; not that there is any doubt in my mind what his decision will be.

Ultimately though, it's going to be up to me to decide, and live with the consequences. We are all responsible for the choices we make, and the sides we take. That is life.

CHAPTER 29

<u>Wednesday, 7.30 pm</u>

I am happy to report that we have arrived home safely and without incident. The good news from PC Blinkerton is that they caught the culprit who stole my bike, and, as it turns out, also damaged our car and caravan. The bad news is my Cannondale was sold to an unknown buyer, before they could nab the thief. If the police had been more thorough checking the roads nearest to Gower Street for blue Vauxhall Corsas, perhaps they would have made the connection sooner, and been in time to recover my bike.

It appears Hannah and I were both right about the perpetrator's motivation: It *was* someone I upset, just as she said it would be; but it transpires it was as much about seeking revenge on Hannah, as it was about taking retribution against me; because *she* had upset him, too. We agree that neither of us should be blamed for his decision to target us. I was right in the sense that there *was* a stalker following us, playing tricks and damaging our things; so I wasn't being obsessive and paranoid, after all.

The offender is unemployed, and well-known to the police: PC Blinkerton would not disclose his address, but did indicate that he lives in the 'general vicinity' of Gower Street. The officer also confirmed that it was my intelligence work in supplying the video footage of the backs of the four Vauxhall Corsas, that led to his identification and arrest. It was my recording of a pint-shaped, Cornish Real Ale Society sticker, displayed in the lower offside corner of the rear window of one of them, that enabled the police to identify the offender's car, featured in The Weir Inn's CCTV. It was then just a question of running the registration number through the Police National Computer, which gave them name of the registered keeper: Mr Gryffyn Townsend, our inebriated tour guide at Godleven Tin Mine.

It appears that Mr Townsend is, as I suspected at the time, an alcoholic. He is also a habitual drink-driver, with several convictions for driving cars on roads with excessive levels of intoxicants in his body. Once his Corsa's registration number was tagged, it was only a matter of time before it passed an ANPR[17] camera, which was set up to send a message to the police advising them of its location and direction of travel. When it did, it was fortunate that a police patrol was nearby, and intercepted him.

Officers not only found Gryffyn Townsend drunk behind the wheel at 10.15 am this morning; he was also disqualified by a court a few weeks ago from driving a motor vehicle for twelve months. At the end of his prohibition he must re-take and pass his driving test. PC Blinkerton told me that the additional offences of drink- and disqualified-driving, and driving without insurance have been added to the proposed charges. These should substantially extend that period of disqualification, as well as result in the imposition of a custodial sentence.

They have to wait for him to sober up before they are able to interview him; but that may take some time, considering the result from the breath-test showed a level of intoxication five times the legal driving limit for alcohol: enough to kill most people. But the selfies on his phone, seized and analysed for evidence on the basis of his suspected trade in dealing in stolen bikes, show him laughing whilst urinating in our caravan's fresh water butt. There is also one of him kneeling down in the car park at Marazion, grinning and pointing at the offensive scratches on our Volvo's door. Whatever he says when interviewed, the officers' own eye-witness evidence, supported by their Bodycam footage of him driving, the intoximeter's readings of his inebriation, and all of the video and photographic material, should be sufficient to convict him.

I don't need to wait for a post-interview update from PC Blinkerton to suspect that if Gryffyn Townsend elects to talk fully and frankly, rather than exercise his right to silence, he will explain how his actions were motivated by revenge: for the complaint Hannah and I made to management about his conduct and inebriated condition in the mine, which resulted in his dismissal from the inter-active museum, and subsequent unemployment.

I genuinely believe I am making fewer outrageous statements, becoming less judgemental or inclined to defend the indefensible. Change is difficult when long-term beliefs and values are challenged; and perhaps it is hampered or halted by the manner of objection. I am gradually learning to listen and accept Hannah's points-of-view and emulate her exemplary standards of conduct, philosophy and moral rectitude. Given time, I am sure that my own behaviour will become more comparable to her high bar, without even having to think about it.

Maybe Hannah doesn't always communicate her crusade effectively, or acknowledge my progress reasonably. She tells me that she often tunes out when I rant. It is possible that her own inattention and over-amplification of opinion, merely resulted in me responding in kind, leading to a self-fuelling, tumbling spiral of mutually provocative behaviour that moved us further apart instead of bringing us closer together.

On a personal, interactive, social level, I shall be less assertive that my way is right, and others are wrong, or that I am more worthy or important.

On a marital level, I hope that Hannah accepts that it is reasonable for two people to think or respond differently to the same stimuli, even if they are husband and wife. It is normal to take opposing sides in a discussion; or have contrasting perceptions of an event that can lead to more holistic, alternative resolutions to dilemmas. Disagreement and difference doesn't have to mean the end of a relationship or a marriage, which in our case is pretty sound on the whole; just like it doesn't have to mean the disintegration of Society. What do *you* say?

Sorry, I must go. Hannah wants to talk to me. She says it's really important...

AUTHOR'S NOTE

I hope you enjoyed reading this humorous tale of Henry's and Hannah's adventures in Cornwall. Whose side did you take, when considering the moral, behavioural and societal events and dilemmas encountered by our hero, heroine, and other characters?

Some of the places depicted in this fiction are themselves fictitious - just products of my imagination. You will not, for example, find a place called Dormouth or Ashbourne in Dorset. There is no Sable Theatre on a Cornish beach, constructed from concrete-reinforced sand, unless someone builds one in the future; neither are there Cornish towns called Addleton or Godleven; nor an inter-active museum called the Godleven Tin Mine, nor a supermarket called Happy Bargains.

If you enjoyed this book, then please recommend it to others.

Finally, a big thank you for buying and reading Taking Sides.

Andrew J Huckman
August 2019

GLOSSARY

1. Boryer: metal bar for drilling holes

2. Banjo shovel: short-handled shovel

3. Kibble: rounded bucket that should snag on mine walls when hoisted

4. Hoggan: pasty

5. Crib: snack

6. Jack: water container

7. Captain: person in charge in the mine

8. Spale: fine for breaking mine rules

9. Hobnail: boots worn by miners

10. Miner's lung: Silicosis - disease caused by dust in the lungs

11. Cage: lift to transport miners up & down the shaft

12. Dips: miners' candles

13. Max Gate: Victoria house designed, built & inhabited by author & poet, Thomas Hardy

14. O.P.: Observation Position

15. Quote from Socrates, philosopher in the 5th century BC: *"The only true wisdom is in knowing you know nothing"*.

16. Quote from Saul Bellow, writer: *"A man should be able to hear, and to bear, the worst that could be said of him"*.

17. ANPR: Automatic Number Plate Recognition (alerts the police to vehicles of interest)

Printed in Great Britain
by Amazon